VANISHED?

A Swedish Crime Novel

Stockholm Sleuth Series

CHRISTER THOLIN

Copyright © 2018 Christer Tholin

Stockholm, Sweden

contact@christertholin.one

www.christertholin.one

2nd English edition 2018

Edited and partially retranslated by Doreen Zeitvogel

Original translation by Dwight E. Langston

Title of the original German edition:

VERSCHWUNDEN?

Published 2016

Cover design by Anne Gebhardt

ISBN of pocketbook:

ISBN-13: 9781717821034

ISBN-10: 1-7178-2103-0

For my wife

Contents

Part I

1

Now it would soon be over. Maybe another half hour's drive. Somehow the trip had lasted longer than he had imagined. He had left Berlin in the evening and taken the night ferry from Rostock to Trelleborg. His single-bunk cabin had been basic; the night, short. The ferry had arrived in Sweden at exactly six in the morning, but the route from Trelleborg to the vacation house had proved laborious. First, there was the 110-kilometer-per-hour speed limit on the freeway. Not all of it was freeway, either, and he rarely even reached the 70-kph speed limit on the county roads. Somehow, he always wound up behind some large freight truck. Oh well, it was almost over. At least, his Audi was purring—the route seemed to suit it just fine.

Martin had placed the driving directions from the owner of the house on the passenger seat beside him. "It's extremely easy to find. Just follow the directions carefully, and be sure to drive very slowly toward the end so that you don't miss the turnoffs," the owner had told Martin when he picked up the key in Berlin. All he could do now was to hope the directions were good and would still be easy to follow once he left the main road. At first, his GPS couldn't even find the address.

At least, the scenery was gorgeous, with lots of forest, lots of lush green meadows, and the occasional lake. There were hardly any towns, and houses appeared only now and then amidst all the nature, and then they were usually painted the typical rust-red and also yellow and light blue. This was Martin's first trip to Sweden, and his initial impressions confirmed the image he had had: pristine nature with lots of quiet. He needed that—to think, above all. And that meant getting clear on how to proceed from here.

It was already over a year since Martin's separation from his wife and his little girl Lara. But the divorce hearing took place just three weeks ago, and that formality had affected him more than he expected. Now it would be signed and sealed, complete with visitation rights. On top of that, his wife—no, his ex-wife—was marrying again, which wouldn't make his relationship with his daughter any easier.

After the meeting with the judge, it became obvious to Martin that he simply could not go on like this. He needed to take a break, to reorient himself. It was then that he happened to notice the following ad: "Vacation home in Southern Sweden: holiday in harmony with nature." He thought it over for another two days, and then he called and booked, which was never a problem during the off-peak season. Yes, and now he was almost there.

"Start by heading toward Gulsten." Fine, he did that. The road grew narrower as it wound its way through the woods. Then the landscape opened up again, and a small town came into view. That had to be Tensta, the nearest shopping locale.

Shortly before entering the town, Martin noticed a sign that read "Koloniområde Öst-Tensta." He turned onto the road, which was narrow but still paved with asphalt. After a few kilometers, the landscape changed. Now it was no longer flat but gradually went uphill. Once again, he entered the woods, just as the landlord had described. At that point, he was supposed to take the third turnoff to the left. But what exactly did "turnoff" mean here? Surely not this tiny road that could barely accommodate a car ... or was that it? All right, he had already passed one. That much was clear. The second was debatable. And so it continued, which unfortunately meant that it was not so obvious where he should turn off and not at all as simple as the landlord had claimed—and that, in spite of the fact that Martin was driving very slowly and carefully checking every junction.

For a long time, the road went on through the woods, continuing gently uphill. Finally, another junction appeared. A right turn would lead to Östergård, but there was no sign for the left turn, only half a dozen mailboxes. What choice did he have? He turned left. In about 100 meters, the asphalt stopped, although the dirt road was entirely passable, and the terrain had leveled off as well. According to the directions, he was supposed to take the second option to the right. Hopefully, something—anything—would appear.

3

Martin had driven maybe two kilometers when he came to a clearing. Here the road forked, with the right turnoff leading to one end of the clearing. There stood a house, yellow in color. He drove up to it. There was a Jeep sitting in the driveway, and on the garden gate, a large sign boasted *"Hjärtats plats."* Martin stopped the car. Should he ring the doorbell and ask?

As he got out of the car, Martin realized that he had no need to ring the bell: there was a woman working in the garden to the right of the house. She had looked up and was leaning on her spade. About his age, she was wearing work clothes and had woven her blond hair into a braid.

"Excuse me, madam, could you please help me?" Martin asked in English. The woman came over to the fence and looked at him inquiringly. She had beautiful blue eyes, and her skin was covered with freckles. Tiny beads of sweat stood out on her forehead.

"You can speak German with me as well," came the answer in fluent German.

"Oh, I didn't realize I had such a pronounced accent."

"It's not that. I happened to notice your license plate."

"Ah, right. I'm sorry to bother you, but I'm not sure I've gone the right way."

"Where are you headed?"

"I've rented a vacation house. It's called, uh ..." He looked at the piece of paper. "... 'Solplats.' Is that anywhere near here?"

"Solplats." She pronounced it "Soolpluts." "Yes, you're not too far off. All you need to do is to drive back a little way to the last junction, take the other road, and then veer right after about three kilometers. It's the third or fourth house on the right, I think. You can't miss it. The name is on it in big letters."

"Great! I'm so relieved. I wasn't sure if I'd even gone down the right dead end. According to this paper, it's the fourth house. But thanks so much for your help—and in German, too. Where did you learn to speak it so well?"

"Oh, thank you. I do a lot of business with Germany."

"No, I should be thanking you. If I take another wrong turn, I'll be back. Goodbye!"

"I'm sure you'll find it. Goodbye!" She had a lovely Swedish accent.

Martin got in the car and turned it around. They waved at each other, and then he drove back to the last junction and took the other road at the fork. He found himself heading back into the forest. Everything went like clockwork after that: first, the road to the right; then the three houses—red, blue, and red; and finally, the fourth house, "Solplats," also painted red. The name was written in large letters on a small sign that sat enthroned on a pole in front of the house. The owner had explained to him that the name meant "sun place." And it made sense: the road ran up the hill, and the house stood on a rather precipitous spot in a clearing. From there, you had a beautiful view across the meadow to a little lake.

The house itself was small, a single story with a nearly black roof and white window frames. The natural garden was covered with tall grass and a few rocks sprinkled here and there. There was no fence, at least not on this side. Martin drove into the small parking space beside the house. He had arrived.

Saturday, September 19

2

Martin was warming his hands on his mug of coffee. Mornings on the terrace were brisk, but the panorama was breathtaking. The lake lay, calm and quiet, between the green tops of the trees. On the near side lay a long stretch of meadow that was home to a herd of deer. Every morning, Martin would watch them, and on one day, there were even several stags. Good thing he had packed his binoculars.

The house itself was furnished for comfort and convenience, and by now, Martin was feeling quite at home. He had spent the first two days settling in and looking around, and now he could devote himself entirely to relaxing and taking walks. He had already done a fair amount of walking, although there were hardly any road signs, so he had to pay close attention to avoid getting lost. The weather had also been somewhat capricious, but he was enjoying it all the same. This area was like a wasteland, with not a soul in sight. Even the neighboring houses appeared to be empty. But that was good—it would give him plenty of room to think.

To Martin, one thing was already clear: he would stay in touch with his daughter and take full advantage of his visitation rights. Back home, he had considered completely breaking off contact to give his wife's new family a chance. But that had been a knee-jerk reaction, and he knew now that that choice would have caused him a great deal of torment. Besides, he didn't think his daughter would accept it. It was true that she was much more attached to her mother, but her father meant a lot to her as well.

Martin had no intention of meddling in his ex's new relationship. He had already done that with his daughter's upbringing—he and his ex had quarreled a lot over that. The image of men that his wife—no, ex-wife—had already conveyed to the four-year-old girl was far too negative. Not all men were chauvinists, after all. But Martin no longer had any desire to discuss that. In the time that he had with his daughter, he would try to give her a realistic image of himself, and that would at least be different from the picture his ex-wife had painted. Oh well, it still wouldn't be easy.

Today, Martin's goal was to shop. The provisions he had bought at a small shopping center in Tensta on his first day there were already running low. This particular supermarket was open every day, and he liked the convenience of not having to worry about what day of the week it was. Meanwhile, he had gotten used to the road through the forest and down the mountain, not to mention the fact that he rarely encountered another car.

Once in Tensta, Martin drove straight to the shopping center, which was situated on the main road. There was a large parking lot that gave direct access to the stores, which lined it in the form of an L. The supermarket was at the short end.

Martin took a shopping cart and trundled off. He found the store's selection somewhat limited, apart from the bewildering array of dairy products. His first time there, he had bought some *Filmjölk* because of the large cow depicted on the carton. It turned out to be buttermilk, which he wasn't overly fond of and which wasn't at all suitable for coffee. This time, he bought *Mellanmjölk,* even though there was no cow on it. The store had a large selection of fish as well, so Martin picked up several jars of herring in different sauces and placed them in his cart.

At the checkout stand, the lone woman ahead of him was embroiled in a discussion with the cashier. Martin recognized her. It was the nice lady who had told him the way to the house. She seemed to be having a problem with her credit card. Since she hadn't noticed him yet, he addressed her.

"Excuse me, can I be of any help?"

The woman turned and looked at him. She had a serious expression on her face, but the wrinkles on her brow soon melted into a smile of recognition.

"Oh, it's you! Hello! Yes, the card reader won't take my card, and I didn't bring enough cash."

"I'd be happy to help. How much do you need?"

"Oh, that would be so kind of you, and I'll pay you back right away. It's not much—just 260 kronor."

"Ah, that's no problem. I have enough." Luckily, he had taken out plenty of cash since he hadn't expected to be able to pay with his card wherever he went.

Martin's blond neighbor explained the situation to the cashier, and both women looked relieved. As Martin handed the attractive neighbor the money, their fingers touched. That brief contact sent a chill down his spine. He froze, unable to do anything but stare. After several seconds that seemed like minutes, he shook himself loose from his petrified state and paid for his purchase. Had the woman noticed his reaction?

Having placed their items in plastic bags, Martin and his neighbor walked to the exit together.

"I'm so grateful to you for helping me out," she said, "and without even knowing me at all."

"It's not a problem. At the very least, it gave me a chance to repay you for your help earlier."

"You're very kind." Her blue eyes were sparkling. "I know! I'll use a different card to get some cash, and then I can have you over for coffee tomorrow. Would that be all right? I can give you the money then. What do you think?"

"I'd love to. What time should I be there?"

"Around three o'clock. Can you find your way to my house?"

"Oh yes, I'm sure. I've almost driven past it several times already."

"All right, then I'll see you tomorrow. I'm looking forward to it!"

"Me, too."

"My name is Liv, by the way."

"Martin."

"Great. In Sweden, we say *hejdå* for goodbye."

"Heydoh." Martin gave it a try.

"Not bad for a first attempt. Hejdå!"

They headed in different directions as they walked back to their cars. Martin turned to look at Liv. She was an attractive woman from the back as well.

Now on his way home, Martin was contemplating their accidental meeting. He was looking forward to their get-together and to spending time with another person. He was a bit lonely, after all, being all by himself in his cabin. Besides, he found her interesting. He wondered if she lived alone.

The day passed quickly. Martin had spent the afternoon in the woods, somewhat longer than he meant to after trying a new path and getting lost. Then, to make matters worse, it started to pour so that he returned home drenched and exhausted. But after a hot shower, he already felt better.

For supper, he made fish and also indulged in a bottle of wine. His thoughts turned to his daughter once more. He missed her, and in that moment, he truly regretted that it had come to this. Maybe he had also made it too easy for himself. Was there nothing more he could have done to save his marriage?

At some point, Martin finally quit making compromises, and he chose to ignore his wife's perpetual complaining to the extent that he could. Yes, all right, if he were honest, you could probably see that as chauvinistic. For the brief time he was home, he had dealt exclusively with his daughter, and otherwise, he had focused on his job. He and a colleague had started a law practice together, and that took a lot of work, especially in the first year. His indifference had infuriated his wife, and there was constant bickering, even over trivial matters. And so, Martin buried himself even more in his work.

And then his wife met Gerhard, and Martin could no longer forestall the end. Not that he had particularly tried. Somehow, he hadn't cared too much because he didn't believe that his wife would ever push to the point of divorce. But she did—and fast, too.

Right, so there he was. Another sip of wine, and he would be ready to drop into bed.

Sunday, September 20

3

The engine failed to properly warm up on the short stretch to his "neighbor" Liv's, but Martin had no desire to walk. The rain was still coming down, and the road was muddy.

Martin was looking forward to seeing Liv again. She was an interesting and attractive woman. He thought of his response in the supermarket the day before, and he wondered whether he would experience a similar sensation today—upon shaking hands, for instance.

He parked the car by the side of the road in the same spot where it had stood before. As he got out of the car, he took the roll of cookies he had set on the passenger seat beside him. It was not the most original gift, but he had no wish to make the extra trip to town to pick up flowers. He then walked up the three steps to the front door. There was no doorbell, just a large ring that functioned as a door knocker, which he now put to use. No response. After waiting a short while, he tried again, this time a bit louder. Nothing. Three times he tried, quite forcefully. This knocker was certainly loud enough. Still, not one thing stirred. Martin looked about. The Jeep was sitting in the driveway, and there was no house within visible range, so she wouldn't be at the neighbor's. Could she be in the shower? He tried again and shouted "Hello!" Nothing.

Martin went over to the Jeep. Locked. Cold hood. He walked around the house. In the back was a half-covered terrace with a table and some garden chairs. Everything was deserted. He went up to the terrace door and peered through the glass. Inside was a small dining table, and beside it was an overturned chair. Something was not quite right here. He knocked on the glass and shouted again. The door swung slightly open: it was unlocked. Martin pushed on it some more and took a hesitant step inside the house. He shouted one more time, though by now he no longer expected an answer.

Aside from the overturned chair, everything here looked normal—a comfortably furnished living and dining room. He ventured farther into the house. Next door was the kitchen, where all was immaculate and tidy. He could see nothing in the way of preparations for coffee, and the coffeemaker was clean. Had Liv forgotten about him? Or had he misunderstood her?

Martin felt uneasy walking around the place uninvited, and he was debating whether to leave when he decided to look on top of the clothes cabinet in the hallway. There lay her car key and cell phone, which was on. Without these items, she wouldn't be gone for long, would she?

The key to the door had been inserted into the lock from inside. Martin tried the handle and found that the door had been locked from inside as well. That meant that Liv had left the house by way of the terrace. Had she gone to a neighbor's home farther off? There was virtually no other option. Or maybe something had happened to her—she had fallen from a ladder or some such thing.

Martin decided to investigate. He looked inside the guest half-bath and then climbed the narrow steps that led upstairs, where there was a full bath and two small bedrooms. But Liv was nowhere to be found. Martin headed back downstairs.

What should he do? Simply leave and try again tomorrow? Or should he wait, after all? Here in the dining room? He could see himself sitting at the table as Liv opened the terrace door. He would say to her with a sheepish look: "Hello there, I decided to let myself in."

No, that didn't appeal to him. Martin exited the house and got in his car, taking the cookies with him. Annoyed, he set them back down on the passenger seat. He then decided to drive to the neighboring houses and inquire there. He started the car and drove farther down the road. Two kilometers later, with still no house in sight, he turned around. At the junction behind Liv's home, there was nothing but forest for several kilometers in either direction. That much he knew. Where could she have gone—on foot, without her cell phone or bothering to lock her house? Not to mention the fact that forgetting a date from one day to the next was hardly the norm.

Martin stopped once more before Liv's house. He got out of the car, this time leaving the package of cookies behind. He decided to knock on the door again. Then, lying to the left of the gate, he noticed a slipper. Its color was plush red, and it was wet. On looking more closely, he detected footprints as well, even if they were faded. And then there was a tire mark that was not from his car, since he had parked on the other side of the road. Could someone have picked Liv up?

The whole thing was starting to give him an eerie feeling. Still, there had to be a simple explanation: being in a hurry, Liv forgot her key and cell phone and knocked over the chair as she rushed out. The slipper may also have been lying there a long time. Although why she went out the back was still unclear—the front door would have been quicker.

Martin knocked again, and when he received no answer, he went around the back. Right in front of the terrace on the sodden grass was some sort of trail that he hadn't noticed before. This was turning more and more mysterious.

He went back inside to have another look around the living room, but even a closer inspection revealed nothing. On the dining table—by the overturned chair—lay a paperback book, apparently a Swedish novel. There was also mud in several spots on the carpet. Had he tracked it in himself? He had to admit that he hadn't been overly careful.

Martin revisited the hallway. There, too, he noticed traces of mud on the linoleum floor. Inside the clothes cabinet hung an array of jackets, including the brown one Liv had worn the previous day. A sporty-looking handbag was hanging there as well. This was getting stranger and stranger. The women he knew would hardly step out of the house without their purse. He took a look inside it. There wasn't much: just a mix of paraphernalia: a hairbrush, lipstick, and a wallet with cash and credit cards. There was also an ID the size of a credit card. Liv Ulldahl was her full name—it was easy to recognize her from the photo. She must have been in a huge hurry.

On the wall beside the cabinet hung an old telephone that had a rotary dial with the phone number on it. Martin wrote it down on a notepad that was lying on a shelf by the phone. He tore off the slip. Now he could call the house later on to find out if Liv had returned in the meantime.

After another thorough look around, Martin finally left the house. But on crossing the terrace this time, his eye caught sight of something red beneath the chair standing closest to the door. It was the other slipper.

4

Dealing with this policeman was a major headache. His English was painfully slow, and otherwise, too, he was hardly the sharpest tack. From the looks of him, there were just a few more years between him and his retirement. And yet, his epaulets sported three stars.

"Maybe Ms. Ulldahl got a ride from someone else," he had just finished saying.

"That's possible, but we had a date at three."

"Well, she could have forgotten."

"Yes, that's true, but it's been at least three hours since she's been gone. Look, I got there at three, and she was already gone. Then I waited at home for two hours and tried again."

Martin had also called several times, but of course no one had picked up.

"She was still out," he continued, "and her cell phone, key, and bag were in the house the whole time. Not to mention the bit with the slippers."

"Mr. Petzold. First of all, what you did is illegal. You cannot just break into someone's house. That aside, I can understand why you're worried, but there's probably a good reason for it all. There's unfortunately nothing we can do at the moment. We would first have to file a missing person's report."

"But that's exactly what I want to do," Martin protested.

"You have to be family a member. And then you have to wait at least twenty-four hours."

"All right, but it seems her family members don't live anywhere near the area. How are they supposed to fill out a report?"

"In a case like that," the policeman replied, "a friend or neighbor could also file a report."

"Then I can do it. I'm a neighbor."

"But you said you lived several kilometers away."

"Right, but it's actually the closest house."

"I see." The policeman was ruminating. "Then you can do it. We just have to wait twenty-four hours."

"Couldn't you at least try to get in touch with her family members?" Martin asked.

"Do you have an address or phone number?" the policeman responded.

"Of course not," Martin replied, exasperated. "But I'm sure you could find that out."

"It's not that simple."

In the end, Martin was able to persuade the policeman to at least give it a try. He left him his cell phone number and address, and they made an appointment for the following day.

Martin had an odd feeling as he was driving back to Solplats. Somehow this day had not turned out as he had imagined, and he had a bad feeling about the whole story. His neighbor's house was totally dark as he passed the junction. He decided to return there first thing in the morning.

Monday, September 21

5

It was the first thing Martin thought of on awakening. He had called two more times the previous evening, with no answer either time. He checked the clock: it was 7:30 a.m. Should he call again this early? He decided to have breakfast first.

After breakfast, there was still no answer, so Martin got in the car and drove to the house again. Everything appeared unchanged. Knocking at the front door brought no response, so he went out back to the terrace, where the door was still open. This time, he decided to do a meticulous search of the house. There had to be some kind of clue.

The purse, cell phone, and key were still in the same place as before. Yesterday, Martin had felt uncomfortable walking around uninvited inside the house. Today, his inhibitions were gone. A night had passed, and he was convinced that something was off, though he also had to admit that investigating the matter was exciting.

Martin went upstairs. The beds were untouched. One of the rooms appeared to be Liv's bedroom. There was a blouse draped over the chair and a pair of pants on a hanger that was hooked on the wardrobe. In the corner stood a suitcase. Martin opened the wardrobe. Hanging and lying inside it was every possible type of garment that would fit Liv.

On the other side of the room stood a chest of drawers. The top drawer contained all sorts of knickknacks, scarves, small bottles, ballpoint pens, and a notepad. Martin was about to open the next drawer when he heard a noise that clearly came from downstairs. He dashed out of the room and shouted: "Hello, is someone there?" No answer. But then he heard the noise again, as though someone were walking around down there. He went downstairs and shouted "Hello!" once more. As he turned toward the living room, he sensed a movement behind him. But before he could turn around, something struck him, and darkness wrapped itself around him.

Martin was freezing. His head hurt. It was pitch black and smelled of must. He couldn't move—his hands and feet were tied. He was lying in some unknown place on something soft.

It took some time for his senses to come into focus, but now he could feel that something was stuck in his hair at the back of his head. A tiny bit of light was filtering through the cracks in the door. Martin looked around. He was able to discern the outline of various objects. Was that a lawnmower? Some poles and sacks were propped against the wall. It was a small room, and he could see that he was lying on a pile of chair cushions, probably for outside furniture. He seemed to have landed in a garden shed.

Now he recalled that someone had assaulted him inside Liv's house. Was the sticky stuff on the back of his head blood? It hurt a lot in any case. Martin struggled to sit, which was not so easy to do with his hands tied behind his back. His feet hit against something hard. Yes, there was in fact a lawnmower standing before him. From the bit of light that shone through the narrow cracks, he could make out what looked like a double door to his left.

What should he do? Call for help? Try to free himself? Of course, there was the risk that the person who had struck and bound him was still nearby, in which case shouting was not such a good idea. He tried pulling one hand free, but they were both bound fast. He thought for a moment. If this was a garden shed, there had to be something here that he could use to cut the rope. He carefully raised himself up and edged past the lawnmower to the door. It was slow going. With his feet still tied, he could do no more than shuffle back and forth. On top of that, his left thigh hurt. Maybe he had fallen on something when he was knocked down. But he made it to the door and was able to lean against it for better support. Slowly, he inched his way along the wall to where the poles were standing. They were actually garden tools: a hoe, a rake, and some miscellaneous items. And there it was—a pair of pruning shears that were hanging on the side of the shed. Except that they were hanging at shoulder height, and he had an impossible time reaching them with his hands behind his back. Only one other option remained: he cautiously took the shears between his teeth and let them drop to the ground. Then he turned around with care and slowly squatted down. Somehow in doing so, he hit the hoe, and the pole fell on his head. One more pain to deal with. He clenched his teeth and held the pole between his head and shoulder so that it wouldn't fall on the lawnmower and make a racket.

Finally, Martin was able to squat down low enough to find the shears. He grabbed them with one hand and felt around. Of course, they had some kind of locking mechanism that he would have to undo. Despite his hands being numb, he found the lever and, after working it a bit, the shears released. He carefully turned them around and positioned them so that he could cut the rope. Squeezing the shears shut in this position was not easy, but he somehow managed to do it. He had apparently placed them correctly, because he felt no pain, and after a bit of resistance from the rope, he was able to push the shear completely through and loosen the rope. Relieved, Martin dropped the shears, freed his hands from the rest of the rope, and rubbed his wrists. That felt much better already. The blood flowed back into his hands with an unpleasant sensation of pins and needles. He quickly undid the ties around his feet.

There. Now he was finally starting to regain some control over his situation. He felt his pants pockets. Yes, cell phone, car key, and wallet were all there, so the assault had not been a robbery. A look at his cell phone showed that he had reception. Should he call the police? Actually, the first thing he wanted to do was to get out of wherever this garden shed might be. Martin used his phone as a flashlight and studied the double door. It appeared to be locked. He shone the light on the other side, where he found one bolt each at the top and bottom and was able to unlatch them both with ease. Now he could push both doors outward, which he did as slowly and carefully as possible. In spite of his efforts, he couldn't avoid making a scraping noise. Hopefully, no one heard it!

Martin peered outside through the crack. It was no longer morning in any case, so he must have been unconscious for several hours. From the crack in the door, he could see a vegetable bed. He slowly stuck out his head and looked around. To the left, he saw Liv's house, with his Audi sitting out front. Whew, at least that much was good. He cautiously stepped outside the shed and tried to determine whether anyone else was nearby. There were no other cars, nor could he see or hear anything else that pointed to the presence of other people. Martin plucked up his courage and crept over to his car. He opened the door, sat down, locked the car, and started the engine. So far, so good. He turned around and hit the gas. Time to get the hell out of there!

Martin was on the phone with that numbskull again. He had driven straight back to his vacation house and first taken a look at the places that were hurting. His head had a wound that had bled quite a lot, and his thigh had a large bruise. Standing in the shower, he had carefully washed the blood from his hair, and then he had put on clean clothes. After that, he raided the refrigerator—he was starving. The clock read two in the afternoon. Once he felt halfway revived and had collected his thoughts, he called the number he had gotten from the policeman at the station. And now, for the second time, he was explaining what had happened.

"Yes, I know I went into the house again. But it was still unlocked. I just wanted to make sure that nothing had happened to Liv. Besides, that's not the point. I was knocked out cold and tied up. That's surely a statutory offense. I'm a lawyer in Germany, and I know that the police have to take action under such circumstances."

"Now calm down—we're taking care of it. I'm sending a patrol car to Ms. Ulldahl's house and to yours after that. We already have your address. You'll probably have to come back here so that we can take your statement."

"All right, thanks."

The patrol car never showed, of course. Instead, the policeman called Martin shortly before five o'clock and asked him to come to the station the next morning. He wouldn't give him any more information but put it off until the following day. Martin was sure the man was about to call it a day.

Martin resolved to have a quiet evening, but that was easier said than done with the day's events going around and around in his head.

6

Martin drove to the police station right after breakfast the following morning. It was not yet nine o'clock when he arrived. The policeman greeted him somewhat wearily and immediately brought him to a back room.

"Mr. Petzold, we need to take your statement."

"Yes, of course, but what did you discover yesterday after sending a patrol car?"

"Let's go through the statement first!"

The policeman gave Martin a penetrating look. The last time they spoke, Martin had failed to notice what bushy eyebrows the man had. Maybe he noticed today because the policeman was frowning and looked almost threatening behind those brows.

"Surely you're not going to keep me in the dark. Please tell me whether they've found Liv!"

"We're going to take your statement now."

This man was evidently stubborn. Martin complied, explaining for the third time what had happened the day before. The policeman recorded everything with a microphone that was attached to his computer.

When he was done, Martin asked him, "Can you tell me now what you found at Liv's house?"

"What I can tell you," the policeman replied, "is the following: in the garden shed, we found some pieces of rope that had been cut through. That suggests that your story could be true."

"Aha. Thank you." They apparently hadn't classified him as a credible witness. "Anything more?"

"Nothing more." The policeman regarded him calmly.

"Excuse me?" Martin was trying to contain himself. "What about Liv? Were there other people in the house?"

"We didn't go inside the house."

Now Martin was at a complete loss. "Why did you not go inside the house?"

The policeman's bushy eyebrows twitched as he gave Martin another of his penetrating looks. "The door was locked."

"Yes, I know. The front door was locked. But I told you the terrace door was open."

The policeman turned to his computer and began typing. "No, the terrace door was also locked."

"What? That can't be. And the overturned furniture?"

The policeman looked at Martin over his monitor. "As far as we could see, everything was in order." He continued typing.

Martin leaned back in his chair. What was going on here? Either the police hadn't thoroughly checked the house, or the person who had assaulted him had put everything back in order.

"So what about Liv?" he asked.

"I couldn't tell you anything about that."

"Now listen here!" This guy was about to drive Martin up a wall. "She has been missing for two days. Don't you think someone will eventually have to file a missing person's report?"

The policeman stopped typing and looked up at the ceiling. He seemed to be contemplating something. Martin waited. His eye fell on the epaulets with the three stars. Why did an old East Frisian joke come to mind just then? One star meant the man could read. Two, that he could do arithmetic. And a grand total of three, that he could do both.

At long last, the policeman turned back to Martin, unfortunately once more with that penetrating look, underscored by those twitching eyebrows.

"Mr. Petzold, that is not your concern, and I would like you to let it be. However, I will tell you this much: Liv Ulldahl is fine. She has left her vacation house and is with her family. You may consider the matter closed." He turned to his computer once more.

Martin was speechless. There was apparently nothing he could do. He rose, intending to leave, but then decided to make one final attempt.

"So that means that you've spoken with Liv?"

"There's nothing more I can say."

"Then you haven't?"

This time, the policeman's eyebrows twitched even more furiously. Annoyed, he replied: "Liv Ulldahl is with her family. That's all I can tell you. Accept it once and for all!"

Martin was forced to admit defeat. "All right, then how does that affect my statement?"

"You entered a stranger's house uninvited and may have been knocked unconscious in the process."

"May have been? What about the wound on the back of my head?"

"Right. That can result from a blow."

"Are you suggesting I made it up?"

"I'm not suggesting anything. But let me give you one bit of advice: stay away from other people's houses! Good day, Mr. Petzold."

Martin left the police station. Somehow that hadn't gone at all as he had imagined.

7

He was puffing and panting, but he still kept up his pace and continued jogging the last few meters to the driveway. Once there, he cooled down and did some stretching exercises. It was critical now to keep fit and maintain his routines. He bounded up the steps to the massive front door, opened it, and stepped across the threshold. He went inside, removed his running shoes, and walked upstairs.

Saga met him on the stairs, barefoot as usual, her braids swinging back and forth. She chirped excitedly: "Papa, we got a call from a man who didn't know any Swedish. I had to speak English with him."

"What did he want?" he asked warily.

"To speak with Mama." Saga brushed a strawberry blond curl from her face.

"What did you tell him?"

Saga ran down the rest of the stairs. "Uh, that she was out of town."

"Hang on—wait a minute! Did he say anything else?"

Saga turned around: *"Nö."*

"What was the man's name?"

"Don't know," she called and kept going.

"Have you done your math homework?"

"Yes!" And she was gone.

He continued up the stairs, down the hall, through the spacious bedroom, and into the bathroom. Who could have called? The last thing he needed right now were more complications. Just one more week. It pissed him off that things had turned out like this. He wasn't at all happy about it. And yes, he had made some mistakes, like wanting to earn too much too fast. In the beginning, things had gone well, but by the time they backfired, there was no turning back. And he knew that he couldn't tell Liv what he had gotten himself into. Their relationship was no longer going well, and if she learned about the secrets he was keeping from her, she would immediately file for divorce. If that happened, he would lose everything.

The sale of the company was his best chance for solving all his problems in one go. Liv had left him no choice. There was no way he could have talked to her about this, and the Russians kept exerting more and more pressure. The appeal period hadn't suited them at all, which left the kidnapping as the only solution. Now his only hope was that Bosse wouldn't screw up, or he would be in deep shit. And that applied to two things. First, Liv would have to drop off the radar for that week, but he also didn't want anything happening to her. He prayed that Bosse wouldn't make any mistakes with the sleep medication dosage and that he would carefully follow his instructions.

He stepped into the shower and turned on the water. Having adjusted it to the perfect temperature, he was enjoying letting it flow from the huge showerhead over his sweat-covered body. He was feeling happier and happier with this bathroom—it had turned out great. Overall, the renovation of the villa had been worth it: it absolutely suited his social position. This was how a business owner should live. And no one would take that away from him.

Wednesday, September 23

8

Martin was back on the freeway again, with Stockholm still 200 kilometers away. He hadn't realized how large Sweden was—Stockholm wasn't even halfway to the northernmost end. It was a good thing Liv resided in Stockholm and not even farther away.

The day before had gone by fast. After his frustrating experience with the policeman, he had decided to forget the whole thing. After all, he barely knew the woman, and it was none of his business. This was also a foreign country. He had no authority here as a lawyer, and he didn't speak the language. Besides, he was on vacation—his goal was to relax. He wasn't about to let himself get knocked down again and then insulted by the police on top of it all.

Martin had tidied up the cabin and afterwards fired up the grill. Once the sun came out, it felt very pleasant on the covered terrace. He had made himself a small salad and grilled a large steak. To go with it, he had treated himself to a Swedish beer, which he bought at the supermarket. He had been skeptical, since its alcohol content was a mere 3.2 percent, but there was nothing else available at the supermarket. The woman at the checkout stand had explained that anything over 3.5 percent could only be obtained in a specialty shop. Still, the beer was drinkable, and you couldn't tell that it was a lighter version. And so, Martin had sat on the terrace, eaten his meal, and enjoyed the view across the meadow to the lake.

After that, Martin had some coffee and read. When it got too cool for him, he moved inside to the sofa, where he nodded off. It was three in the afternoon when he awoke, and the sun was still shining, so he decided to go for a walk. Along the way, he tried out a new path through the woods and, after a good half hour, was surprised to find himself back at Liv's house. At least, he hadn't gone that way on purpose. He was at the rear of the house, which meant that there was a second path leading to and from Liv's place—whatever relevance that might have.

The tool shed stood to Martin's right, while the terrace lay straight ahead. He deliberated for a while, observing the surroundings the whole time. Since nothing had moved, he risked taking another look. The tool shed was still unlocked, and the double doors were ajar. He detected no change inside. Even the cut pieces of rope were still lying next to the lawnmower.

What surprised him, however, was the state of the house. The terrace door was in fact locked. The previously overturned chair stood upright beside the table, and otherwise everything looked to be in perfect order. Even the terrace furniture had been put back in place. The red slippers were inside the house by the door, and from what he could tell by looking through the window, Liv's jacket no longer hung inside the cabinet in the hallway. There were no cars in sight. All of this confirmed the policeman's statements.

As he headed back to his cabin, Martin simply could not let the matter go—and that, despite his decision that morning to stop worrying about it and to focus on his vacation. Had Liv returned and fetched her things? If so, then who knocked him down? And why, above all? Or why hadn't she called him? It didn't add up in his view.

Back at the cabin, he had turned on his computer and gone on the Internet. The rest was easy. He googled the name Liv Ulldahl—and lo and behold, Sweden had web pages that listed every resident, complete with address, age, and phone number. Fortunately, Ulldahl was not an everyday name. In all of Sweden, that particular combination of first and last name occurred only once: Liv Maria Ulldahl, thirty-six years old, resident in the vicinity of Stockholm. She lived in the same house as one Thomas Lind, thirty-eight years old.

Martin had then gotten up his courage and called the house. After several rings, a girl answered the phone. Luckily, she spoke English—unusually well, in fact, for what he guessed was a girl around the age of ten. He had asked for Liv and received the answer that she had gone out of town. The girl's father was not at home, either. Martin hadn't dared ask her anything else.

Later, he had spent the evening thinking about the whole scene, unable to find a moment of peace. And yes, he had to admit again that he found the pursuit exciting. Anyway, since the assault, he had become personally involved, and besides, staying at the cabin the entire time had started to bore him. He confessed that he had another motive as well: he wanted to see those lovely blue eyes again.

By the time Martin awoke the next day, he had reached a decision: he would drive to Stockholm and get to the bottom of this story. His vacation time would certainly allow him to make a detour to Sweden's capital. If it turned out that Liv was all right, he would at least have had the chance to see the capital city. If she were not all right ... well, then he would have to see.

He had booked a room in a smaller hotel, packed a few things, and set off after breakfast. So there he was on the freeway again, driving at 110 kilometers per hour. At least, his GPS had no problem with the hotel's address, which meant that he could focus on driving and only needed to follow the "lady's" instructions. The one thing bothering him was the wound on the back of his head, which hurt the minute he leaned back on the headrest. Although the wound itself had healed, the spot was still tender. That was why he had kept the gauze bandage on, though he intended to remove it once he got to the hotel.

9

Martin's hotel room was small and simply furnished, but it was clean and sufficient for his needs. He unpacked his bag and focused on the bandage. From what he could see of the back of his head in the mirror, the wound was dry and hidden by his hair. That meant that he could now do away with the bandage. There was still some dried blood in his hair, so he decided to take a shower and wash it thoroughly. Now that he was in the city, he wanted to look decent.

Just as Martin had stepped out of the shower and started blow-drying his hair, he heard his cell phone ring. Still dripping wet, he ran into the room and pulled the phone out of his jacket pocket. He could see from the screen that the caller was his partner from his law practice.

"Hi, Jürgen."

"Hey, Martin. Sorry to bother you during your vacation, but I need your advice about the Wernicke case."

"No problem. Can I call you back in fifteen minutes? I just got out of the shower."

"OK, got it. I'll call back in twenty."

"Thanks. Talk to you then."

Martin went back to the bathroom and finished getting dressed while he waited for Jürgen's call. Finally, his cell phone rang again.

"Hi, Jürgen."

"Hey. Are you done getting dressed?"

"Yeah, I can talk now."

"So how are you doing up there in the far north? Aren't you bored in the woods?"

Jürgen had been skeptical on hearing Martin's vacation plans. Of course, Jürgen was the type who was more likely to want a lot of socializing and action on his vacation. He took regular trips to Mallorca, where he would throw wild parties on Ballermann, the island's party mile. It wasn't Martin's kind of thing at all.

"No, it's not even vaguely boring. I managed to get myself embroiled in some story that's been keeping me on my toes. That's why I drove to Stockholm today."

"Oh yeah? Let's hear it! What kind of story?"

Martin described to his partner how he had met Liv, how they had made a date for coffee, how she suddenly vanished, and how he was knocked unconscious while looking for her.

"Have you fallen for this woman, or what? Why are you getting so caught up in it?"

"No, I just thought she was nice—that's all."

"OK, then let the police handle it."

"They're not doing much of anything. They finally sent a patrol car to her vacation house after I was knocked unconscious there. The problem is that they found the door locked and the house all cleaned up. They also claim that Liv is back with her family in Stockholm. But when I called there, the daughter told me her mother had gone out of town."

"And that's why you're in Stockholm now?"

"Right."

"And what are you planning on doing there?"

"I don't know the specifics yet. In any case, I'm going to drive to the address to see if Liv is there. If she is, then that takes care of it."

"Well, good luck with that. I think it's great at any rate that you're not spending your entire vacation sitting around in that cabin. Stockholm is bound to be more interesting. Now about the Wernicke case ..."

This particular case involved a dispute over the boundary between two properties. Martin had originally taken it, but because of his upcoming vacation, he had passed it on to Jürgen. Jürgen, however, did not get along too well with Mr. Wernicke, and he wanted to advise him to drop the lawsuit. But Martin still believed that the suit stood a good chance of success, and he managed to convince Jürgen to pursue it.

"Thanks, Martin," Jürgen said after their discussion. "I'll talk to Wernicke again. He never mentioned the bit about the earlier fence. I'll keep you posted, although I can't imagine a whole lot happening before you get back."

"Hey," he continued, "about the thing with Liv ... If you really want to do something about it, shouldn't you get help from some local sources? I mean, you're all by yourself in a foreign country with a language you don't understand. Seems like it would be hard."

"Yeah, that's true. It is kind of awkward having to deal with everything in English. It's just that I don't know anyone here. Although what did you mean by help?"

"Well, I had someone professional in mind. You know how when we're stuck, we sometimes hire a private investigator for the case. Find someone like that in Stockholm. I'm sure it will cost a little something ... and, anyway, why are you so intent on sticking your neck out all the time?"

"That's true about the PI. I hadn't even thought of that. That could be a good option—thanks for the tip. But now I'm going to go see if Liv is home, after all."

They said goodbye, and Martin promised to call if anything new turned up in the Liv affair. Jürgen seemed to take a great interest in it, and Martin felt much better after talking to him about it. Jürgen never doubted his story at all—unlike the police, who evidently assumed it was all in Martin's head. Jürgen, on the other hand, had taken every bit of it seriously from the start. And Martin loved the tip about the private detective. Jürgen was right: he needed the help of someone who could speak the language and who knew his way around there. A couple of days' worth of assistance would hardly cost a fortune.

10

Martin climbed the last step out of the underground station and made his way to the hotel. He had gone sightseeing and had been going around Stockholm all afternoon. He was extremely impressed by the city: lots of water, lots of green, and not a single skyscraper. He had found a tourist brochure in his room and had taken it with him. It explained that Stockholm encompassed sixteen islands that were linked to each other and the mainland by bridges. He had taken the underground—or *tunnelbana,* as the natives called it—and gone to the Old Town, which was known as Gamla Stan. According to the brochure, it was on a small island in the heart of Stockholm. This island had also given the city its name: "Stockholm" translated as "Pile Island," from the fortification that was built in the thirteenth century by German workmen. One point of interest was that the island divided the fresh water from the salt water. Lake Mälaren, Sweden's third largest lake, was situated to the west of the island, while the waves of the Baltic Sea splashed against its shores on the other side.

Martin had walked all over the Old Town and was fascinated by its narrow alleys and the water all around. Until then, he had had no image at all of Stockholm, and he was truly enthralled. He had also been unaware that Stockholm was called "the Venice of the North," and he found it a fitting expression—the place was teeming with bridges.

Toward the end of his stroll, Martin crossed the bridge from the Old Town to the mainland and took a walk along Strandvägen. There was a quay wall here, and a number of boats of various sizes were either moored there or setting sail for the Baltic Sea. The promenade itself was lined with large trees, and the other side of the street featured a row of strikingly lovely nineteenth-century buildings, each with a unique design but all blending together: their height and style were perfectly harmonized, and everything looked very well maintained.

From these impressions alone, Martin decided to spend a few more days in Stockholm. Of course, his search for Liv was the other reason. Up to now, he had had no luck with that, but after his phone call with Jürgen, he had driven to Liv's Stockholm address, which his GPS had found right away. The house, which could easily be called a villa, was located north of Stockholm in an area with huge plots of land and a number of ostentatious homes and small castles. The villa itself had its own access road and was three stories high, with numerous small oriel windows and balconies and a gorgeous gable roof. Although the house was constructed of wood, it appeared solid and dignified, and it was in good condition despite its age. The front yard was also large and well cared for, with a spacious lawn and a number of trees.

Martin rang the doorbell several times, but no one answered. It looked as though no one was home. There was no car in sight, although he had no way of checking whether either of the two garages was occupied.

And so, Martin drove back to the hotel empty-handed, and on the way, he made up his mind to follow Jürgen's advice. The young lady at the hotel front desk was very helpful and promised to call some private investigators for him. And it seemed she succeeded, for the next day, as Martin was standing before the royal palace in the Old Town, his cell phone rang.

Having moved away from a group of chattering Japanese tourists to take the call, he could hear the voice of a man introducing himself in English. It was the head of a security agency that also conducted investigations for private individuals. Martin outlined his concerns, and the man on the other end explained the fee structure to him. The minimum charge would be for two days at 10,000 Swedish kronor per day plus expenses. That was no small sum, but Martin had reckoned on about that amount, and now he had gotten in deep enough that the money was no longer an issue. Besides, he wasn't exactly poor. Once Martin had agreed to the cost, the man made arrangements for him to meet with an associate that evening. The associate would call on him at the hotel at around 8:00 p.m. Martin was excited about the meeting.

11

She slowly came to and looked around. It was still the same room. Her head ached, and she was awfully thirsty. On the small table beside the bed stood a glass and a bottle of water. Still dazed, she propped herself up. Her hands trembled as she poured the water into the glass.

She was about to drink but then stopped short. Something was making her sleep all the time. Was there something in the water? Or in the food that was sitting there the last time she awoke? She looked about. There was no sink, and the toilet had no flushing mechanism but was a dry toilet instead. She had no choice: drink the water from the bottle, or go thirsty. But she had to drink something. She would see if she went right back to sleep again if she drank. At least, then she would know for sure that there was something in the water.

After drinking two glasses, her thirst was quenched. What day was today? And what time of day? It had to be daytime, because there was light coming through the shafts of the barred window. Even if it wasn't much, it was noticeably more than the last time she awoke.

She still couldn't believe that he had done this to her. How could she have been so mistaken about him? All right, she had always known he was ambitious, but that was what had held them together for so long since she, too, wanted to do more with the company. But that he simply wanted to sell it now ... She had fought it for a long time but had then given in. If only she hadn't signed! Now she sat there, trapped, with the appeal period about to expire. That bastard!

She thought back to how they had met. He had been so charming, always so carefree and easygoing. She had felt so comfortable with him. Her parents had also liked Thomas, even if her father had sometimes nitpicked—but he had done that with all her boyfriends.

The wedding was a dream, with her in that fabulous wedding dress, the festivities on the island in the Archipelago, and Thomas at her side. They had gotten along fine after that as well, always agreeing on everything. So when did it all change? Thomas had long since stopped being carefree. He had grown distant and no longer talked about what he was doing. What had gone wrong? How had it come to this? The children probably thought she was still at the vacation house. Hardly anyone would miss her. Damn! How could she have been so stupid?

She rose and walked over to the steel door. She jiggled the handle, but the door was locked tight. She pounded on the cold metal with both hands and shouted for help. No answer. That hadn't brought any results the last time, either.

She looked around. There was no way out of there. The window wasn't an option, and the rest was just concrete wall. The room had to be in a cellar somewhere. At least, it was warm in there. But there was no sound from the outside, and other than the bed, the camping toilet, and a small table, the space was utterly bare. Food and water arrived only while she slept, and she sadly never managed to stay awake for too long. He had to have repeatedly given her some kind of sleep inducer, which would also explain the headaches. But what could she do?

She found it impossible to grasp what he expected to gain from the kidnapping. Even if the appeal period had expired and the company been sold, there was no way he could believe that she would simply return to her life with him.

Or was someone other than him behind the whole thing? Was she abducted for the purpose of extracting ransom? That thought was even more menacing. After all, she hadn't seen who had drugged her with the chloroform. Still, that would be an odd coincidence that it happened now, of all times, just as the appeal period was about to end. And exactly one day after they had argued and she had announced that she would exercise her right to appeal.

She hardly knew which version she preferred: that her husband had done this to her or that a stranger had abducted her. The first would be the greatest disappointment of her life—what a betrayal! The second was fraught with uncertainty. Would she ever make it out of there in one piece? Would her husband want to pay the ransom money, especially now? That question alone showed her lack of trust in him. In the end, though, it seemed most likely that he was in fact the perpetrator. And if that was so, the relationship was over.

Damn, what a pile of crap! The tears welled up in her eyes. She felt totally sidelined and helpless. Never before had she been so low as now.

She was starting to feel drowsy again. The stuff must be in the water ...

12

The door to the elevator opened, and Martin walked up to the front desk. Standing there was a tall man, who now turned around.

"Martin Petzold?"

"Yes, that's me," Martin answered in English.

The man replied in German. "I'm Lars Olsson from the company Secure Assist."

"Oh, you speak German? Very pleased to meet you."

Lars had large hands, and his handshake was clean and strong.

"Would you like to go sit in the restaurant? Are you hungry?" Martin asked.

"Yes, I'd be glad to. I could use a bite to eat."

Martin led the way to the restaurant, with the detective walking beside him. He noticed that Lars was dragging his left leg a bit.

"Did you injure your leg?" he asked.

"It was a work-related accident," Lars answered, "from a long time ago."

Once inside the restaurant, they found a table in a corner, where they could talk undisturbed. The detective was casually dressed in jeans and a polo shirt. He had hung his leather jacket on an empty chair and now sat down. Even seated, he appeared unusually tall.

After the waiter took their orders, Martin said to Lars, "It's none of my business, but may I ask what sort of work-related accident it was?"

"No problem. A lot of people ask that." Lars smiled to himself. "I was with the police force for ten years and was shot during an arrest. My knee has been stiff ever since."

"Oh, I'm sorry to hear that. Is that why you now work as a private detective?"

"Yes. After my rehabilitation, I was switched to desk duty, but I didn't like it. So I looked around for other options. I've been with Secure Assist for three years, and it's a lot more exciting."

The man came across as honest. He had friendly blue eyes, and his angular chin gave him a straightforward look.

"May I ask what sort of cases you handle for Secure Assist?"

"Oh, it varies a lot," Lars explained. "Most of our work is with companies that are having security issues or that need the lowdown on private individuals. And then, there's always one type or other of the standard life partner surveillance to uncover possible infidelity issues."

"Well, then my case will be different."

"Could be. So far, I've only been given a brief description. From what I understand, a woman has suddenly vanished. We do get that kind of thing once in a while, where we have to track someone down, but it's usually when the person is in debt and is trying to abscond."

"I see. No, it doesn't seem to be that sort of thing."

"So tell me," Lars said, "please tell me the whole story—from the beginning."

Once the waiter had served their drinks, Martin complied with his dinner partner's wish and told him about his vacation, his acquaintance with Liv, and what had happened after that. He did his best to leave nothing out. The detective paid close attention without interrupting, his blue eyes riveted on Martin the entire time.

"... right, so after I found no one at the house, I decided to get help since I don't know my way around here at all and I don't speak the language. And that's why we're sitting here now."

Lars leaned back in his chair and was staring at the wall. Was he skeptical? Did he not want to take the assignment? Martin sat and waited.

After some time, the detective leaned forward again—an impressive movement, given the size of his body—and looked Martin in the eye.

"What I can offer you is to do an Internet investigation and to observe the family at the same time. Depending on how that turns out, we can contact their acquaintances or speak with the family directly. Best case, we find Liv Ulldahl. Does that work for you?"

"Yes, that sounds good. I would also like to be closely involved with the work. Maybe I could even help with certain parts. I don't have anything else to do."

"We should be able to swing that."

"The fact that you know German is also obviously a big plus. How did you come to speak it so well?"

"My mother is German. We spoke her native language a lot at home."

"Ah, that's why."

"So from what I can tell, we're in business," Lars said. "My boss has already explained the financial aspect to you. The only thing left for you to do is to sign the contract."

Lars took a roll of documents from his jacket and laid the contract out before Martin. It consisted of two copies of two pages in English. Martin read through the contents. Everything was in order, and the price was also correct. He signed both copies—Secure Assist had already signed.

Lars took one copy and reached his large hand across the table.

"Here's to working together!"

Just then, the waiter arrived with the food. Martin had ordered fillet of chicken, and Lars got something cold—it looked like raw ground beef with an egg on top.

"So since we'll be working so closely together, I have a request." Lars looked at Martin and paused.

Martin wondered what it could be. "Yes?"

"I think my German is pretty good, but I have a problem. The formal mode of address is hard for me. I've never used it correctly, and it doesn't exist in Swedish. Do you think we could use the informal version of 'you' when speaking to each other?"

"Yes, absolutely. I'm not that formal, either." That was no problem at all for Martin.

"Great, then call me Lars!"

"Martin. Cheers!"

"Skål."

Now that that was settled, the two men turned to their food. In answer to Martin's questions about his life, Lars explained that his father came from Norrland, in the northern part of Sweden, where they still had a vacation home. In Lars's childhood days, his family had spent the summers there, usually with his relatives from Germany. The sun never set there in the summertime. Martin couldn't begin to imagine that.

Over coffee after dinner, the conversation turned once more to the case.

"Martin, do you have any theories about what happened to Liv?" Lars asked.

"No, I don't have any real theories. But from the start, it seemed to me that something was off. I mean, would they have knocked me unconscious otherwise? Or am I missing something?"

"No, you're right. That part of the story struck me the most. If that hadn't happened, we should definitely be able to find a plausible explanation."

"You mean something like Liv forgot about her date with me for some reason and suddenly had to go out of town?"

"Yeah, exactly. Maybe someone came by before you were supposed to meet. She rode off with the person, came back afterwards, and then got ready for her trip."

"Maybe. But what woman leaves the house without her purse, wallet, and cell phone?"

"Yeah, that is strange, but if she didn't go far and the person was a close acquaintance ... No, I'm sticking to the fact that the assault on you is the most striking part."

"Do you have any doubts about it? I'd be happy to show you my wound."

"No, no, I have absolutely no reason to doubt it. I'm just trying to analyze the situation. I don't think you would be taking such a strong stand on the matter otherwise. Or ... or

50

have the two of you gotten a little closer than what you've let on so far?" Lars gave Martin a piercing look.

Martin could feel himself getting warm as his face flushed red. Why did this question embarrass him? There was absolutely nothing to hide.

"No, honestly, I've told you everything. I admit that I took an instant liking to Liv and was looking forward to seeing her again. But that's all there is to it. And in the meantime, I've even learned that she has a family ..."

"OK, sorry to ask these questions, but I always like to know how things stand with my clients' motives. For most of them, the issue is either fear, money, or hurt feelings. In your case, though, none of that fits."

"That's true. To be honest, I'm not entirely sure myself why I've stuck with it to this extent. On the one hand, I'm sure it has something to do with liking Liv. On the other, the fact that I was assaulted in her house and bound hand and foot in the garden shed—that sort of thing has never happened to me before. I'd love to know the reason for it."

"Yeah, I can understand that. So let's go through it one more time. What could have happened?"

Martin thought it over. Lars was good. He didn't let up.

"Someone could have abducted her," Martin suggested.

"Yeah, but then why did he come back the next day and knock you down?"

"I don't know. Maybe the abductor noticed that he had forgotten Liv's things—her bag, cell phone, and such."

"That's possible. But then that doesn't sound like a pro."

Lars was right. It was definitely the work of an amateur.

"So, Martin, in essence, we're saying the following: we don't believe that Liv knocked you down and tied you up."

"No, never."

"Which means that whatever the reason for Liv not being there the first day, there had to be someone else in the house, someone who knocked you unconscious and tied your hands and feet. Since he failed to notify the police, he must have been there illegally. I'm assuming it was a man since the person managed to drag you from the house to the garden shed. After that, he put the house in order, locked the door, and took all of Liv's personal items with him. If that was in fact the kidnapper, he may have wanted to cover his tracks."

Martin had to agree. No matter what angle they took, they couldn't come up with a better explanation.

Lars had to go, but he promised to get in touch the next day. The two men said goodbye.

Martin was pleased. His impression of Lars had been good, and he was eager to see what the following day would bring.

Thursday, September 24

13

The minutes ticked away, but nothing happened. Lars simply sat in the car and watched Liv's house.

He had been there since seven in the morning. The father—Liv's husband—had taken the two children to school. That was at about 7:40 a.m., and the school was just five minutes away. After that, the husband had driven to his company in Täby, and Lars had followed. He appeared to be some company bigwig, judging from his reserved parking space right outside the door, which was not the norm in Sweden. Lars had waited there for an hour, and since the man never showed again, he had driven back to the house. For he had noticed something interesting: as the children were leaving the house, a woman briefly appeared and handed them a container to take along. He assumed that it held their sandwiches or whatever kids brought as breaktime snack these days. But that didn't matter. It was much more important to find out who this woman was. He hadn't gotten a good look at her, but from what he could see, she had long, dark hair. That was why he had assumed she wasn't Liv and had decided to follow the father and kids. But now he wanted to know exactly who she was.

Unfortunately, there was nothing to see, even with binoculars. There was no one at the window or in the garden. According to the people search-engine records—

there were several good sites, and Lars had already checked three—the only adults living there were Liv Ulldahl and Thomas Lind. Could Liv have colored her hair or even been wearing a wig? Lars didn't think so.

Something about this case was odd. The German guy was right about that, at least, even if Lars didn't fully buy his motive. He was definitely smitten with this woman Liv. Something may even have happened between them. After all, our friend Martin had turned pretty damn red when Lars mentioned it. Oh well, that shouldn't make any difference to him—the lady appeared to have vanished in any case. Or not. They would see.

Lars had Elin, his colleague at the office, do an Internet search on the Ulldahl-Lind family while he took care of the observing. So there he sat, waiting to see if anything would transpire. This part of the job was never fun for him: patience was not his strong suit. But, as always, every job had its downside. With the police, it had been the lousy administrative work, all the stuff you had to fill out and report on. He didn't miss that at all. But the field operations were great. And he also missed his colleagues—here he was mostly on his own. The upside was that his salary was somewhat better, which came in handy, especially now that Lisa had just gone on maternity leave. Besides, Lisa was much calmer since he had switched to detective work. Before, she was often afraid for him. And anyway, with his injured leg, he had a hard time keeping up whenever the need for physical action arose.

But now Lars had waited long enough. The time had come to act. He got out of the car and walked up the driveway and the five steps leading to the front door. The door had both a bell and a large knocker. He decided to try the bell. The ding-dong sound was loud and clear, though it was only after the second try that Lars heard the approach of footsteps. The door opened slowly, and the black-haired woman came out. She appeared to be Asian and was no older than twenty. This was definitely not Liv. Her dark eyes studied him with a searching and uncertain look.

"Hello. I'm looking for Liv Ulldahl," Lars began.

"Not here," she replied softly. She had an accent.

"When could I see her? Will she be back later?"

"No." She was about to close the door.

"Wait! It's important. Liv Ulldahl ordered something from me, and I was supposed to deliver it today." This trick usually worked, and this time was no exception. The door opened again.

"You can give to me." The woman held out her hand.

"No, I'm sorry, that won't do. I have to give it to her personally."

She apparently didn't like that. Her look betrayed disappointment. "Why?"

"Liv insisted. It's something valuable. When will she be back?"

"Do not know. You can call?"

"Yes, I have her cell phone number and have tried it a number of times, but her cell phone appears to be turned off. Do you have another number for her?"

"Maybe. One moment!"

She shut the door. All Lars could do was hope that she would return. He was in luck. She opened the door and gave him a slip of paper. Before he could even say thank you, the door shut once more. She was evidently glad to be rid of him. On the slip of paper was a number, written in large, round figures. That was something, anyway.

Lars went back to the car and reflected on the woman he had just seen. She had to be an au pair. The Ulldahl-Lind family appeared to have plenty of dough, and an au pair would represent the least of that. Still, she came across as being very uneasy. He knew that his size could often have an intimidating effect, but he could usually make up for that by being friendly. It didn't work in this case.

Back in the car, Lars immediately entered the number. It wasn't a cell phone number—that much was clear. The area code was for the south of Sweden. Lars let it ring a long time. No answer and no voicemail.

Lars called Elin and asked her to find the address to the number. She called back less than two minutes later—Elin was effective. It was the number for the vacation house. No wonder no one picked up. He then asked Elin what she had found out from the Ulldahl search, to which she replied that it would be worth his while to stop by the office. She didn't want to say anything more—she was keeping him in suspense. Lars started the car.

14

They were sitting in the hotel restaurant again, this time for coffee. Following a tip from Lars, Martin had taken a three-hour boat tour through the Stockholm Archipelago. He didn't regret it. There were thousands of islands, abundant forest and cliffs, and a host of pretty houses that nearly always blended with the landscape. It would have been even more pleasant with company, but Martin enjoyed it all the same, especially since it was a sunny day. Lars had called at around noon, and he and Martin had agreed to meet here at the restaurant.

Lars wasted little time on formalities. Instead, he immediately started spreading out a long series of web page printouts.

"This is an interesting family, Martin. Liv Ulldahl is married to Thomas Lind. I don't know what it's like in Germany, but in Sweden both spouses can keep their own last names. They both come from wealthy families. They own several companies, the major ones being a construction company and a property management firm. Their combined fortune is estimated at several hundred million Swedish kroner. That's many millions of euros."

Martin hadn't anticipated this. The villa was impressive all right, but neither Liv nor the summerhouse had smelled of big bucks.

"The construction company is the largest," Lars went on. "They build grandiose houses throughout Scandinavia and also in Germany. This company is from Liv Ulldahl's family. She inherited it from her parents, who both died in a car crash five years ago. Liv was their only child. Both parents were in their early fifties." Lars indicated the relevant articles as he spoke. Most were written in Swedish, but a few were in English.

"That," Lars added, "makes the Ulldahls, and especially Liv, clear targets for kidnapping and ransom demands."

Martin nodded. "That's true, if they have that much money. But then shouldn't they have appropriate protection? I noticed nothing along those lines at either the summerhouse or the villa."

Lars agreed. "Yes, in another country, the Ulldahls would definitely have had that. In Sweden, the people are still somewhat naive about the dangers facing the rich and famous. You'd be amazed at the type of people you can run into in Stockholm—right in the middle of town, without any type of protection: government ministers, actors, wealthy business owners. The only ones under constant guard are the members of the royal family, although as far as I know, there's never been an assassination attempt on any of them."

"All right," said Martin, "but I would think that the summerhouse belonging to such a wealthy family would be different from Liv's."

"Right. They have that, too."

Lars laid some more printouts in front of Martin.

"The Ulldahls have a total of five houses in their possession, or I should say five that we know of. First, there's the villa in Danderyd here in Stockholm. You've already been there. Then there's a gigantic property in the Archipelago, complete with a villa and adjacent buildings, all of it right on the water. Take a look!"

Lars showed Martin a photo of a large estate with a jetty, an enormous motorboat, and its own private swimming area.

"And then they own another house in the mountains near Åre, a popular Swedish ski resort." There was also a picture of that, a modern house in the countryside, surrounded by mountain peaks.

"Number four is a finca on Mallorca." The photo showed a picturesque blue sky over a Spanish country estate that was nestled among the hills.

"And finally, there's the summerhouse in Småland— where you first met Liv." Lars had brought a picture of that, too, and Martin recognized Liv's house.

"Wow, I wasn't expecting this." Martin still couldn't fathom it. Had Liv been staying at one of the other residences, he would probably never have met her. But why was she staying in the small vacation house?

"How does the little summerhouse fit in with the others? And why was Liv there, of all places?" asked Martin.

"Good question. We don't know yet. But vacation houses of that sort are a tradition in Sweden and are usually passed down within the family. They're often filled with memories, which is why the families never sell them."

"Like your family's summerhouse in Norrland?" Martin remembered their conversation from the previous evening.

"Exactly. I'd never sell that, either." Lars was firm on that point.

Martin was thinking things over. Then he said, "So there's still the question as to why Liv was at the summerhouse in the middle of September, when school had already started—and all alone, no less."

Lars knit his brow. "Yeah, that is a bit strange. And it gets even stranger when you see what's going on with the Ulldahls at the moment."

Now what? Martin held his breath.

Lars pulled out two more printouts from his case. "It looks as though they're about to sell the construction company. We found two articles on that in the financial papers. One of them even maintains that they've already signed their names to the deal. If that's true, then Thomas and Liv are selling the company to a Russian firm. I find that pretty unusual."

Martin took a look at the articles, but they were in Swedish. "Sorry, I'm afraid I don't understand any of it. Could you translate some of it for me?"

Lars summarized the articles for Martin. Liv was the company's principal owner and the chairman of the board. Her husband also sat on the board of directors and owned thirty percent of the stock. The article gave no reason for the sale, although one of the journalists speculated that Thomas and Liv had not been comfortable with the way the business was being run. Liv's parents had apparently taken a very hands-on approach, and it was only after their deaths that Liv and her husband got involved. They may have discovered that the business didn't particularly suit them, although the company had no major problems. According to the second article, the sales and performance figures were steady and even slightly on the rise.

Martin took some time to let it all sink in. "All right," he finally said, "then let me summarize what I've understood so far. Liv comes from a wealthy family. After the death of her parents, she takes on the management of the business but then decides to sell it after a while. At that exact point in time, she drives—all by herself—to their remote summerhouse, where she vanishes without a trace. So what do we get from that?"

"Let me briefly tell you a few other things."

Lars gave an account of his observations that morning and of his encounter with the young Asian woman.

"When we put it all together," he concluded, "we come up with two explanations: an innocent version and a serious one. The innocent one is that Liv disappeared of her own choice to escape the journalists, who would be plying her for information on the company sale. The alternate explanation is our hypothesis from yesterday: abduction for the express purpose of extracting ransom. What we didn't know yesterday was that you could extract quite a bit from the Ulldahls. That version would also explain why the family has said nothing about Liv's whereabouts. Either the police are involved or the family is trying to solve the issue themselves by paying the ransom. In either case, neither the family nor the police would want to admit anything to an outsider."

Martin took a sip of coffee. "I'm totally with you on the second version. The first still leaves us with the question as to why someone knocked me unconscious."

"Maybe Liv had to leave suddenly because the journalists had caught wind of where she was. Could be a bodyguard picked up her things and thought you were a paparazzo or an intruder."

"And then tied me up in the garden shed?"

"I admit that doesn't fit. But we shouldn't commit to the kidnapping version just yet. There may still be an innocent explanation."

"Agreed. I don't want to get stuck on it, either. I don't need to worry if it's the innocent version. I just want to keep investigating in case there's a problem. So let's assume there's been a kidnapping. What can we do? Or would we be better off staying out of it? I mean, do you think we could be jeopardizing a potential negotiation and delivery?"

"That depends on what we do. But you're right. We need to be careful."

"Well, I have no intention of getting involved in a kidnapping affair, but I'd still like to know what's going on here. Is there any way we can find out without creating too much of a disturbance?"

Lars said that he could easily understand Martin's concern.

"Absolutely. We haven't made direct contact so far except for my conversation with the au pair, and that won't attract attention. I think we should keep things as they are: just stay passive and observe. Besides, we can certainly find out more through the Internet. My colleague Elin is already on it."

"OK, I've paid for two days, anyway, which means that we'll continue tomorrow in any case. And if you come up with as much tomorrow as you did today, then it will be worth it. But what specifically should we do now?"

"First, let me talk to Elin. Something new may have come up in the meantime. Then I'll plan the next few steps. I can call you tomorrow morning to discuss things. Would that work?"

"Yes, great! Maybe I could also take on an assignment."

"I'm sure we can come up with something for you. OK then, it's a plan."

Lars rose to his full height and stretched his bad leg. The two men took their leave, and Lars exited the restaurant.

Martin watched him as he headed toward the door, his movements a bit awkward because of his stiff leg.

"Good man," Martin thought. "He came up with a ton of information. And in such a short time."

15

Lars had just relieved his colleague Marie, who wasn't at all happy that he had arrived so late. She needed to bring her children to a sports event, and Lars was supposed to have taken her place an hour earlier. But what could he do? His boss had told him that the conversation with Martin took priority. And had it been up to him, he wouldn't be there at all. This particular surveillance was utterly dull. They had been at it for an entire week already, with no results. It had to do with a company that suspected one of their associates of selling some company secrets to a competitor. So far, though, they had no evidence of any contact. The associate in question was still at the office, and Lars was supposed to observe what he did after work. Oh well, at least, it gave him a chance to give Elin a call.

Elin picked up right away. "Elin."

"Hey, Elin, it's Lars. I was wondering if you had learned anything new."

"Does the Pope wear a funny cap? What do you think I do here? Polish my nails all day?"

Man, she could be cocky. Sometimes she got a little stressed.

"No, Elin, I don't. I just know that you're also working on other cases."

"Well, fine. Just a sec!" That seemed to pacify her. Lars had obviously come up with the right response, although he knew that in reality she probably had no other cases at the moment.

There was a rustling sound, and then Elin was back on the line.

"So first of all, there's the issue with all those houses. Liv and Thomas bought some of them on their own, like the villa in Danderyd and the cabin in the mountains. But the finca in Mallorca and the estate in the Archipelago were inherited by Liv from her parents."

"OK, and the summerhouse in Småland?"

"Liv inherited that from her grandmother—eleven years ago, in fact."

"Right, that fits. Does that mean that the grandmother wasn't that rich?"

"No, she wasn't. Both the fortune and the construction company were from the father's side of Liv's family. The grandmother in question was on her mother's side. She was a kindergarten teacher, and her husband was also a teacher. They both lived in Jönköping, so not too far from the summerhouse."

"So the summerhouse belongs exclusively to Liv?"

"Yes, the same as the properties on Mallorca and in the Archipelago. On the other hand, Liv and her husband Thomas each own half of the houses in Danderyd and Åre. On top of that, her husband has a summerhouse in Dalarna that he co-owns with his sister and brother. I didn't know that before because at first I only searched for properties belonging to Liv."

"Good work, Elin."

"Thanks, Lars." She softened. "There's more." Elin giggled.

"Let's hear it!"

"I called the house on Mallorca and spoke with the manager or caretaker. The Ulldahls were last there in the spring. The manager is usually informed whenever they plan on going there, but he wasn't aware of any such plans."

"Great! Did he just come out and tell you that?"

"Well, no, it wasn't quite that easy. Maybe you remember that I speak a little Spanish, which definitely helped. So I pretended to be a travel agent and asked if the house was available for rent. Of course, it wasn't, but that opened the way for a conversation."

"Good job!" Lars needed to keep Elin in a good mood, and she needed the compliments. But all that aside, she was genuinely effective.

"Thanks, I'm good, aren't I?" She giggled again. "Unfortunately, I had no luck with the places in Åre or the Archipelago. No one answered. The house in Dalarna has no phone service. Don't know how to get any further there."

"I'll deal with the house in the Archipelago and the one in Dalarna, Elin, if you can find out whether anyone is living in the ski cabin. I'm sure you'll find a way."

"I'll come up with something."

"Can you also email me the address of the house in Dalarna?"

"What do you think I am? Already done. Just check your email!"

"Thanks! Have a great night! Call me as soon as you hear anything about Åre."

"Right. Talk to you then."

16

His cell phone rang. This late at night? The screen showed it as being Lars. There was also a warning that Martin needed to charge the battery. Earlier that evening, he had spoken with his partner Jürgen and had forgotten to charge the phone after the call. Of course, Jürgen had been glad that Martin had followed his advice and hired a private investigator. What Martin had learned in that one day was also the subject of their long talk. Jürgen now thought he should stick with it for a while.

Martin picked up the phone. "Hello, Lars."

"Good evening, Martin. Hope I'm not calling too late?"

"No, no problem. I haven't gone to bed yet."

"I tried several times earlier, but the line was always busy. I also want to get an early start tomorrow. I have news for you."

Lars summarized Elin's findings. "Elin is now trying to find out if there's anyone staying at the ski cabin. She's very clever. She'll find a way. Liv is apparently not in Danderyd, so all we have left are the houses in the Archipelago and in Dalarna. Dalarna is the Bavaria of Sweden in a way. That's where the small red horse figurines come from, the ones they sell in every souvenir shop. It's about a four-hour drive from Stockholm, which is why I think it's unlikely that Liv is there. But tomorrow morning, I'll be driving over to the house in the Archipelago to see if anyone is staying there. What do you think?"

"Sounds good. How will you get there? Do you have to take a boat?"

"No, it's on one of the islands that's reachable by car. You drive over the bridge to Värmdö, and then you take a car ferry. It will probably take an hour and a half, provided I don't have to wait too long for the ferry. I should hopefully be back around noon, and I'll give you a call at that time."

"You know, I'd also like to do something to help. Do you think I could check out the house in Dalarna?"

"Hmm, that's a long way out in the woods. I'm not too thrilled with the idea of having you poking around there all by yourself. Besides, I don't think Liv is there. The house belonged to her husband's family, and she has better options."

"Yes, but if she's not there, then nothing can happen. And I'd also love to do something. Stockholm is nice, but I didn't come here to sightsee."

"Right, well, if you absolutely want to, but you'll be on the road all day. Maybe you'd better plan on spending the night."

"That's no problem. That way, I'll get to see more of Sweden."

"OK, I'll email you the directions. Your GPS won't be able to find it. And if you can't figure it out, give me a call!"

"OK, great! Any tips on what I should do when I'm there, Lars?"

"It's important to maintain a hands-off approach, Martin. Be sure to park your car a good distance away and then walk from there. Keep an eye out for any indication that someone is staying at the house. You can also talk to some of the neighbors, assuming there are any. If you find anything at all—for instance, if there's a car there—call me! Do not do anything before talking to me, please!"

"OK, got it."

"Good. Then we'll hear from each other tomorrow. Have a good trip, and lots of luck!"

"Ciao."

Martin hung up and placed the phone on the charger. He would be needing a fully loaded battery tomorrow. He was looking forward to the coming day so that he could finally be doing something again, even if nothing came of it. To search for the house on his own and look around there would be exciting.

Martin took another beer out of the minibar and thought about the best way to organize his trip: four hours to drive there, two to find the house and look around, and then he would find a place to eat. It was possible to do all of that and drive back in one day. But it would be a long day, and the thought of eight hours of driving didn't exactly send him into raptures. He decided to check out in the morning and spend the night in Dalarna. He was on vacation, after all.

Friday, September 25

17

Martin's GPS had indicated two possible routes, so he decided on the longer route with a larger section of freeway. It was supposed to be quicker than the shorter route by county road. Of course, it took him half an hour to get through the rush hour traffic. This was obviously not the vacation season. Friday was a regular workday, and at eight in the morning, there was plenty of action on the streets. After finally making it out of Stockholm, Martin headed straight north, past the airport and through several cities with funny names: Uppsala, Gävle, and Falun.

The second half of the route passed into much higher altitudes, similar to the Central German Uplands. There seemed to be a lot of winter sports activity here. Shortly before leaving Falun, Martin noticed a ski jump and a large number of parking spaces to his right. For some reason, the name Falun rang a bell. Hadn't the Nordic World Ski Championships taken place there the year before?

Martin then stopped in a place called Bjursås to fill his gas tank and have lunch at a small restaurant. That went fairly quickly. You went up to the counter, picked out your meal and drinks, paid at the end, and carried everything on a tray to a table. The food was all right. He had opted for the famous *köttbullar,* or meatballs. Oddly enough, they were served with cranberries—a strange combination.

After lunch, he still had an hour's drive. Shortly after Bjursås, he had to exit the county road, and at that point the roads got narrower and narrower. He now found himself on a dirt road in the middle of the forest. Martin was glad he had gotten directions from Lars. His GPS hadn't been able to find it, so he had driven to the nearest village and followed Lars's directions from there. Unfortunately, he only had them on his cell phone, which was a bit inconvenient because of the small screen. Nor did the fact that it was raining make things any easier.

Martin had been following the dirt road for more than eight kilometers now, and only once did he pass a small cluster of houses. Otherwise, there was nothing but forest. But the road was fairly straight, and apart from the occasional small rise, it was also flat. It seemed to run between two mountains, which was probably why it was called Dalvägen. Martin had looked that up. It meant exactly what he thought: Valley Road.

Here came another couple of houses up ahead. You could always tell from the mailboxes, which were mounted on a wall specifically constructed for that purpose and which served all the properties in the area. The wall was right on the main road, and from there, several small roads led to the individual plots. Here, too, the houses were set far apart. He could see only two showing through the trees—all the others must have been situated farther back.

Martin stopped by the row of mailboxes, some of which were held shut with rubber bands. Those houses were probably vacant after the summer months, and the rubber bands were supposed to discourage junk mail. Above the wall were the words "Dalvägen/Moskogen." That was right.

But there were no names at all on the mailboxes. They were simply numbered 1 to 12. That was bad, because he was looking for 16 Dalvägen.

Should he keep driving? Maybe "Dalvägen/Moskogen" still had a part two, even though the directions said it was the second settlement after about ten kilometers on the dirt road. Martin picked up his cell phone to call Lars. Crap—no connection. Well, no wonder. He was out in the middle of nowhere.

Martin took a closer look at the mailboxes. Sure enough, on one of them—the one with the number 6—was a small sticker that read "Melander, Dalvägen 12." So he was right, after all. Number 16 must be close by.

Martin looked around. Two small roads, just wide enough for a car, branched off from the dirt road on the other side, and there by the two roads were some small signs with the numbers 8 and 10. Martin kept driving. After a while, there were more small turnoffs, not all of them with numbers. Finally, he saw the number 14. Martin decided to park the car there. He drove a short way down the little road and left his Audi there. He pulled on his rain jacket, walked back to the dirt road, and followed it farther down. Another dead-end road appeared, but unfortunately with no number. After the next turn came a sign with the number 18. So the road before it had been the right one, after all.

Martin walked back and followed the turn onto the dead-end road with no sign. After about 200 meters, the forest opened into a clearing, and he found himself before a cabin. It was constructed of sturdy wooden beams and painted black with green shutters. Farther to the left was another small house that probably had only one room.

There was also a shed. They were all built in the same style, with the same black color. The whole place looked utterly deserted. There were no cars, everything was locked, and the property was all tidied up. Martin walked around, peering through the windows, but the buildings were all dark inside, and there was no one in sight.

All right, so this was probably it. He and Lars hadn't expected Liv to be there, anyway, assuming this was the right house. There was no number, no sign with a name, and no other clues as to the owner. And trying to find the neighbors was futile—it seemed the homes were all vacant summerhouses.

Martin felt disappointed now. He hadn't imagined that his search would end up so solitary and fruitless. He slowly walked back to the dirt road.

Shortly before reaching it, he heard the sound of a motor. Through the trees, he could see a black pickup truck come off the narrow road on the other side of the main dirt road, turn onto the same road, and hit the gas. Someone apparently lived there. As Martin came to the dirt road, all he could still make out were the taillights of the pickup truck. What should he do? He decided to try the neighbor's house, the one that the pickup truck had come from. That sign also had no number.

Martin got back in his car and veered onto the narrow road, driving cautiously because the road made a number of turns. He had expected a house to appear after several hundred meters, but that wasn't the case. Not for another three kilometers would he see the house in the distance. At that point, there was a slight widening of the road, so he decided to leave the Audi there. He wanted to avoid driving onto the property.

As he walked the final hundred meters, Martin was glad he had worn his boots. The ground was rather muddy.

18

Liv awoke once again. She still felt somewhat dazed from the sleep medication and needed a few minutes to clear her head. Then she sat up. On the small table before her were a plastic water bottle, some sandwiches, and a glass. She stared at the glass. This couldn't be. Had he found it? She needed to check right away. She walked over to the window, opened it, and reached through the bars. She carefully felt around to her right—and there it was. She took hold of the glass and slowly pulled it in.

Yes, her plan had worked. The glass was nearly half filled with rainwater. It wasn't much, but it was better than nothing. She drank it down in one gulp. Then she placed the glass back in the air shaft in front of the window. She had set it so that no one could see it from inside. That way, she had bought herself time—time when she wasn't asleep. Each time she had awoken, she was thirsty, and every time she had drunk from the bottle of water, she had soon grown drowsy again. Now she should be able to get by for a while without drinking. Besides, it was still raining. That meant the glass would fill some more.

Finally—she could dig into the sandwiches. She was

hungry, but she felt better with a bit more control over the situation. Once she was done eating, she planned her next move. She was betting on her kidnapper expecting to find her asleep, so she arranged the blanket and pillow on the bed so that it would look at first glance as though she were wrapped inside the covers. Then she positioned herself on the other side of the door, although she quickly realized that she needed something to use as a weapon. She looked around. Unfortunately, there was very little in this room. Then she hit upon an idea: the small table.

She set the glass and plastic water bottle on the floor. What could her kidnapper have thought when he saw the glass was missing? That had been the weak point in her plan. There was a chance he could have looked for it or become suspicious in some other way. But he didn't. The plan had worked. He had merely put a new one in its place.

Liv picked up the table and swung it around in the room. Yes, you could definitely slam someone with that. It might be a bit heavy, but she would only have to swing it once. Now, however, it was time to wait.

For a long time, nothing happened. Liv must have been waiting at least an hour when she heard an engine start outside and a car drive off. She opened the window to hear better. The car was apparently leaving, because the sound of the engine rapidly faded until she could no longer hear it. The rain also appeared to have stopped. She checked the glass—a small mouthful of rainwater had collected inside it. Liv drank greedily. She wouldn't be able to go far on that before having to resort to the water bottle again.

She leaned against the wall. What did this mean now? Someone had just driven away. She didn't know how long the drug lasted—probably several hours. Worst case, that meant it would be another few hours before her kidnapper returned to check on her. Crap, she couldn't hold out that long without water. It didn't matter. She would try.

Liv shut the window and sat down beside the door with the table close at hand. Then she waited. With any luck, someone would soon come. When that happened, she would put every ounce of strength she had into the blow. She knew it was her only chance. She would see what she did after that. Of course, if there were several guards, her chances were bleak. Never mind. She would have to risk it, anyway.

Suddenly, she heard a noise at the door. Were there two guards, after all? If so, it was a good thing the other had driven away—she would only need to worry about one. She got in place, reached for the small table, and prepared to strike.

The key turned. Liv held her breath. Slowly, the door opened. The guard could now see the bed. Hopefully, the crumpled blanket would fool him. Yes, the man stepped into the room. Liv saw a blue parka and swung. The blow didn't hit as planned—the table was too heavy. But she caught him on the shoulder, and the force of the blow made him lose his balance, fall, and land near the bed. Liv didn't lose one moment. She threw open the door, dashed out, and slammed it behind her with a loud bang. The key was still in the lock, so she quickly turned it. Done. The guard was locked inside. Her sole hope now was that no one else was there.

Liv looked around. She found herself in a large basement with shelving on the walls. It was a big mess, with cartons, bottles, old furniture, and lampshades strewn around. There was a strong smell of must. Some steps led upwards, and there was another door on the same level. Maybe that one led outside. Liv tried the handle. Locked. But there was even a key here. She turned it, and the door opened, though with some difficulty. No, this was just another room in the basement, smaller than the one she was in and utterly filthy. She closed the door again. All that remained were the steps that led upstairs.

It was a stone stairway, so at least it couldn't creak. At the top was a door that was halfway open. Liv peered inside. There was a corridor with a kitchen at the end. This was the only way out. She looked around and cautiously continued. Not a sound could be heard, but her heart was pounding so hard she could feel it in her throat. Someone, she thought, must be lurking around every corner. But when she looked, there was no one there. Once she calmed down, she went to the kitchen sink and turned on the faucet. She drank directly from it—for a long time. How good that felt! It tasted like iron, but at least it contained no sedatives.

It was the same view from almost every window: the house was apparently in the middle of the forest. It was quite large for a summer cabin. There was even an upper story, but Liv had no wish to explore. She just wanted to get away from there. Who knew when the other guy would return?

The furniture was old, and the house was messy and not exactly clean. There was an open bottle of whiskey on the coffee table. And then she spotted her things: her leather jacket, shoes, and purse, complete with her wallet, all her credit cards, and her ID. Oh, and then there was her cell phone, but of course the battery was dead. She pulled on her jacket, slipped on her shoes, and took her cell phone and purse. She opened the front door and hurried down the three steps to the yard. There was chaos here, too: old cars and machines, broken lawn furniture, all lying around helter-skelter. But then she spied her Jeep. She ran over to it. Locked. She looked inside her purse and in the pockets of her jacket. No, the key wasn't there. It must be somewhere inside the house. She would have to go back in and look. She didn't like that, but the car was important. Reluctantly, Liv returned to the front door.

19

Martin was coming to. He could not have been out for long. He had fallen and hit his head on the bed. His forehead ached, and his shoulder hurt. He was lying on the cold floor, a small table beside him. Someone had used it to knock him down. Was this becoming a habit? Slowly and painfully, he raised himself up.

Martin thought he had found Liv. First, he had recognized her car and then the leather jacket in the living room. The front door had been open. He had moved stealthily around the house, not knowing who was there. When he first opened the door to this room, he was sure someone was lying in the bed. Now he pulled off the covers—but there was no one there. It was a damn trap!

What was going on here? Liv must have been here. Had she been locked up?

Martin stood up. His body ached. Maybe Liv was still in the house. He pounded against the door with his fists.

"Liv Ulldahl, do you hear me? It's me, Martin Petzold. Please help me!"

He called three more times. Then he heard Liv's voice on the other side of the door.

"Do you speak German? Who are you?"

"I'm Martin Petzold. We met at your summerhouse. I loaned you money at the supermarket. Please let me out!"

"You? Why did you kidnap me?"

He—kidnap her? Martin was speechless.

"I've been looking for you for five days. You vanished without a trace. I had nothing to do with your kidnapping."

Liv thought it over. The German man had been nice. She couldn't really imagine him kidnapping her. But then why would he take such a risk now?

"I saw a pickup truck driving off. That had to have been your kidnapper. You can't leave me at his mercy after I got you out of here. We both need to get away from this place."

That made the difference. Liv unlocked the door and took a step backward just in case. Martin looked her over. She was pale, her hair was totally unkempt, and her T-shirt was dirty. But it was Liv, with the same blue eyes and freckles.

"It's good to see you," he said. "Come on, let's get out of here!"

Liv looked at Martin, relieved. He really had come to help her. She gave him a quick hug and mumbled: "Thanks! Sorry I hit you."

"It's OK. You couldn't have known who was coming in."

They headed up the stairs as Liv told him, "I found all my things. The only thing missing is my car key."

"We'll take my car," he answered. "I parked it down the road."

As the two of them exited the house and set off, they could hear the sound of a car making a rapid approach.

"Damn, someone's coming. Quick—into the woods!"

Martin motioned to Liv, and they ran behind the house and dove among the trees. There was a narrow path there.

Martin tried to muffle his voice: "We'll stay under cover until we get to my car. Follow me!"

They followed the path into the woods for a while and then turned right through the trees. The ground was muddy and almost impassable, which meant that the going would be slow. "Let's try to not make any noise."

Liv nodded. They made their way slowly around the house. By now, the car had arrived: it was the black pickup truck.

"Shit!" Martin was cursing.

Liv gripped his shirtsleeve. "Shouldn't we try to escape through the woods instead?"

"Do you know your way around here?"

"No." Liv looked about. "How far is it to my summerhouse?"

"Liv, we're in Dalarna, right near to your husband's summerhouse."

"What?" Liv's eyes widened, and she held her hands to her mouth in disbelief.

Martin looked at her. "To my car?"

She nodded, and they continued moving cautiously through the woods. They could hear the driver getting out and going up to the house. It would not be much longer before he noticed that Liv's things were missing. Then he would go down to the basement, and ...

They made slow headway as they neared Martin's car. As Martin looked back, it seemed to him that they were out of danger and could now come out from under cover. Once on the road, they were able to walk faster. Martin's shoulder ached with every step, but now it was simply a matter of clenching his teeth. Just as he was unlocking his car, he heard a sound from the direction of the house. The man had come out the front door and was bellowing something Martin couldn't understand. Liv looked at him in horror, and they climbed into the car as fast as they could. Martin started the engine, but it still took some time to turn the car around because there wasn't much room and he had to back up twice. Finally, he managed to drive off.

Just at that moment, Martin heard a revving sound from the pickup, which was coming up behind them. He looked in his rearview mirror: the truck was already closing in. Martin hit the gas. The car responded and lurched forward. Martin drove at top speed as Liv clung in fear to the armrest and kept looking forward and back.

"Faster! Please!"

"I'll try."

Martin stepped on the gas. Before them lay the main road. He knew he wouldn't make the curve at that speed, but he still kept driving at the same pace. A quick glance in the rearview mirror showed the pickup truck immediately behind them. Its engine was loud, and the black steel fenders in front of the hood were getting dangerously close.

At the junction to the main road, Martin braked slightly, hoping to make it onto the road without landing in the ditch. He gripped the steering wheel with all his might, and the Audi swung around. It looked like they were going to make it.

The pickup, however, had other plans. It had no intention of making the curve. Just as the Audi was making the turn, the pickup veered slightly to the right and rammed it from the side. The tail end of the Audi hurtled toward the woods. Liv shrieked, both airbags deployed, and Martin stepped on the brakes with everything he had. The car came to a halt perpendicular to the main road.

Before Martin could recover his senses, the door flung open, and he found himself staring down the barrel of a rifle. The man holding it was bellowing something in Swedish. Martin couldn't understand a word, but what the man wanted was clear. Martin got out of the car and raised his arms, with Liv crawling out behind him. She said something to the man, who briefly bellowed back, after which Liv said nothing.

The kidnapper was wearing a green parka and had pulled his collar way up. He was also wearing a baseball cap. Between those two things, most of his face was hidden. All that was visible was his tousled dark hair and large, red nose. The man waved his hostages over to the pickup with his rifle. Then he opened the hatch over the truck bed and said something in Swedish. Liv climbed in, with Martin following close behind. She explained to Martin that they were supposed to lie down and that the hatch would then

81

close. Feeling for his hand, she took it in hers. The pickup smelled of cement and leaves, and the truck bed was cold. It was pitch black.

The pickup started up, turned around, and drove off. A few minutes later, the hatch reopened and the man led Liv and Martin into the house, down the stairs, and into the cellar. Still pointing the rifle at them, he motioned them to sit down on the bed. Then he looked around the room, cursed, kicked the table so hard it went flying through the doorway, and left the room. The key turned in the lock.

Martin and Liv looked at each other. Liv was crying as she rested her head on Martin's shoulder. Martin placed his arm around her. He had no idea how to comfort her. The situation seemed hopeless.

20

Lars hit the red button and put down his cell phone. How many times had he tried already? Either Martin's battery was dead or his cell phone was off. The call kept going to voicemail.

Lars had also called the hotel. Martin had checked out early that morning, so Lars assumed he had driven to Dalarna. Why hadn't he called? He had to have arrived some time ago. Lars called Elin.

"Elin."

"Hey, Elin. It's Lars. How are things today?"

"Everything's A-OK. You?"

"I haven't been able to reach our client, which is strange. We spoke on the phone last night, and he insisted on taking on the summerhouse in Dalarna. According to the hotel, he checked out this morning. But now his phone goes straight to voicemail—it doesn't even ring."

"Maybe he found his bride, and they don't want anyone bothering them." Elin giggled.

"Well, that would be the least of my problems. I hope the explanation really is that simple. Listen, did you have any luck with Åre? The seaside property in the Archipelago was totally dead—not a soul there."

"Åre wasn't that simple. When I finally managed to get the right caretaker on the phone, he didn't want to give me any information. But I did find a taxi driver who was willing to drive to the cabin and knock on the door. Cost me 800 kronor—hope that's OK. He said he'd call today."

"Good job. We'll charge the amount to expenses."

"OK. I found a couple more articles on the Ulldahls. I'll email them to you right now."

"Thanks. Anything interesting?"

"Not really. We already know most of it. Oh, wait! Maybe there is something. In one of the articles, someone mentioned hearing something about a low sale price for the construction firm. But no one else has confirmed that."

"Aha, well, this sale keeps getting weirder and weirder. Listen, is the boss in the office?"

"Yeah, wanna talk to him?"

"That would be good. Can you put me through?"

"Sure, hang on. Talk to you later."

The phone picked up after three rings.

"Hi, Lars. You wanted to talk to me?"

"Hi, Tobias. Yeah, I have a slight problem." Lars told Tobias about the houses and how they had gone to check them out.

"Are you saying that you sent him to Dalarna alone, out in the sticks?" Tobias was a city person. For him, everything outside of Stockholm was the sticks.

"No, Tobias, I didn't 'send' him anywhere. At first, I didn't even want to bother with the cabin in Dalarna, but Martin insisted on doing something, and he was intrigued by the idea of visiting a different part of Sweden."

"I still don't like it, Lars. When we take on an assignment, we're the ones who do the job, not the client. He could tag along if he absolutely wanted to, but this is not good. Why didn't you at least have him do the Archipelago? We could have even sent Elin along."

"Yeah, you're right, that would have been better. Somehow we're always smarter in hindsight."

"You just didn't feel like driving to Dalarna, did you?"

"No. I just didn't think it would be too productive. First, there was the long drive, and second, I figured the cabin would be the least likely place to find Liv. Sorry. Not my best call."

"Well, let's hope the guy turns up again in one piece. But if you haven't heard anything by tomorrow morning, then you'll need to go and clear it up."

"What do you mean?"

"You'll have to drive over there and look for the guy! But not alone. You're taking someone with you!"

"OK, fine. But tomorrow is Saturday."

"Lars, you botched this one. I don't give a damn what day it is—you need to iron this out."

"Yeah, fine, that's no problem on my end. I didn't mean it that way. I was thinking more of my colleagues. Marie definitely won't do it. She's already working more than she wants to. Torbjörn and Palle are involved in a big surveillance job. Best case, I could ask Anders."

"No, he flew to Gothenburg today and won't be back for another week. Ask Elin! She's itching to do some fieldwork, so this would be her first chance."

"OK, thanks, Tobias. I'll do that."

"Good luck! Hopefully you won't have to go there at all."

They hung up. Lars hadn't expected Tobias to respond that way, but Tobias was always good for a surprise. And if Lars were honest with himself, the idea of Martin making that trip hadn't appealed to him, either.

Still no luck. Lars would try Martin a few more times and then ask Elin.

21

Thomas's cell phone was vibrating. He checked the screen: Bosse again. He didn't like that at all. What did he want, anyway? Thomas rejected the call.

The head of HR had just presented him with her salary suggestions for the beginning of next year. In Thomas's view, they were way too high.

He interrupted the presentation. "Why are we budgeting a three percent increase? Inflation is negative."

85

And why, Thomas wondered, had she gotten so dolled up today? Her outfit was a blatant case of overkill: suit, silk scarf, frilly blouse.

The HR manager turned to face him. "Thomas, as I showed you earlier, our wages are well below market average. I think we could afford to even things out a bit this year."

"Christina, we've already had this conversation multiple times. We provide so many other benefits that I think we're all right having our wages below average. I've already said this repeatedly. Anyone have another opinion?" He looked around the circle.

Two of his colleagues were shaking their heads. They agreed with Thomas. But then the head of finance made a move to speak.

Right at that moment, Thomas felt his cell phone vibrate. It was a text message.

"Yes, Olof?" Thomas turned to the CFO.

"Maybe we could identify the specific employees who are well below average and hike them up by two to three percent. We were already talking this over with Liv."

Thomas looked at the message. Bosse had texted that he urgently needed to talk to him. What a pile of crap.

Thomas was not interested in Olof's idea, and he now needed to break things off.

"Great. Christina and Olof, the two of you can come up with a proposal. Let's postpone the decision until then. Can you two have this done by the end of next week?"

They nodded. Thomas rose and excused himself, explaining that he needed to take an urgent call. He hurried out of the conference room and down the hall to his office, carefully closing the door behind him.

Bosse answered immediately: "Thomas, I'm getting out!"

"What? Are you out of your mind?"

"No. This is not what we agreed on. All hell has broken loose here."

"Slow down, Bosse! What happened? We were just on the phone not that long ago."

"Shit. Right. I come back, and your broad is gone. Run off with the same shithead I whacked over the head in Småland."

"I don't believe it. How did he get there?"

"I don't get it, either. I had to ram his car and use the gun to herd them in. Damn it all, this is not my thing."

"Is anyone hurt?"

"Nah, they're still in one piece. But his crate is totaled."

"OK, Bosse, good job. Where are they now?"

"In the cellar."

"Both in the same room?"

"Fuck, yeah, it's not like we're running a hotel." Bosse's volume was rising.

"Calm down, Bosse! I was just asking—it's fine. What's up with his car?"

"What about it?"

"Is it still sitting on the road somewhere?"

"What, do you think I'm dense, pal? I towed the car and stuck it in the yard. I've had my hands full here."

"OK, great! What kind of car is it?"

"The same one that was sitting at your broad's place— an A4 with a German license plate. Fuck, man, I'm hangin' here with two prisoners, and you're sitting in Stockholm, all nice and warm."

"Bosse, chill out! I'm just trying to get a picture of the situation. You've done everything right, but now we have to figure out what's next."

"I don't have to do a damn thing, pal. We never discussed this shit. Finish it off yourself. I'm not into this anymore."

"Whoa, Bosse, slow down! We can't just finish things off—you know that. Then we'd both be in trouble. Give me a couple of hours. I'll find a way. Just one more question: were you wearing a mask when you took them both in?"

"You've got some nerve, dude. I come into the house, the stupid cow has taken off, and I hear a car start. I go after them with the truck, and after that, everything went super fast. And you think I remembered the damn mask? It was in the shit cabin."

"That's fine, Bosse. I just want to know whether they saw your face and would recognize you."

"Uh, probably not. I had my collar all the way up and my cap on."

"That's good. Thanks. Did you talk to them some more? Maybe try to find out what this guy was about and how he got there?"

"Look, chum, you think I wanted to hang out and have coffee with them? After all this shit? I barricaded the door, and that was it."

"Great, then everything's hunky-dory. Listen, let me try and figure how to solve this problem. I'll call you back at six, OK? And I'll double your pay."

"As if that's enough. I'll be here at six, but I'm not promising you a thing. If you don't come up with something good, I'm outta here." Bosse hung up.

Thomas let out a long, deep breath. What a pile of crap. Couldn't anything ever go right? How was he going to get out of this mess? But Bosse had responded well to the situation—that much Thomas had to admit. That's if it all happened as he described. Bosse had a definite tendency to exaggerate. He was pissed, though. That much sounded real.

Still, there were some things Thomas didn't get, like how this German guy managed to find the hideout. He must have followed Bosse—there could be no other way. Had Bosse maybe not given an accurate account of what went on in Småland? Or maybe the German guy had managed to free himself quickly and then follow Bosse. Bosse had Liv's car hooked up to his trailer, and the car would have been easy to identify. But then Bosse would surely have noticed Martin tailing him—at least, by Dalarna, where there were not that many cars on the road, especially cars with German plates. The timing didn't work, either. Why would the German guy wait several days before freeing Liv? Thomas couldn't understand it. Somewhere, Bosse must have missed something. Maybe he'd had one too many whiskeys again.

It didn't matter. What Thomas needed to do now was more important. He would take the rest of the day off. He had to find a solution.

22

Lars had just set out for home when Elin called. He still hadn't gotten a hold of Martin. It didn't look good.

"Hey, Elin."

"Lars, the taxi driver called. He said the cabin is dark and deserted."

"Yeah, OK, that's what I thought. Thanks. Good work."

"Always glad to help."

"Listen, Elin."

"Yes, Lars?" Elin's voice had a sense of suspense.

"I know you've been wanting to do an assignment outside the office, right?"

"Yeah, for sure. You got something for me?"

"Yeah, although it's not yet 100 percent sure. I may have to drive to the cabin in Dalarna, and I need someone to come with me."

"Because of the German guy? Hasn't he called yet?"

"No, it's like the earth has swallowed him up."

"OK, but I don't know what the boss will have to say about this. He's always been hesitant whenever I've wanted to work in the field."

"I've already dealt with that. Tobias agrees."

"Great! Thanks, Lars!"

"There's just one problem, Elin."

Elin said nothing. She seemed to be waiting.

"If we do end up going, it will be tomorrow morning."

"Tomorrow morning? On a Saturday? And you tell me this now, half an hour before quitting time?"

"Yeah, I know. I understand if you already have plans. But I need someone to come with me."

"Oh, so for that I'm good enough."

"Elin, please! Tobias suggested you himself, and I think it's a great idea. I like working with you, and you know the case inside out. Please don't leave me hanging!"

"Well, OK, since you asked so nicely, I won't be that way. But you owe me for this."

"OK, thanks, Elin. There's a chance that we won't be going. Martin may still call. But if I haven't heard anything by 8:00 a.m. tomorrow, we're heading out. I'll come pick you up. Does that work?"

"Yeah, OK. What do I need to bring?"

Elin always wore sports clothes, but that might not be enough this time.

"We may have to crawl around in the woods, so waterproof outdoor clothing. And an overnight kit in case of an emergency."

"You know, this keeps getting better and better. I do have other plans on Sunday."

"I said in an emergency."

"OK, gotcha. See you tomorrow."

"Ciao."

Great, Lars thought to himself, at least that was taken care of, although Elin didn't exactly make it easy. What would driving up with her be like? Hopefully, she wouldn't bitch the whole way.

Lars still had to break the good news to his family. They were sure to be thrilled, especially his wife Lisa. His oldest daughter had a soccer game tomorrow, and Lars was supposed to take her. Lisa would now have to take that on, and Lars knew how much she loved that.

23

Elin was making herself comfortable on the couch. She had put on a loose-fitting jogging suit, made a couple of pieces of cheese toast, and poured herself a glass of wine. She was waiting for Maja, who would normally have been home by now but had texted that she was running late. That's what Elin loved about Maja—you could always rely on her.

That obviously wasn't the only thing she loved about her. Elin smiled. Maja was also seriously good in bed. They had been together for two years now, and it was Elin's first relationship with a woman. She had tried having a relationship with a guy a couple of times, but somehow it never worked for her. Then she met Maja, and that did it. The same was true for Maja, even though she had another relationship going on at the time. But she knew what she wanted, and she broke up with the other woman. After that, Elin moved in with Maja—and she didn't regret it one bit. Life with Maja was great. She was also a few years older than Elin, and that felt good. Elin could lean on her.

Of course, Elin's entire circle of friends knew about her relationship, although her parents had no clue. They thought she was just living with a female friend. Elin had also kept quiet about it at work. Private detectives were a rugged bunch, and she could do without their stupid comments.

There was the sound of a key turning in the door. Elin leapt up, ran over, and threw her arms around Maja in a stormy embrace. Maja smelled good—she had just showered.

"Geez, love, do you mind if I take off my jacket?" Maja protested as she fended Elin off. They gave each other a long, passionate kiss. Finally, Elin let go of Maja so that she could set down her bag and remove her jacket. She unzipped her boots and slipped them off.

"I made cheese toast," Elin said. "You want a glass of wine with it?"

"No, I'd rather have a beer. I'm thirsty."

"How was your class?"

"Great! I had three new participants, and one of them was amazing. He gave me a serious workout."

Maja taught judo and karate, and Elin also attended one of her classes once or twice a week. That was where they had met. Elin had thought it couldn't hurt for a woman to know a bit about self-defense, especially a woman who wanted to be a private detective. When she combined that with her IT degree, she saw herself as made for the job, but her boss Tobias was apparently not convinced. He was an old-school type who liked to bank on people with prior experience in related professions, like police work. Unfortunately, Elin couldn't claim that for herself.

Maja sat down on the couch and picked up a piece of cheese toast.

"How was your day?" she asked.

She took a big bite out of the cheese toast. Looked like she was hungry, too.

Elin could no longer contain herself and burst out with the news.

"Guess what? I've got my first assignment tomorrow. Lars needs someone to go with him to Dalarna to search for a client. He's gone missing somehow."

"That's great! And your boss approved it?"

"Yeah, Lars hashed it out with him. Amazing, isn't it?" Elin beamed at her.

"Congratulations! Maybe this is the breakthrough you've been waiting for, even if I will miss having you around tomorrow." Maja shoved the rest of the sandwich in her mouth.

"I hope so. I've already laid out all my stuff for the morning. Lars thought we might have to crawl around in the woods."

"Did you pack your knife and baton?"

"Absolutely!" Elin had a jackknife that in its open position could hold its own with a hunting knife. She also had a baton like the ones the police carried. Both were dangerous weapons. And best of all, she knew how to use them—Maja had shown her a thing or two.

"What do you all know about this missing man? Do you have any leads?" Maja asked.

"Not a whole lot. There's a summerhouse in Dalarna that he wanted to drive to, but after that, he didn't call anymore, and we haven't been able to reach him since. That's why we want to go look for him tomorrow."

Maja took a hefty swig of beer. "I know the two of you can do it. And then my little Amazon will be a real PI."

Elin chuckled. She loved when Maja talked like that. "That's right! If all goes well tomorrow, then Tobias won't be able refuse me anymore."

"I'll keep my fingers crossed for you. But now it's time to get comfy, don't you think?"

Maja gazed at Elin with her dark eyes. Elin melted, and the two of them embraced.

24

Martin was observing Liv as she slept. She had gone into shock after their failed escape attempt, sobbing like a child and lying on the bed in a fetal position. She was still lying that way, with her hands tucked under her chin and her arms and legs pulled tight against her body. Martin himself had an impossible time sleeping, never mind that there was only one bed. He was agitated and had a whole heap of questions, but so far, Liv had been unresponsive.

It was warm in the room, so Martin had removed his rain jacket and boots. He had also relieved Liv of her leather jacket and shoes. That was before she fell asleep and had been able to help. But Martin still felt warm, so he took off his sweatshirt and picked up the water bottle. He walked over to the window and opened it. The guy with the gun was no longer in sight, whatever that meant. Martin hoped he wouldn't just leave them to their fate, given that their chances of escape were as good as zero. He peered upward through the window bars and looked outside from below, but he could see nothing. The air shaft was too high. They were obviously below ground.

Liv stirred. She had turned onto her back and was now more relaxed. Up above, Martin detected the sound of a car starting, so he moved as close to the window as possible to hear what was going on up there. It sounded like the pickup. The car drove off, and the noise of the engine faded away, so Martin guessed that they were now alone. Whether that did them any good was another question. He opened the bottle of water and started to drink.

"No! Stop!"

Martin froze.

Liv had sat up and was staring at him. "There's a sedative in the water. I've done nothing but sleep for almost the entire time I've been here."

Martin set the bottle down and screwed the cap back on.

"I see," he said. "But there's nothing else to drink here, is there?"

Liv shook her head. "Great combination, isn't it? An overheated room and nothing to drink but a sleeping potion."

Martin examined the heater, which had a standard electrical element. You could turn it off on the side and also regulate it by adjusting the knob. He turned it to the lowest setting. "Well, then we're better off freezing a bit rather than drinking this stuff, right?" he asked.

Liv nodded. "Good idea."

Martin walked over to her and sat down beside her. "You feeling better?" he asked

"Not really," Liv replied. "But crying and sleeping did me some good. I feel calmer now. Sorry about all that."

"No problem. But Liv, could you please tell me what's going on here? Do you know this guy?"

"No. I honestly have no idea what's going on. That day at my summerhouse when ... when ..."

"The day we had our date?"

She thought a bit. "Yes, it must have been that day. Exactly. I was just about to start preparing things for coffee, and I was on the terrace when someone was suddenly standing behind me and pressing a cloth to my face. I think it had chloroform on it. I ... I managed to fend him off for a short while, but then I blacked out. When I came to again, I found myself here. I yelled and pounded on the door, but no one answered. I was hungry and thirsty, so I ate the sandwiches and drank the water. After that, I soon fell asleep. That happened a couple of times. I became completely disoriented and had no idea what time or day it was. You said you've been looking for me for five days? What does that mean? What day is today?"

"Friday. Our date was supposed to be Sunday."

"My God, I've been here that long?" Liv's chest caved in, and Martin could see the tears welling up in her eyes again. He put his arm around her. That seemed to calm her.

"Thank you, Martin. That feels nice." She leaned against him. "Then I realized the sedative was in the water, because he didn't bring the sandwiches every time, but I would get tired anyway. And I was always awfully thirsty when I awoke. I don't know if that had something to do with the sedative or if it was because the sandwiches were so salty. Or maybe it was just too warm in here. Anyway, I came up with the idea of using the water glass."

Martin looked at Liv. There was a questioning expression in his eyes.

She pointed to the window. "I set the glass outside the window over there and managed to collect some rainwater. When I awoke this last time, I was able to drink that instead, which is why the bottle is still full now. That way, I managed to stay awake, and my plan was to take out the kidnapper with the table. But I got you instead. I'm so sorry! Does your shoulder still hurt?"

"Yeah, a little. But that's not my worst problem right now. Liv, do you have any idea who might be behind your kidnapping?"

Liv shook her head.

"I know about the sale of your company," Martin continued. "Could that have anything to do with it?"

Liv looked at him in disbelief. "You're extremely well informed."

"Yes, that's a long story. I've also experienced a few things since Sunday."

"Do you want to tell me about it?"

Martin told her everything: about his visits to her house and how he was knocked unconscious and bound hand and foot; about his frustrating experience with the police and the clue that led him to Stockholm; about his success with Lars and their latest findings; and about why he had driven to Dalarna and how he had first found her husband's summerhouse and then this cabin.

Liv listened intently, her blue eyes fastened on him the whole time. Once he had finished, she gave him a huge hug.

"Oh, Martin, thank you. It's just incredible what you've done—and you don't even know me."

"Well, I was determined to get my 200 kronor back."

She pushed away from him and stared. "What?"

"I loaned you money—at the supermarket. I'm joking, of course."

Now Liv understood and laughed a heartfelt, honest belly laugh. It had a good ring to it, and Martin joined in. It was a release for both of them.

"Right, exactly! That's how it all started. Martin, you asked me about the sale of my company. It's true. My husband was pressuring me to sell the company. At first, I gave in. I also wasn't sure whether the company was right for me, but it's not doing badly. In any case, my husband had found a buyer, and we were just about to sign when I started having doubts. I didn't like the people, I didn't like the price, and I didn't want to sell, after all. So we added a clause that I could revoke the contract within a period of two weeks, no questions asked. At that point, I wanted to take some time to think things over again."

"And that's why you were at the summerhouse? Why there?"

"I inherited the house from my grandmother, and I have a lot of fond memories of it—I spent many of my childhood summers there. My parents were always working, which is why I spent my summer vacations with Mormor, the Swedish name for the grandma on the mother's side. My husband had always wanted me to sell that house, but for me, that was an absolute no, even if I was hardly ever there these past few years. But it was lovely being there again. And it quickly became clear to me that I would object to the sale of the company. I told my husband that, too, when I phoned him on Saturday. We had a big fight over it, which was also the reason I took the wrong credit card to the supermarket. It had expired, and I had laid it out with the intention of throwing it away. But after our fight, I was so upset that I wasn't thinking and simply stuck it in my purse."

Martin thought a bit. "When does the objection period end?"

"On Monday."

"So in other words, you had a fight with your husband in which you told him that you had decided against the sale, and the next day, someone kidnapped you and kept you sedated for days on end?"

Liv stared at the floor as she played with one of her blond curls, a look of doubt on her face.

"Yes, I've also wondered whether my husband had something to do with it. I don't want to think ill of him, and I can't imagine that he would do such a thing. But it is a striking coincidence."

"Yes, and there's also the fact that he and his siblings own a cabin very close to this one. Did you know about it?"

"Yes, we've been there a few times, but just briefly to visit his sister's family when they were there on vacation. We never used the cabin ourselves. But you're right. The fact that we now find ourselves locked up near that cabin, of all places, unfortunately fits the version with my husband." Liv knit her brow, with all its freckles. "So what do we do now? Do you see any way of getting us out of here?"

"Not on our own." Martin waved his arm around the room. "These are concrete walls, the window has bars, and we're dealing with a steel door with a strong lock. The way I see it, we have just two possibilities: either this guy will make a mistake—but I don't think he will, because our escape attempt should make him even more cautious; or—and this is what I hope will happen—the private detective I hired will find us. He should be missing me at any rate, and he knows where I went. Maybe he'll find this hideaway the same way I did. By now, both our cars are probably sitting in the yard. That should be a clear giveaway. The only thing I don't know is when he'll make it here. It may not be until Monday, which means that there will be next to no time left for you to object."

"Oh, that doesn't matter. I can live without the company. I just want to get out of here and back to my children."

"How old are they?"

"Saga is ten, and Hampus is eight. I miss them."

Martin swallowed. For a while, they were silent. Then Martin finally spoke.

"All right, so what's our strategy now? Do we try to stay awake? That means we'll be dying of thirst. Or do we take turns sleeping? Under no condition should we give this guy a chance to go in and out while we're both drugged."

Liv got up from the bed and walked over to the window. Reaching her arm through the bars, she pulled in the water glass. It was empty. Disappointed, she put it back.

"Maybe it will rain some more later on," she said. She went back to the bed. "I think it's a good idea to take turns sleeping. Are you very thirsty?"

"No, I can hold out a while."

"All right, then I'll drink now." Liv took the bottle, opened it, and paused. She looked at Martin.

"It's a funny feeling. I mean, drinking the stuff when you know it will put you to sleep. And when you don't know what will happen while you're out."

"I'll watch out for you."

"Thank you, Martin. But don't place yourself in danger again! I hope nothing bad happens while I'm asleep."

She hugged him briefly and drank, leaving the bottle half full. Afterwards, she lay back down on the bed and pulled the covers over her. Martin wished Liv good night, and less than five minutes later, she was fast asleep, leaving him alone with his thoughts.

Martin desperately hoped that Lars would try to find him. They had a good understanding, and Lars had also told Martin some things about his own personal life. Martin found it interesting that Lars, like Liv, had such pleasant childhood memories. Both in the same way, too: vacations at their summerhouses, the one in the north, the other in the south of Sweden. Was that a coincidence? Or was that typical of Sweden? In any case, there was plenty of space here, and many families owned summerhouses. In Germany, that was more often the exception.

Martin's own childhood was not especially positive in retrospect. His parents had not had much money, and vacations were rarely a part of their lives. All he could remember were a couple of times in Bavaria at a small pension. He was the youngest of three siblings. The others were older by five and seven years, which meant that he was usually left out of their games. He had never been especially athletic, either, so he had no hobbies like soccer, and he was usually one of the last to be chosen for the school team. He made the most of the situation, though. Despite his parents' and siblings' lack of support, he finished his law studies, and his law practice did extremely well.

Funny how distant it all seemed now. And there he sat, a prisoner, when his plan had been for a time of rest and relaxation. Instead, he had been knocked down twice, and his greatest hope now was to come out of it all in one piece.

Saturday, September 26

25

Lars was cursing. "I was afraid of this. There's nobody here."

He and Elin had found the cabin right away: Dalvägen 16. They had walked around the house and inspected everything, but it looked like no one had been there recently.

"Where the heck did his flashy ol' sports car drive off to?" Elin looked at Lars questioningly. Lars gazed down at her from above. Elin had a fine-boned, small build, something no one would ever believe from just talking with her on the phone.

"I don't get it, either. To some neighbor's nearby?"

"Yeah, that could be anywhere around here. There are a whole bunch of little roads that veer off to the right and left."

"Well, at least we know that the Porsche turned off onto Dalvägen. And back at the turnoff, the sign said it was a dead end, didn't it?"

"Yup."

"So let's go back to the mailboxes and take another look around."

They walked back to the dirt road where they had parked their car. It had all started out so well. Since Martin was still unreachable, Lars had picked up Elin as arranged, and they had made good time. Elin was in a good mood throughout the whole ride. She was cheery and enjoying the chance to work in the field. She had done a great job preparing, even printing out all her research and bringing it along. She had also asked Lars about his equipment after grabbing the small metal case with his paraphernalia. She had him explain everything: the lock pick, the night vision goggles, the GPS tracker, the walkie-talkies, etc.

Then shortly after they left Falun, Elin proved herself to be truly with it. A red Porsche had passed and pulled ahead of them. Elin immediately noticed and started searching through her files. She found the correct printout and excitedly confirmed her suspicion: the Porsche was registered under the name of Thomas Lind—the license plate matched. On learning that, Lars did his best to keep the Porsche in his sights, which was not so easy since it was completely ignoring the speed limit and was much faster than his Volvo. Even though Lars and Elin figured it was probably heading to the same place, they still preferred to err on the side of caution. The Porsche did in fact turn onto Dalvägen, but Lars and Elin chose to wait by the turnoff to avoid being too conspicuous on the dirt road. That turned out to be a mistake, because the Porsche wasn't at the cabin, after all.

Lars examined the mailboxes but could detect nothing unusual. As was so common in Sweden, the numbers related only to the mailbox positions, and there were virtually no names and addresses.

Elin had walked farther up the road, and she was now calling Lars over.

"Did you find something?" he asked

"Yeah, look! There are shards of glass from a car on the ground here, and there are also a lot of tire marks."

Lars examined the spot. "Yeah, it looks like there might have been an accident here. There's even damage on both sides of the road. I hope Martin wasn't involved in it, but that could explain why he hasn't called. Maybe he's at the hospital in Falun."

"In that case, he must have had some incredibly bad luck to have crashed into the only other car for miles around on a road this small."

"Yeah, and they don't drive that fast here. But if alcohol had anything to do with it …"

"Let me show you something else. Right at the spot of the accident, the road veers off to the right, and there are a ton of tire marks there. There must be a fair amount of traffic here. And look! There are fresh tire marks on top of them. They could be from our sports car, couldn't they?"

She was right. There were clear traces of fresh tracks in the mud. Judging from their width, the tires that made them were wide, but they didn't belong to a freight truck. Lars studied the road some more. The marks appeared to go on for a while, but he could see no house.

"Listen, Elin, I'd like to take a closer look at this, but I don't want to risk losing the Porsche. Let's split up. I'll keep going down this road on foot to find out where these tire marks lead. In the meantime, you drive back to the start of Dalvägen."

"OK, and what do I do there?"

"You wait and keep an eye on anyone driving in or out, and you write down every single license plate number. If the Porsche drives out, tail it!"

"Even if you're not back yet?"

"Even then! Can you swing that?"

"I'll try. We'll see what I can get out of your Volvo. This is getting exciting!"

"OK, we can keep in touch by phone. Hang on a minute." He pulled out his cell phone. "Oh, crap, there's no service here."

"What about the walkie-talkies?"

"They don't have a long enough range. It's almost ten kilometers to the start of the dirt road. We would need CB radios for that."

"Why don't we have any?"

"Because they're pretty big and clunky, and we don't normally need more than a range of six to eight kilometers."

"Gotcha. So then we'll only be able to maintain contact once you're back in range of the cellular network."

"Maybe the walkie-talkies are a good idea, after all. I'll take one, and you take the other. I may get within range for those sooner than for the cellular network. That could save me a few kilometers of trekking."

"Well, a little movement would be good for you after the long drive."

"Right. Too bad I have an injured leg."

"Oh yeah, sorry. Didn't think of that."

They tested the walkie-talkies and then set off down the road in opposite directions.

Lars hadn't expected to go so far into the forest. He must have already walked two kilometers, but the tire marks kept going and going. And no wonder: there hadn't been a single turnoff.

There was the sound of an engine from up ahead. The car seemed to be coming closer. Lars figured it would be better to stay out of sight, so he took a few steps deeper into the forest. He hid behind a tree, curious to see whether the Porsche would appear. From his hiding spot, he peered in the direction of the engine sound.

No, it was not the Porsche but a large pickup truck with black fenders in front of the hood and an extra set of headlights on the roof. And right behind the pickup came the Porsche. So it had come here, after all.

Lars was trying to decide: should he follow them and try to contact Elin? Could be that Liv's husband had simply picked up a neighbor and was driving with him back to his own cabin to have him fix something. But Lars still wanted to know where they had come from just now, so he decided to keep walking.

It was another ten minutes before Lars finally spied a house between the trees. With vigorous strides, he walked onward until he came to a yard where chaos seemed to be the dominant theme, with weeds and junk battling for supremacy. Lars went up to the house and looked in one of the windows. There, too, chaos reigned, but the overall effect was of emptiness. The door was locked.

Lars took a closer look at the yard, where he noticed a number of tire marks in the mud. Some of them led to a big shed that almost looked like an old barn. He walked diagonally across the yard to the large double door, which was secured with a chain and padlock. The sides of the shed, however, were constructed of nothing more than a single layer of crude planks that had seen better times. They had all kinds of cracks and holes. Down below to the right, one of the boards had been broken off, so Lars made use of the gap to peer inside. He recognized the two cars parked beside each other. He lay down on the ground to get a better look— good thing he was wearing his outdoor clothes. Then he took his flashlight from his side pocket and shined it into the shed. There stood a Jeep and an Audi A4. The Audi had a German license plate.

26

They had been on the road for at least an hour, although it was hard to gauge the time. The truck had rocked back and forth quite a bit at first, but now it drove more smoothly and at a faster speed. Martin figured they were on the freeway. This time, they had a large piece of chipboard and a blanket as a pad, so at least they weren't lying on a cold truck bed. Of course, there was neither heat nor air, and it was also dark. But they had been given two bottles of water with the seals intact, which meant it was unlikely they contained sleep inducers. Their kidnappers probably wanted to avoid having to carry them from the pickup truck once they arrived at the destination.

The night had passed quickly. Down in their room, the man with the rifle had provided them with two sandwiches, a bottle of water, and another mattress. Soon after that, they lay down and quickly fell asleep. In the morning, they had to wait a while before their guard arrived. Meanwhile, Liv told Martin first about her parents and then about her children. Martin headed up his story with tales of his separation from his wife and of his daughter.

Some time later, they heard engine sounds, and after that, everything happened very fast. Two men suddenly entered, both of them armed and masked. Martin and Liv had to hand over everything they had: cell phones, watches, and wallets. They were led upstairs and had to crawl back into the pickup. They were not allowed to speak, and of the two men, only one—the one from the day before—said anything at all, and then only the bare essentials in short commands.

As a result, neither Martin nor Liv had any idea what was happening or where they were being taken. They were both worried. It was clear to them that with the way things stood, it would be virtually impossible for Lars to find them. Their sole hope now was to be released unharmed on Tuesday, as soon as Liv's objection period had expired. The best-case scenario, then, was three more days of imprisonment.

Liv lay curled up in a ball beside Martin and uttered not one sound. She had placed a great deal of faith in the notion that the private detective would rescue them. But with how things looked right now, it was clear to her as well that their chances for freedom were slim.

27

Lars hurried back to the main road as quickly as he could. Maybe he would be in luck, and a car would come by and pick him up. He assumed that Elin was tailing the Porsche as planned, which meant that he would now have to figure out how to catch up with her. That was why he was all the more surprised to see his Volvo parked beside the mailboxes, with Elin sitting inside it.

Lars opened the door. "What are you doing here?"

"Hey, Lars. So nice of you to finally come." She grinned at him, teasing.

"Didn't you see the Porsche? It tore out of here, along with a pickup truck."

"I've got it all under control. Don't get so riled up!"

"Elin, you should be following that Porsche. Speaking of having things under control!"

Elin glared at him. "Can't you first listen to what I've done before drawing a bunch of hasty conclusions?"

They stared at each other a while. Then Lars finally yielded.

"OK, so what happened?" he asked.

Elin was content and smiled to herself. She scrunched her little snub nose.

"Get in the car!"

Lars walked over to the front passenger seat and got in. He was fuming inside, but what else could he do?

"So, happy?"

"Yup. OK, so listen! I was standing down by the junction when I suddenly heard a car approaching. I got out of the

Volvo, positioned myself by the side of the road, and was making hand signals. The pickup just zoomed on by, but the Porsche stopped. I asked the driver if there were any nearby restaurants. He said he didn't know of any. While I was doing that, I bent down and stuck one of our GPS trackers inside his wheelhouse. I had figured that tailing him might be hard since Porsches are a lot faster. Besides, I didn't want to leave you alone here. Smart, huh?"

Lars was flabbergasted. That was a great idea.

"Yeah, I have to hand it to you: nice work. Did you also activate the tracker?"

"Does Dolly Buster hit the bed on her back? Seriously, Lars, do I look like a moron? Besides, you showed me how to do it on the ride up here. The only thing I couldn't get to work was the search program, because you didn't give me the password for the laptop."

"Wow, you did amazingly well, Elin. I'm proud of you. So let's turn on the computer right now!"

He grabbed the laptop and hit the power button. Elin started the Volvo, and they drove off.

"So what happened on your end? No sign of the German guy?" she asked.

Lars looked up. "Yes, there was. I found his car—it has to be his: an Audi A4 with German plates standing next to a Jeep, and both of them hidden in a shed. The Audi was badly smashed on one side, so I'm guessing it was involved in an accident. I wrote down the license plate number for the Jeep. You have Liv Ulldahl's vehicle info, don't you?"

"I'm sure I do. It has to be in those papers somewhere. Take a look through the stack ... So was there no cabin?"

"Yeah, there was. I even climbed inside through one of the windows, which luckily was easy to open. It was pretty chaotic inside, but there was no one there. The problem is that I didn't come up with anything concrete. But there is a room in the cellar with a steel door that can be locked. There was a bed and mattress inside it, but otherwise nothing. It's possible that someone was being held prisoner there. And if that's the case, then that person is now being brought to a different location. I'm assuming that Thomas Lind was the only person in the Porsche. Did you see anyone else in the pickup truck?"

"No, just the driver. But it did have a large covered truck bed."

"Exactly. OK, I got the program going. It's searching ... yup, the tracker is functioning. It's working great. Brilliant work, Elin! They're not all that far ahead of us."

"Good." Elin smiled with satisfaction. "So that means we're tailing them?"

"Yup, exactly. Let's just hope they don't split up. The only one we can track is the Porsche, and my guess is that neither Martin nor Liv is in it."

"So Lars, what do you think is going on here? I mean, what role is Liv's husband playing? Is he even involved? Or is he trying to free his wife?"

"Well, it doesn't look like a rescue attempt, and it also doesn't look like a ransom payment. If Martin or Liv or both are in the pickup truck, that would mean that they're lying in the truck bed, which means that they're being held prisoner. And since the Porsche and the pickup truck are traveling one right behind the other, it looks to me like the two drivers are in it together."

"But why would Lind kidnap his own wife?"

"I don't get it, either. Hang on, I've found the right printout. Right, so the Jeep belongs to Liv Ulldahl, which means that either both of them were kidnapped or they ran off together. But then Martin would have called off the job, wouldn't he?"

"Yeah, who knows what goes on in people's heads."

"You're probably right. It doesn't matter. I don't see where we could look for them here. We'll keep tailing the two cars for starters. Hit the gas a bit—it would be great if we could get a visual of the pickup truck."

28

More than anything, Thomas would have loved to hit the gas so that he could pull the whole thing off as quickly as possible. But he had to be careful to not overtake the pickup truck. He was also slowly getting tired. And no wonder. Since yesterday, he had had a pretty full plate. First, he had gone back and forth on how to solve the whole story as originally planned. But there was no chance of that anymore. That German guy had screwed it all up. Who the hell even knew who he was? Did Liv have something going with the guy? If so, then only she was to blame for the consequences.

In any event, the German guy knew where they were hiding Liv. After all, he had found his way there—however he managed that one. That made the German a risk. And by now, he had had plenty of chances to chat with Liv, which meant that Liv now knew where she was and only had to put two and two together.

No, there was no longer a legitimate way for Thomas to get out of this. He would have to make a clean break. And that would have to include Bosse, who, when Thomas called him at 6 p.m., had done nothing but whine that Liv and Martin had now seen his cabin and also knew his car. He wanted out. It wasn't easy getting him to calm down. Thomas had told him a little about a new plan he had come up with, and he had promised him that everything would turn out all right. The first step would be to relocate the two captives, and he already had a new place. Bosse had bought the story but had insisted that Thomas help him move the two hostages. And Thomas had to admit that it would be hard for one person to deal with both captives, so it made sense for both Bosse and him to be there.

And now they were on their way to the new hiding place. Thomas had scouted it out earlier that morning. He knew there were a lot of summerhouses south of Gävle and that they weren't being used at the moment. He had broken into one of the cabins and checked it out. It would work for his purposes.

Thomas had taken care of everything else the night before. It was just great what all they had stashed away at the construction company. That was what had convinced him that he could wrap this up on his own. It was hardly a fun time, but he didn't want to involve even more people. His new contacts in Russia could certainly have settled all of his problems with ease and professionalism, but that would mean getting entangled in yet another dependency. No, he would have to pull this off by himself.

There were still a few things he needed to take care of to make it look like Bosse had performed the kidnapping alone, which would include demanding the ransom money from Thomas himself. After that, Thomas would be free of his problems and could finally start all over again. It would be worth it. It would have to be worth it. He could see no other solution, even if he had never wished for things to turn out this way. Liv was his wife, after all, and he still had feelings for her in spite of their differences. But that didn't matter. What had his mother always said? You had to make sacrifices if you wanted to achieve anything. And Thomas was ready to do that. The time had come for his streak of bad luck to end.

29

According to the GPS, they were not that far behind the pickup truck. Once on the freeway, they were able to narrow the gap between them. They had driven to Gävle and then turned onto the E4 motorway heading to Stockholm. Soon after that, they exited the freeway again and found themselves back in a wooded area. The blinking dot on the screen had come to a standstill a few minutes earlier, and it looked as if the Porsche had reached its destination. Unfortunately, they hadn't managed to close in enough for a visual, so Lars could do nothing more than hope that the pickup truck was there as well.

Although the GPS showed the tracker's location, because of their need to remain undetected, Lars and Elin would have to find their way there without it. Up to that point, it had been easy: first, there was the county road to Falun and then the freeway. But after that, with the countless turnoffs, it became more difficult. Now, however, it was getting easier again as they neared their goal.

"Slow down, Elin. I don't want to attract attention."

Elin let up on her speed, but Lars could see that she was not happy. Her aim had been to catch sight of their quarry.

"It has to be right around here," Lars said, "up ahead on the road to the right. But we're not turning in there. I'm guessing that leads to a house, and we don't want them to notice us. Better to keep driving a bit. We can park over there on the left."

Elin followed his instructions and then turned off the engine. "Now what do we do?"

"We'll sneak up there and watch. We'll take the binoculars with us. We need to find out for sure whether Martin and Liv are there."

The two of them set off down the road. Many of the houses were right on the street, but neither Lars nor Elin saw any cars. Either the residents were out, or he and Elin were looking at vacation homes that were vacant for the time being. They turned onto the narrow road that was supposed to lead them to the GPS tracker. Here, too, the houses stood on either side of the road, and most of them were quite small. The plots, however, were large enough that the houses had a fair amount of space between them.

After Lars and Elin had walked about 200 meters, they finally spotted the end of the road. There stood a house on a large parcel of land, and in front of the house sat both cars.

"Elin, move to the side—quick! We'll walk across the properties from here."

Together, they left the road and crept through the undergrowth. The land that the houses stood on had been left in its natural state, with the trees and bushes almost as dense as the forest. As was the norm in Sweden, there were no fences here. It was anyone's guess as to where one property began and the other ended, although the dividing line usually ran along the poles for the power and telephone lines, which always led from the road to two adjacent houses.

Lars and Elin did their best to remain out of sight and eventually arrived at the neighboring lot. There, they came upon a stack of firewood piled in a circular form and crowned with a tarpaper covering that came to a point in the center. From there, they had a clear view of the two cars and the house behind them. They crouched down to the left of the stack, and Lars pulled out the binoculars.

The pickup truck was parked with its tail end facing the house. The Porsche stood next to it and was facing the other way. A light was on inside the house, and they could make out the silhouette of a person walking around the room.

Lars and Elin kept quiet and remained hidden. After some time, the light went out and the door of the house opened. Two men emerged, and through the binoculars, Lars could see that both men were carrying a rifle and wearing a mask. Lars held his breath. Elin squeezed his arm. He raised his index finger to his lips, and Elin nodded.

The two men walked to the pickup truck, and one of them opened the hatch. One by one, two people climbed out of the truck, their hands in the air. The first was Martin without a doubt. The second was a woman with shoulder-length blond hair—probably Liv, although Lars couldn't see her face. The four of them slowly entered the house: first, one of the men; then Martin, followed by the blond woman; and finally, the other man. The door closed behind them. Since the light in the house was now off, Lars was unable to see what was going on inside—it was darker in there than outside.

He turned to Elin. "Did you see that?"

Elin nodded.

"I recognized Martin. And the woman had to be Liv. Elin, it's time. We need to call the police. Go back a ways, maybe to the nearest house, and call 112. Tell them that two people are being threatened with guns and that they were taken out of a car and escorted into the house. But no names for now!"

Elin nodded once more. "But I have to give them mine, don't I?"

"Of course. Otherwise, they won't take your call seriously."

"What do you plan on doing in the meantime?" she asked.

"I'll sneak up to the house. If it looks like an emergency, I may have to step in. But I hope we can just let the police handle it. Tell them to hurry!"

Elin dashed off.

Lars crept on all fours, first to the pickup truck and then to one of the cabin windows, where he cautiously peered inside. There was no one in sight. The view was of the main room of the cabin: a living room, kitchen, and dining room in one. To the right, by the rear wall beside the kitchenette, was an open door. Behind that were probably additional rooms into which all four people seemed to have disappeared. Lars waited. It was a good five minutes before anyone returned. He quickly drew back his head to avoid being seen. Then he squatted down and watched through the lower part of the window. One of the men had just come into the room, followed by the other. All of a sudden, the second one hauled off and bashed the other with his gun, and the first man collapsed in a heap. Lars stared as though riveted to the scene—this kept getting better and better.

The second man was now bent over the one on the floor and binding him with duct tape. Then he dragged him over to the kitchenette. He laid the other man's rifle on the dining table, took his own gun, and headed for the front door. Lars needed to hide, so he leapt around the corner of the house. He had barely made it to the side of the house when he heard the door open. As he peered around the corner, he saw the man walk to the Porsche and open the door. He laid his gun in the car and took a silver case from the back seat. Then he carried the case to the house and disappeared inside, leaving the front door open.

Lars waited a moment, but the man didn't return. Lars then slunk over to the window and peered inside to see what was going on. The man had apparently disappeared into one of the back rooms again, and the case was nowhere in sight. Lars waited. He was feeling great. His adrenalin had surged, and he was tense but focused—just like old times.

Finally, the man came back. Lars pulled away from the window and crept over to the door, positioning himself behind the panel. He had made up his mind. It looked like the man—probably Thomas Lind—was planning to abscond. He was unarmed and apparently felt completely safe. The moment had come to intervene.

Lars heard the man's footsteps coming closer, so he prepared himself. As the man turned to close the door, he was startled to see Lars standing there. But it was too late. Lars executed a perfect karate chop, landing it right on the carotid artery. Good to know he could still do that.

The man slumped down without a sound. Lars pulled some cable ties out of his pocket and used them to tie the man's hands behind his back and bind his legs. Then he grabbed him by the armpits and dragged him into the house. He laid him beside the sofa and removed his mask. Yes, that had to be Thomas Lind. At least, he was breathing—Lars had feared he had struck him too hard.

Lars then cautiously made his way to the kitchenette. There was the other man, still bound and lying on the floor. Lars took the rifle from the dining table and walked through the open door to the rear of the house, where a corridor led to several rooms. He opened the first door. It was a child's room with a large teddy bear and a Playmobil landscape. There was no one in it. He went to the next room. This one was a bedroom with a double bed. And lying upon it were Martin and the woman, both bound and gagged and both of them staring at Lars, wide-eyed. Lars fetched the knife from his pocket, flicked it open, and went over to Martin first. He set the knife down, and with a single, quick tug, he ripped the duct tape from his mouth.

"Wow, thanks! Thank God you're here, Lars."

"Listen, Martin. I've managed to incapacitate two men. Were there only two, or are there more?"

"No, we only saw two. Until this morning, it was only one."

"OK, good. Let me cut off your ties." Lars retrieved the knife and cut carefully through the tape to avoid injuring Martin. "Is that Liv?" he asked, when he was done.

"Yes. She also speaks German."

Lars turned to the woman and set about freeing her as well.

"*Tack så mycket!*" Liv exclaimed, relieved and grateful.

Martin pulled the rest of the tape from his wrists and stretched his limbs. Both he and Liv looked worn out.

"We've informed the police," Lars told them, "although I have no idea how long it will take them to arrive, and I'd rather get you out of here right away. Our car is about 200 meters from here. Can you manage that?"

Both Liv and Martin nodded. Lars started making his way to the door, carrying the rifle with him. Martin and Liv pulled on their jackets, which had been lying at the foot of the bed. They followed Lars through the hallway and into the living room.

"Now don't be frightened! The two men are lying on the floor in here, but they're both tied up and unconscious."

As Liv and Martin followed Lars through the living room, they glanced at the men on their way by. On seeing the second, Liv stopped in her tracks and clasped her hands to her mouth in horror.

"No! That's my husband. How could he do this to me? It doesn't make sense."

Martin placed his arm around her. "I'm so sorry, Liv," he said. "But that is what we were thinking. Do you want to talk to him?"

"No! I want to get out of here. Let's go to the car, like Lars suggested."

Lars carefully scanned the area before stepping outside. Since all was clear, the three of them hurried down the road to the main street.

"Lars!" Elin met them on the road as she was coming from the neighboring property. "Is everything all right?"

Lars answered her in English: "Yes. These two people are Martin and Liv. This is my colleague Elin. She's the one who called the police." He turned to Elin. "What did they say? When are they coming?"

"They didn't give any specifics except to say that they would send a patrol car right away. What happened to the two guys?"

"Both out of commission. Let's get to the car."

All four of them walked in silence as they headed to the street and then veered right to go to the Volvo. Martin and Liv got in the back.

"What do we do now?" Elin asked.

"We wait for the police to arrive. At that point, we'll probably have to make our initial statements."

Liv felt her jacket. "I don't have my cell phone. Or my wallet."

"Same here," Martin added.

"You can use my cell phone," Elin offered.

Liv gratefully accepted. She wanted to call her children.

After pondering the situation, Lars said: "I'm going back in there one more time. I want to make sure there's no chance those two guys can free themselves. I can look for your cell phones at the same time."

"Are we safe here?" Liv was feeling uneasy.

"Yes, I think so. Lock all the doors, and if someone comes, Elin will simply drive off. Understood?"

Elin answered for all of them. "Yeah, understood."

Back at the cabin, Lars found the two men still unconscious. Their ties had held fast, but to be safe, Lars also bound the man in the kitchenette with cable ties, which were harder to break than the duct tape that was binding his hands and feet. Then he dragged the man to the sofa, tied both men to its legs, and made sure there were no sharp objects within reach. Once that was done, he searched for the wallets and cell phones but found nothing. Then he noticed a parka lying on one of the armchairs. He felt inside the pockets—yes, there was something there. He dug out two cell phones and two wallets, shoved them in his pockets, and left the house once more.

Just as he made it to the pickup truck, the patrol car pulled up. Lars laid the rifle on the ground and slowly walked toward the patrol car. The car stopped, both doors opened, and two policemen got out and drew their weapons.

"Hands behind your head! On your knees!"

Lars did as he was told. He knew the procedure. One of the officers went over and frisked him. He found the cell phones but no firearms and seemed satisfied. He picked up the gun.

Lars decided to speak. "I'm Lars Olsson, private detective. My colleague was the one who called the police. The two kidnappers are inside the house, and both are tied up. As far as I can see, there's no one else there. We've freed the hostages."

"OK. Stay with my partner. I'll check the house."

The first policeman walked to the front door. Lars stood up with considerable effort and started moving toward the police car. He had barely taken three steps when he heard a deafening blast. A shock wave gripped him from behind and catapulted him within inches of the patrol car. Suddenly, all was still. Then he heard a loud peal, like the sound of a giant bell. He saw smoke and blazing particles floating above him. The other policeman came out from behind the car door and helped him up. The policeman was talking, but Lars could hear nothing. He turned around. The house was in flames, and the front wall had fallen on top of the pickup truck. Burning objects were strewn all around, and a bush had caught fire. The policeman pulled Lars away from the flames and behind the patrol car. Then he pointed to the road. He was holding his radio to his mouth and appeared to be speaking with someone, but all Lars could hear was a loud clanging sound. Right at that moment, there was a second blast as the pickup truck's tank was blown to bits. Lars's breath was knocked out of him, and he was thrown to the ground again. Then something struck him from behind, and everything went black.

30

It was a total inferno. Everything was on fire. At first, Elin had been relieved that the patrol car came so quickly. She had introduced herself to the police, described the situation, and shown them the way to the cabin. Her main concern had been how long she should stay—she was slowly getting hungry. Martin and Liv had also wanted to leave. But then, all hell broke loose: first one explosion, then a second. The flames and smoke could even be seen from the street. Elin didn't hesitate for a second but immediately took Martin and Liv in the Volvo and drove back up the road to the house.

Upon their arrival, there was third blast: a ball of fire was rising into the air right where the Porsche had stood. The patrol car was in front of them, and between it and the Volvo was a large piece of metal. Elin quickly drove over to the neighboring house, left the Volvo there, and flung open the car door. The air was so thick with smoke that it burned and stung. She raced toward the burning house, and as she passed the metal piece, she noticed two men lying behind it. One was the policeman; the other was Lars. She knelt down beside him and carefully turned him over. He was breathing but unconscious, and the back of his head was bleeding. She had to get him out of the danger zone.

"Martin, can you help me?" She looked back. Martin had gotten out of the car and was looking around in disbelief. Liv was still sitting in the car as though frozen, apparently unable to budge.

"Yes, coming!" Martin finally got himself to move.

"Come on—we have to get Lars to the car! Help me pull him over there. But be careful! I don't know how badly he's hurt."

Together, they lifted Lars by his upper body and dragged him to the Volvo. There, they laid him down, and Elin placed him on his side, bent his knees, and tucked one arm under his head. That was how you did a stable side position, wasn't it?

"OK, now we still have to get the policeman!"

They ran back. The officer was in the process of getting up. He seemed to have just come to.

"Are you OK?" Elin asked.

The policeman stared at her blankly. He was still in shock.

"Martin, will you take him to the car? I'll get the patrol car out of here. Otherwise, it will also get blown to bits."

Martin helped the officer to his feet as Elin examined the piece of metal. It had to be the hood from the pickup truck. She figured she should be able drive over it. Time was running out. There was not much left of the house, and what did remain was in blazes. Both cars were in flames as well, and the fire had spread to several trees and bushes, one of which was dangerously close to the patrol car. Elin went to open the door, but the handle was too hot, and she yanked back her hand and blew on it. Then she pulled the sleeve of her jacket over the other hand—her right one—and opened the car door. She got in and sat down. Luckily, the key was in the ignition, so she started the car and put it in reverse. As she glanced in the rearview mirror, she could see Martin helping the policeman over to the neighboring property. The officer was limping and leaning on Martin.

Now the coast was clear. Elin started off slowly in reverse, and as soon as she felt the car moving straight back, she hit the gas full throttle. The car lurched backwards and rocked across the hood of the pickup truck. Then the tires landed firmly back down on the dirt road. Elin drove a bit farther down the road and onto one of the properties, now safely away from the fire. She climbed out and ran back to the others. The policeman was leaning against the Volvo.

Elin spoke to him in Swedish: "Are you hurt?"

He gave her a dazed look. "Uh, no, not badly. Sprained my foot. Must have twisted it somehow. And my shoulder hurts where it got hit by the piece of metal."

"Did you call the fire department and ambulance?"

"Yes, I'd already done that before the second explosion." He was fidgeting with his walkie-talkie. "I tried to get through again, but the walkie-talkie is broken." He looked in the direction of the fire. "My partner is inside the house. He had just gone in when it blew up. We have to find him!"

Elin turned to look at the flames. "I'm sorry. I'm afraid there's no one left to save. We should try instead to get even farther away." She translated the last sentence into English for Martin.

"Yes, but what about Lars? He may be suffering from internal injuries." Martin looked uncertain.

"I'll call the emergency number again. Maybe they can tell us when the ambulance is supposed to arrive." Elin felt for her cell phone. "Oh, right, Liv, do you still have my cell phone?"

Liv looked about and found it on the seat beside her. She handed it to Elin, who called 112 and explained the problem.

"It sounds like they're on the way," Elin told them. "We can wait a little longer, but if the fire comes any closer, we'll need to lay Lars on the backseat and drive on out of here."

The others agreed.

Liv seemed to be coming out of her stupor. "Who set the place on fire? And was my husband still inside the house?"

Elin and Martin gave each other a doubtful look. Then Elin asked the policeman, "Do you know if the two kidnappers were inside the house when it exploded?"

He thought for a moment. "I don't really know. I wasn't inside, but the man—your colleague—said that both of them were in the house. And then my partner went in, and that was when the blast happened."

Elin translated for Martin, who turned to Liv: "I'm so sorry. It doesn't look good."

Liv nodded calmly.

From the street came the sound of a siren, and a fire engine drove up soon afterwards. Everyone breathed a sigh of relief. The fire truck drove up to the metal plate, and four men climbed out and immediately began to unwind the hoses. It wasn't long before the water was spraying. The firemen first tackled the trees and bushes to prevent the fire from spreading. The house and cars were beyond saving, anyway.

One of the men came over to Elin and the others and told them to move farther away from the fire. Elin explained the situation with Lars. The fireman spoke into a walkie-talkie and then turned back to Elin.

"The ambulance should be here any moment. You stay here with the injured man. The others should take the car and leave the immediate area."

Elin translated for Martin, adding, "Martin, can you take the Volvo down to the main road? I'll stay here with Lars and meet you there as soon as the ambulance arrives."

Martin got into the car with Liv and drove off. The policeman limped over to his patrol car. Soon afterwards, the ambulance arrived, and Lars was laid on a stretcher and loaded into the vehicle.

"Where are you bringing him?" Elin asked.

"To the hospital in Gävle," the paramedic replied and asked whether anyone else was injured. Elin showed him the burn on her hand and told him about the limping police officer. The paramedic nodded and said that a second vehicle was on its way. Then he climbed in, and the ambulance drove off.

There was the sound of more sirens approaching, so Elin headed for the Volvo. The entire length of the street was filled with flashing blue lights as another fire truck, two police cars, and an ambulance sped toward them. Things seemed to be slowly coming under control.

31

It was a dreary trip back to Stockholm, with everyone absorbed in their own thoughts. They had stopped at a gas station and picked up some sandwiches and drinks to take care of their most pressing needs. The police had been very understanding, taking only brief initial statements and jotting down their personal information. The second item was complicated by the fact that Liv and Martin were missing their IDs. They had either gone up in flames along with the summerhouse, or Lars had found them. However, under the circumstances, no one had thought to search his jacket pockets. Luckily, the police had accepted Elin's ID of Liv and Martin and let them go. They would take the official witness statements later on in Stockholm.

Elin had insisted on driving despite her bandaged hand. It was her left hand, anyway, and the ball of that hand was all she needed to manage the steering wheel.

She attempted to lighten the mood. "Oh, I'm so looking forward to going home. The first thing I'm doing is taking a nice, warm bath."

"Yes, I'd love that, too," Martin said. "But it just occurred to me that I don't have a hotel room, anymore. And my suitcase is in the Audi—in Dalarna."

"Oh, shit!" Elin exclaimed. "I didn't even think of that. But we can find you a hotel room and also stop off at a store and get you a few things."

"And Martin, you're obviously welcome to stay with us," Liv added. "We have a guest room with everything you could possibly need. I can lend you clothing as long as you're not uncomfortable with that. My husband must be about the same size as you, and the closet is full of clothes."

Martin thought it over. As much as he liked Liv, he needed some time to himself right now. The notion of meeting her children and wearing her husband's clothes— the clothes that belonged to the kidnapper, who had probably just died—was anything but appealing. He turned to Liv and looked her in the eyes.

"Thank you for your offer, Liv, but I'm not sure that's such a good idea. I mean, you're going to want to spend time with your children, and you have a lot to come to terms with. I wouldn't want to get in the way or be a burden on you. Let me first get a hotel room. We'll get together in the morning. What do you think?"

The tears welled up in Liv's eyes, and she cleared her throat. "Yes, you're probably right. But if you can't find a hotel room, you'll come stay with us, all right?"

Martin nodded. "Agreed. Elin, let's find a shopping center. Are they even open on Saturdays?"

"Of course! This is Sweden, the welfare state that takes care of everyone, especially the retail customer. All the stores are open on weekends."

Elin took her cell phone and called information. She was able to book a room at the same hotel where Martin had stayed before.

Sunday, September 27

32

The flames were drawing closer and closer, and the foot of the bed was already on fire. Liv had to tuck in her legs as Martin struggled with the duct tape that was binding her. Unable to rip it apart, he tore off one layer, only to find a new one beneath it. The tape was not just tying her hands and feet: it had her bound fast to the bed as well. Martin had to save her. Liv was shrieking "Martin, help me!" The room was getting hot. Martin ripped off another layer of tape, but now it was stuck to his hand. He tried to tear it off, but no matter how hard he tried, nothing worked. Just then, the ceiling caved in, and the flames engulfed them. He screamed.

Martin opened his eyes to find himself on the bed in the hotel room, drenched in sweat and gasping for air. Through a slit in the curtain, a ray of light streamed in and blinded his eyes. He took a deep breath, rose from the bed, and slowly paced around the room to calm himself. What a dream he had had. It seemed his subconscious still needed to grapple with the events of the past few days. Hopefully, that wouldn't be happening too often. But if he thought about it, the dream was a good reflection of his feelings: he had tried to save Liv, but without success. Martin had not yet fully grasped what had happened, but he assumed his attempt to free Liv had set the previous day's events in motion. Had he not searched for and found her, she would either have freed herself, or they would have released her after the appeal period had expired. It was only because of his interference that three people were probably dead now. He would rather not think about it at all.

Martin went into the bathroom to shower and get dressed. His new things were comfortable and fit well. They were casual clothes that he and Elin had picked up on the fly at the shopping center. They had dropped Liv off there, and she had arranged for a ride home from a woman friend.

Elin had been genuinely thoughtful toward Martin. She had helped him purchase everything and had even paid for two nights at the hotel. She had also slipped 500 kronor in his hand so that he wouldn't be totally penniless the next day.

Martin took the elevator to the ground floor to go to the breakfast buffet. He enjoyed that a great deal. There was a good selection, and he liked the different types of muesli most of all. It was nice being comfortably seated at a table again and having a variety of dishes to choose from.

He had only been held hostage for a day, but that was enough for him. Liv must be experiencing the same thing even more intensely. After all, she had been locked up much longer: six days in darkness and confusion, with nothing but sandwiches to eat and a sedative in the water. All things considered, she had managed to keep a remarkably even keel. It was only yesterday that she finally succumbed to exhaustion, but that was no big surprise.

Martin poured some more milk in his coffee. Swedish coffee was much too strong for him—it only tasted good with a lot of milk. He reviewed his situation. He was supposed to return to Berlin on Wednesday, though he could certainly put that off. Jürgen was sure to understand. Then his car was in Dalarna, along with his suitcase. The rest of his luggage was in the summerhouse he had rented in the south of Sweden. On top of that, he now had no ID or driver's license or credit card. Definitely an interesting predicament. Nothing like this had ever happened to him before.

Now finished with breakfast, Martin took the elevator back up to his room. He wanted to call Elin to see if she had heard any news about Lars, but since he had no cell phone, the hotel phone was his only option.

Elin picked up immediately.

"Elin."

"Good morning, it's Martin. Hope I'm not calling too early."

"Hi, Martin. No, I've been up a while. Just got off the phone with Lars."

"That's great. How is he?"

"Well, things don't seem too bad. But he won't be coming home until tomorrow. He has a fractured collarbone and a concussion. Other than that, just a couple of scrapes."

"Oh, good, that's not too bad. And how is his mood?"

"Well, how can I put this? He still sounded somewhat worn out. He also can't remember the last few minutes before the explosion. All he knows is that he went back into the house a second time, but he doesn't know how he came out. He only learned about the explosion and the fire from the doctor."

"OK. Can he have visitors?"

"Sure. But his family is coming today, so that might be a bit much all at once. I promised I would pick him up when he gets out tomorrow."

"Can I come with you?"

"Absolutely. No problem. Oh, that's right—I have some good news. Lars found your wallets and cell phones. They were in his jacket, although he doesn't remember how they got there."

"Oh, that's great! That makes my life a lot easier. I was wondering how I was going to get home without papers and a driver's license."

"You'll get it all back tomorrow."

They hung up after agreeing to touch base again the next day. Martin was doubly relieved. He was glad that nothing serious had happened to Lars, and it was also great to be getting back his most important belongings. Everything else would sort itself out.

33

The headwaiter showed them to a table in the corner with a view out over the water. The restaurant was inside a historic seventeenth-century building that was known as Stallmästaregården. The ceilings by the entryway were low, and everything appeared extremely old and exclusive. The entryway also featured a hearth with a crackling fire, and another lovely fireplace was warming the large dining room.

Liv and Martin had arranged to meet for dinner that day, and Liv had picked him up. She arrived in an i3, the electric car by BMW and, as Liv put it, "my No. 2 car, very practical for city driving."

The drive from Martin's hotel took no more than ten minutes, and there was a parking spot immediately in front of the restaurant. Martin noticed that the place had hotel rooms as well—a possible alternative in case he needed to extend his stay. It seemed cozy and almost family style to him.

Liv looked stunning. She was wearing a dark-blue suit, black stockings, and high leather boots. Her hair was freshly washed and fell in curls about her shoulders. Her makeup was subtle and tasteful. On the surface, there was not a hint of the torment of the past few days. Martin felt slightly uncomfortable in his casual clothing, but what could he do? For now, he had nothing else.

They took their seats and ordered something to drink. Martin decided on a beer. Liv chose juice.

"Sweden has very tough laws about drinking and driving," she explained. "That's why I never drink alcohol when I take the car."

Liv was rearranging her silverware and then took the napkin and folded it several times. She seemed nervous.

Martin gazed at her intently. "How are you doing, Liv?"

She stared at the table. Her hand reached for the napkin again. The corner of her mouth twitched. Finally, she looked up and said: "Not well, to be honest. I'm a total mess."

Martin noticed her eyes beginning to mist. "I can understand that," he said. "It's a lot to deal with all at once. How did things go with the kids?"

"I haven't told them a thing. They were happy to see me back home again. I … I told them their father was away on an urgent business trip. That's a common occurrence. But it was … it has been very hard for me to keep up the facade. They asked me a number of times if everything was all right."

"Liv, I'm very glad to be here with you, and I think it's wonderful that we've finally had a chance to meet under more pleasant outward circumstances. But if you'd rather be alone or at home, I completely understand. In no way should you feel obligated. We can leave right now."

Liv reached for Martin's hand and held it tight.

"No, Martin, please—no! I was glad to get together with you. I need to speak with you."

She gazed at him with her big, blue eyes. She kept holding his hand, even grasping it. Martin placed his other hand on top of hers and loosened her grip. He cradled her hand in both of his.

"Liv, please relax! I'm happy to stay here with you. Just tell me what's on your mind."

Liv eased her grip. "Thank you, Martin. I wanted … it's hard to know where to begin. You know that my friend picked me up yesterday."

Martin nodded.

"Of course, she wanted to know what happened. But I couldn't bring myself to tell her. I have so many questions myself. I have no idea … so I said that I had an accident with the Jeep. I just couldn't talk about all that. Can you understand that?"

Martin nodded once more.

"That's why I wanted to meet with you today. I have to talk to someone, and you're the only one who ... the only one I don't have to explain everything to from the beginning. You were there for most of it."

"Yes, I think it will do us both good to talk about it. I haven't been able to simply file it away, either." He thought of his dream.

Liv was about to go on when the waiter came with the drinks. He asked if they were ready to order, but they hadn't yet looked at the menu. Martin had been given a menu in English but decided to go with Liv's suggestions. They chose the smoked char for the appetizer and the roast venison with autumn chanterelles for the main course. Martin ordered a glass of red wine. Liv stayed with juice. The waiter happily collected the menus and went his way.

Liv turned back to Martin. "Martin, tell me honestly. My husband is dead, isn't he?"

What was he supposed to say? The matter was clear, but why did he need to tell her? He decided to be open about it, anyway.

"I'm afraid there's not much hope. You saw yourself how he lay there in the cabin, bound hand and foot and unconscious. And Lars told the policeman that both men were in the cabin just before the explosion. I can't think of any reason why Lars would have freed them and then lied to the police. I'm sorry, Liv."

Martin watched her as she took it all in. Liv glanced at the table. Then her blue eyes settled on him once more. She didn't seem at all surprised by his answer.

"Thank you, Martin. But our marriage had already turned sour for quite some time. We had a whole string of differences, mostly about our businesses. Still, that he would resort to these measures ... that never even occurred to me. After the kidnapping, there's no way I would ever want to live with him again. Maybe it's better this way, although it will still be a shock to the children. Not that he was the best father in the world, but they were obviously attached to him."

"What I don't understand," said Martin, "is how the explosion happened to begin with. Was it an accident? Or was it planned?"

"I think it was planned," Liv responded. "And that makes everything even worse. He wanted to kill us."

"You mean your husband caused the explosion? But where did he get the materials for that?"

"You know that we own a construction company. Sometimes we need to use explosives. I'll have someone take stock tomorrow to see if anything is missing."

Martin swallowed hard. This was adding a whole new dimension to the kidnapping.

"Liv, this is my fault, isn't it? If I hadn't come looking to free you, it would never have come to this."

"You must not think that way! You're not the one who kidnapped me, and you're also not the one who blew up the cabin. That was my husband. He's the guilty one. You tried to help me, and for that I'm extremely grateful to you. I mean, think about it: they would have released me on

Tuesday, assuming that was the plan. I still suspected that my husband was behind it, and I would not have rested until the truth came out. And then what? Take my husband to court? Or simply part ways? Even though what happened is terrible, maybe I'm better off without him."

"Maybe. It's just that three people died in the process." Martin paused and then said: "There was something else I wanted to ask you. Were you at all familiar with the cabin that exploded? Why did they take us there?"

"No, I don't understand why they moved us there. Maybe Thomas didn't want the explosion to be near his summerhouse. Someone might have made the connection. That's probably not true of the cabin that blew up. In any case, I'd never been there before. My husband never told me about it, either. And lately, he was on the road a lot and looking at lots of houses. His goal was to buy houses and convert them into apartments for refugees. That was another disagreement we had. You can make an awful lot of money that way since the communities have an urgent need right now for refugee housing, and they'll take whatever they can get. That means that you can dictate the price. There are companies that charge horrendous rents for such places. Thomas wanted to do the same. I was against it. First of all, I didn't think it was right to exploit the situation, and then I also saw the potential danger of having it backfire on us at some point. In Sweden, you can make yourself very unpopular if you heap up riches at the expense of the people."

"I see. And your husband wanted to do that through the property management company?"

"Yes, we had divided things up. He had the primary responsibility for the property management business, and I dealt with the construction company. Originally, it was all one business, but after I inherited it from my parents, we split it into two companies. That's also why I thought it was unfair that we were now selling my share."

"Well, that's no longer an issue. Tomorrow you can raise your objection, and then at least you won't have that problem anymore."

Liv was shifting back and forth in her seat. Finally, she said: "I wanted to speak to you about that. Maybe you could advise me. Somehow, I'm no longer so sure I even want to raise an objection."

Martin looked at her, perplexed. He hadn't expected that. "Why not?"

"Thomas is no longer with us, which means that the dispute is ended. But now the responsibility for both companies will be riding on me, and I'm afraid it will be too much."

Martin leaned back in his chair. He knew why Liv was asking him. He had no vested interest in the matter and was consequently able to form an objective opinion.

He thought it over. Then he said: "That's something you'll have to decide for yourself. I'm not familiar with the details of either the business under consideration or of your life. But if you ask me, what you're saying now seems a bit rushed."

Martin paused.

Liv nodded encouragingly. "Please continue!"

"Well, from what I've understood so far, the construction company is your domain, the part that you identify with more than the rest. Is that right?"

"Yes, I've managed to learn the ropes, even though it was hard for me at first. But now it runs beautifully, and I get along well with the team. I've also gotten better and better at making business decisions."

"All right. Well, in my opinion that would be the No. 1 reason to not sell. Instead, you might want to think about how to get rid of the property management company."

"Yes, that's right. Although I would first have to find a buyer, whereas the contract for the construction company already exists."

"Exactly. Which brings me to my second point. You mentioned that the selling price for the construction company had been set much too low."

"Yes, that's my suspicion. Maybe not much too low, but I believe we could get more."

"Then if I were in your place, I would raise an objection. It may sound simpler now to go through with the sale agreement and to content yourself with the new situation. But you might be angry about it later—about the low price and about the fact that you sold the part that meant the most to you. On top of that, your husband would still be getting his way postmortem. Sorry to put it like that."

"That sounds convincing. I think you're right. Maybe I'm just feeling overwhelmed at the moment and trying to make things easier on myself. But if I do that, I need to think about how to organize my work in the future."

"Can't you hire a general manager for the property management company? That should ease the burden in that area."

"Yes, of course. That is the standard solution, and that's easily done. We simply hadn't planned on it earlier because we both wanted to be in charge. But now I need to hand over some of the responsibility. Martin, thank you for your advice. You've been a big help. I'll still sleep on it a bit more, but I think I'll go about it that way."

"Great, I'm glad I could help. I'm happy to be there for you tomorrow, too, if you need me, although I had planned on going with Elin to Gävle."

Martin told Liv about his phone call with Elin, how Lars was likely to be discharged tomorrow, and that they had located their cell phones and wallets.

"That's wonderful, Martin! Tomorrow I'll also see to it that our cars and your suitcase are brought to Stockholm. And I will most certainly take care of all your expenses: the hotel, the private detective, and the car repairs."

"But Liv ..."

"Yes! No arguments! You had to pay for all that because of my kidnapping, and it won't hurt me one bit."

Martin gave in reluctantly.

Liv smiled. "But now, let's not discuss this anymore and enjoy our meal instead!"

The waiter had just arrived with the appetizer, which looked utterly delicious.

Monday, September 28

34

Lars still looked somewhat battered, but he was in good spirits. He was glad to be going home again. His left arm was in a sling, and he was wearing a clavicle strap on his upper torso.

Elin had packed Lars's things and had already gone to the car. Martin was sitting on a chair beside the hospital bed. There were two more beds in the room, but both of the patients were somewhere else at the moment.

"By the way, Lars," Martin was saying, "Elin was a great help, not only during the fire but to me personally as well." He was telling Lars how masterfully Elin had acted and what she had done to help him.

"I'm glad to hear that." Lars would pass the information on to his boss. This would definitely not be Elin's last assignment.

"Elin told me you couldn't remember the last few minutes before the explosion," Martin said.

"Actually, it's all come back to me now. After my family was here yesterday, I was able to remember again."

"So what exactly happened in the cabin?"

"The second time I went in?"

Martin nodded.

"Nothing at all unusual. I checked the bindings, tied the two men to the couch, and then looked for your things. Once

I found them in the parka, I left the house and was heading back to you all. At that point, the police car showed up. One of the officers went into the cabin, and then it blew up."

"Liv thinks her husband placed the explosive device inside the house. They apparently have access to explosives through their company."

"Yeah, that seems likely. It looks like her husband wanted to remove her from the scene. He had already knocked out the other kidnapper and tied him up."

"Oh, I didn't know that. I thought you put them both out of commission."

"No, that would have been too hard. They were both armed. I was lucky. After the other man was tied up, only Thomas Lind was left. That was when he fetched the silver case from his Porsche and brought it into the cabin. The explosives must have been inside the case. Of course, I didn't think of that then. He also left his gun in the car, which was why I risked bringing him down."

Martin shook his head. "Pretty cold-blooded to just plant an explosive device to blow up your own wife, your sidekick, and another person."

"How is Liv taking it all?"

"Surprisingly well. Apparently, her relationship with her husband wasn't that good anymore. But she never expected him to go this far."

"Why did he even do it?"

Martin told Lars about the planned sale and the objection period.

"So that means that Liv will be raising her objection today?"

"I think so. We spent a lot of time discussing it last night."

"So ... is there something going on between you two?" Lars winked.

The directness of the question made Martin uncomfortable. He could feel himself blushing.

"I do like her a lot. And she's grateful to me for putting myself out for her. But I don't think there's any more to it than that."

"Elin told me that the two of you blend well. And even if this sounds a little macabre, Liv no longer has a husband ..."

Martin thought back to their parting the night before. Once they had moved on from discussing more serious issues, their conversation had been very pleasant. Liv had visibly relaxed, and they had engaged in a lively exchange on every conceivable topic. She had told Martin about her childhood and her parents, and Martin had spoken of his time at the university and his law practice. On saying goodbye, they had kissed—a quick kiss on the lips. Martin was himself unsure of how much it meant.

Now Martin rose and walked to the window. Below, he could see the large parking lot and Elin making her way back.

"I don't know. It's all a bit much and not the best time for such things. Besides, we live in different countries. Liv has her family and her businesses here, and I have my law practice in Berlin. I just don't foresee any common prospects, even if I wanted to."

"What is it they say? Where there's a will, there's a way." Lars had gotten up and was standing next to Martin.

Martin sighed. "Yeah, but I'm not so sure about the will part."

"Your will or hers?" Lars gave him a mischievous look.

"Both."

Lars patted him on the back. "It'll be fine. But what are you planning on doing? Are you staying in Stockholm for now?"

"I'm actually supposed to be back at work on Thursday, but I think I'll put it off until next week. My Audi will probably arrive in Stockholm today, and it still needs repairs. So we'll see!"

Martin had already called Jürgen and informed him of the situation, with the warning that he would probably not make it back that week.

"Well, then you still have a few more days to work on your will." Lars grinned at him.

Martin couldn't help grinning back.

35

His bodyguards were sitting at the next table. He was sitting alone. There was a bottle of vodka in front of him, and his meal had just been served. Classical music was playing softly in the background—Shostakovich perhaps? He liked this restaurant and came here several times a week. That was also why he had a reserved table here. There were definite advantages to being known. The disadvantage, of course, was the security aspect. He was often accompanied by some pretty creature, but today he was by himself. Today, he had also come early, which explained why there were so few guests.

His phone buzzed—a Swedish number.

"*Da.*"

"Igor here. Can you talk?"

"I'm eating right now. Any news of our friend?"

"He was blown to bits with the cabin."

"How unfortunate for him. Yes, I saw your message. What happened with our deal?"

"Scrapped. By way of objection—today."

"As we feared. Not good."

"What now?"

"Plan B."

He hung up, cursed, and reached for the vodka.

Part II

Monday, November 16

36

Martin was en route to his office. The hearing had gone well, and he was sure they would win the lawsuit. Most of his cases were settled out of court, but this one had to be pursued to the end. Still, things were looking good.

Only now he was stuck in traffic. From the Neukölln District Court to Charlottenburg was actually not that far, but the traffic along Reichpietschufer was moving at a crawl. There had probably been an accident at the Potsdamer Straße intersection.

Once again, Martin's thoughts returned to Stockholm and naturally also to Liv. It had been nearly six weeks since he had come back home. He missed her. Yes, he had fallen in love. She was a strong, independent woman who ran a large company and had not allowed September's events to beat her down. That impressed him. And then there were those big blue eyes and that snub nose with all those lovely freckles …

By now, the traffic had inched along a few meters more.

Liv and Martin called each other often, most recently this past weekend. She missed him, too. He knew he meant something to her. In the week following the kidnapping, they had grown much closer and developed a certain intimacy—a lot of touching and kissing, although Martin had restrained himself. He didn't want to push for fear that conditions were not yet ripe. It would be too easy to destroy the tender seedling of their relationship. He preferred to leave the initiative to her.

He was also getting to know Liv's children, although it was the worst time imaginable since they had just learned of their father's death. It was only natural that they wouldn't be overly open to spending time with him, and communicating in English didn't make things any easier.

Martin hadn't attended the funeral. It seemed inappropriate to him. Liv agreed, although originally she had hoped he would be there.

Meanwhile, Liv had raised her objection and returned to the business full of verve. She had also begun the search for someone to manage the other company. And she had asked Martin if he wanted to spend the Christmas holiday with her. Of course, he immediately said yes and was looking forward to it. They had already decided that he would stay at her place. He hoped that the situation there would be relaxed enough by then that they could fully come together, even if their prospects for a common future were totally unresolved. Liv would not want to abandon her businesses, and although he could see himself living in Stockholm—the city genuinely appealed to him—it would mean giving up his practice. In Sweden, he wouldn't be able to work as a licensed lawyer. What would he do then? Go to work in some company's legal department? Or even work for Liv? No, neither of those were decent options. Still, in spite of all that, he had set about learning Swedish: two evenings a week at the adult education center. What was it Lars had said? Where there's a will …

The traffic suddenly started to move, first slowly and then gradually picking up. There were three cars sitting by the side of the road at the Potsdamer Straße intersection. Probably a rear-end collision. The police were waving the other cars through to prevent the gawkers from creating another slow-down and potentially causing a new accident. Martin drove by quickly without even looking—that was luckily not his problem. His Audi was running like clockwork. The repair shop in Stockholm had done a good job.

Ten minutes later, he was back at the office. They only had the secretary for half a day, so she was already gone. Jürgen, however, was sitting in his office with the door open. He looked up as Martin passed by.

"Hey, how did it go?"

Martin stopped. "It's looking good. With today's witness statement, we should win. The other side will have to have an amazing ace up their sleeve if they want to turn this around."

"Sounds good. When's the follow-up?"

"Next week."

Martin went into his office. The secretary had placed several documents on his desk. He set down his things and went into the small kitchen. There was just enough coffee left in the pot to pour himself a cup.

Now armed with his coffee, he returned to his office and proceeded to go through the documents: two statements he had dictated and that needed to be signed and a lengthy letter on one of his cases. He started to read.

He had just finished the first paragraph when his cell phone rang. It was Liv. He was glad, except that she normally didn't call at that time. They usually spoke on the weekends or in the evenings.

"Hi, Liv."

"Martin, can you talk?" She sounded upset.

"Sure, no problem. Did something happen?"

Liv was sobbing. Martin had a bad feeling.

"Liv, calm down. Talk to me! What happened?"

She took a deep breath. "Saga's been kidnapped."

"What?"

Saga, Liv's ten-year-old daughter, was a bright young girl who spoke good English, which was why Martin had been able to converse with her. Her brother Hampus only knew a few snippets.

"How do you know she was kidnapped?"

"I got a text and then an email with a picture. They'll be making their ransom demand tomorrow."

"How long has she been gone? How did they kidnap her?"

"Someone must have grabbed her at school during one of the breaks. One of the teachers called me at noon and asked if Saga had gone home. She was suddenly missing, but she hadn't signed herself out. I called Mai-Li, who said that Saga wasn't home, so we started to search for her—until the text came in."

"Have you called the police?"

"No, the kidnappers wrote that under no circumstances should I involve the police. They would be watching me."

"Yeah, they always say that. I would contact the police, anyway."

"No, I want to wait a bit longer. I don't want to risk it." Liv paused. "Martin?"

"Yes?"

"Martin, I'm sure you have a lot to do. But would it be possible ... could you come here?"

He would make it possible. Only how would he be able to help? He didn't know much about kidnappings.

"Martin, please! I need you."

"Of course, I'll come. But I hope you realize that I can't solve this for you. We'll be needing professional help."

"I know. Thank you for coming. I need you here to talk to—and for support."

"All right, Liv. I'll try to make it there today."

"Oh, thank you so much! That's great. But please don't tell anyone about this."

They said goodbye and hung up. Martin was horrified. He felt genuinely sorry for Liv. First, there was her own abduction, then her husband's death, and now her daughter's kidnapping. That was a lot all at once. He could hardly believe it.

He immediately got on the Internet and booked his flight. He had no problem getting a ticket—Monday evenings were not that popular a time. He sent Liv a text with his arrival time and flight number. The flight was through Norwegian and would depart at 9:30 p.m., which left him plenty of time to go home and pack. But first, he would have to talk to Jürgen. He hoped he would be all right with covering for him again.

Tuesday, November 17

37

Liv had called ahead for a taxi for Martin, and the driver, who was holding a sign with Martin's name, was waiting outside Terminal 5. They drove through the dark night, taking the freeway toward Stockholm and veering off to Danderyd about ten kilometers before. Twenty minutes later, at a quarter to one in the morning, they turned into the driveway to Liv's house.

Liv was already standing at the front door. On seeing her, Martin leapt out of the car, bag in hand, and ran up the steps. Liv smiled and pulled him into the house.

"Come in—it's way too cold outside. I'm so happy you're here, Martin."

She threw her arms around him and gave him a big hug. Martin dropped his bag and responded in kind. As Liv leaned against him, he could hear her starting to sob: "My poor little Saga. I'm so afraid."

Martin stroked her back. Liv was sniffling, so she let go for a moment to wipe her nose with a tissue.

"I'm so sorry. I always seem to be crying when we're together."

"That has a lot to do with the circumstances. I would have happily come to see you for other reasons," Martin replied. "Has anything new come up?"

Liv looked at him with tears in her eyes. "No, nothing."

She pointed to the wardrobe. "You can hang your jacket in there, and then I'll show you to your room. Do you want something to eat?"

"Yes, that would be nice. I only had a sandwich earlier."

"We have some leftover lasagna. I can heat it up."

"That would be great, thanks."

Liv set the plate of lasagna in the microwave. "Would you like a glass of wine with it?"

"Will you have one with me?"

"Yes, I could do that. It would probably do me good."

The two of them sat down at the kitchen table. Liv fetched a bottle of wine and poured them each a glass.

"How was your flight?" she asked.

"Oh, it was fine except that just before landing, the plane ran into some turbulence."

The microwave made a dinging sound, and soon Martin's meal was sitting before him.

"Liv, while I eat, could you tell me one more time exactly what happened today—or rather, yesterday?"

"Yes, of course." Liv took a sip of wine. "It started off like any normal day. I took the children to school and then drove to work. Mai-Li was supposed to pick them up. Saga had school until two and Hampus until noon. Then just before noon, the teacher called me and asked if I knew where Saga was. She hadn't signed herself out or shown up to her math class, and the math class had started shortly before eleven. I said I would check on the situation, so I called Saga's cell phone—she's had one for a year now—but it was turned off. I left her a voicemail and also texted her. After that, I immediately called Mai-Li, who had already arrived at the school to pick up Hampus. She had no idea where Saga might be. I asked her to keep an eye out for her on her way home and to also look around the house to see if she was there. She was supposed to call me right back. At the time, I thought Saga might have been feeling ill and had simply walked home. It takes fifteen minutes to walk to our house, and there are two or three different ways to get there. Then at half past twelve, Mai-Li called to tell me that she couldn't find Saga anywhere. That was when I started to get worried, since nothing like this has ever happened to us before. I immediately drove home and searched up and down the route to the school. Saga's cell phone still wasn't answering. Then I searched the house again myself. I was about to call the school when I received a text—from Saga's phone."

"And what did it say exactly?"

"It was just one short sentence: 'Check your email!' I found that strange. It wasn't like Saga at all. Of course, I immediately checked my email, and I noticed one that had a picture of Saga."

"Do you mind if I take a look?"

Liv fetched her iPad and showed Martin the email. It had a photo of Saga asleep, probably in the back seat of a car. Below that, in Swedish, was the body of the text. Martin studied the sender's address: rskvotne222@bip.net. Not much help.

"Could you translate the text for me?" he asked.

"Yes, of course: 'We have Saga. Nothing will happen to her as long as you carefully follow our instructions. No police. We are watching you. We will contact you tomorrow. Don't slip up!' That's it."

Martin had finished his lasagna, and his hunger was satisfied. He drank some of his wine and set his glass back down.

"So what did you do then?"

"I was utterly spent. At first, I just sat there, paralyzed. A while later, I called the office and had them cancel all my appointments. Then I contacted the school to tell them that Saga was sick. I had talked to Mai-Li and asked her to speak to no one about it. And we told Hampus that his sister was spending the night at a friend's. After that, I milled about here all afternoon in an effort to distract myself. After all, there was nothing I could do. Finally, I decided to ask you here, so thank you for coming, Martin."

"Liv, there's something I need to tell you. In my opinion, we need help, which is why I called Lars before my flight took off from Berlin."

Liv stared at him, dumbfounded. "The private detective? But I asked you to speak to no one."

"Yes, I know. And I didn't say a word about the kidnapping. But I trust Lars. He won't do anything we don't want. And he used to work for the police, which means that he knows more about kidnappings than we do, including what you can and cannot do."

"So what did you tell him?"

"I only hinted that I might have an assignment for him. He said he could meet us at nine in the morning."

Liv thought it over. "But if I am in fact being watched, then it's not a good idea. Even if he's not with the police."

"Yes, that's true. That's why I thought we could meet at your company. That way we could disguise our discussions as a business meeting, and you could explain things to him in detail. What do you think?"

"All right. I like that better. But let's not decide until after the meeting whether and how we plan on using his services."

"Right, of course. And ultimately, it's your decision. I can only make suggestions."

Liv seemed content. They finished their wine, and then Liv showed Martin to his room.

38

Lars took another piece of toast and was spreading marmalade on it. Lisa was busy dressing the children. The youngest was off to kindergarten and the older one to school.

"Please keep still, Olivia!"

Lisa was struggling with the zipper on her daughter's anorak. She finally managed to close it. Then she turned around and went back to the kitchen nook. Other than a small half-bath and the entryway, the ground floor of their townhouse had only a single large room with the kitchen in the front, the living room in the back, and the dining table in between. The kitchenette was located around the corner, and in the middle of it was a small island with four stools. That was where Lars was sitting right then.

"When are you heading out?" Lisa asked him.

"I have to leave right away. I'm meeting Martin, the German guy, at nine. He's back in Stockholm."

Lisa stiffened and slowly turned around. "Are you referring to that incident with the explosion?"

"Yeah, but it has nothing to do with that. He wanted to talk to me about some new thing."

"Lars, you're not going to get involved in anything that dangerous again! You promised me."

Lisa had been rather shaken on hearing about the explosion. And yes, it was true: had Lars stayed in the cabin just a few more minutes, he would not be sitting there now. He had been extremely lucky. Lisa had been so happy back when he quit the police force. The risk had always seemed too great to her. This incident had made her aware of the same potential for danger in his job as a private detective, and she didn't like it one bit.

"No, don't worry. First, I just want to hear what he wants."

Lisa walked over to Lars's stool and put her arms around him.

"Lars, please. I've had enough of these surprise phone calls informing me that you're in the hospital. I really don't need it."

Lars kissed her. "Yeah, I know. I'm careful."

"All right. Well, we need to get going."

Lisa hugged him once more, walked to the front door, and pulled on her boots. A cold gust of wind blew into the house as she opened the door. Outside, it was just a few degrees above freezing and also raining.

"Out you go, you two." She urged her children out the door. "Out into this lousy weather!"

And the three of them took off, closing the door behind them. Lars was now alone.

Lars was well aware of Lisa's opinion of dangerous assignments. And he understood. But this last case with Martin had been fun. There was some real action going on there, and Lars had had a chance to get physically involved. It was exciting, and he had succeeded in freeing Martin and Liv—and that made him proud. He was curious to see what Martin wanted today, although he figured it had to involve Liv again, since Martin had texted him that they would be meeting with her at her company. The company was in Vallentuna, north of Stockholm. That was good, because it would let him avoid the bulk of the rush-hour traffic. His townhouse was in Hässelby, northwest of Stockholm, but he would still need three quarters of an hour for the drive.

Lars placed the plates and coffee mugs in the dishwasher, put away the food, and brushed his teeth. Then he grabbed his keys and wallet and put on his jacket. It finally no longer hurt him to do it. He had dispensed with the clavicle strap two weeks before, and his collarbone had mended well. But for almost ten days after that, he was still having a hard time with a lot of movements. It was only in the last few days that the problems had fully resolved. His doctor had also told him he could gradually start exercising again next week. Lars liked to practice weight training on a regular basis, and he missed that. Six weeks of nothing but sitting around was not his style. He felt incredibly flabby.

Lars went out of the house and locked the door. His Volvo was standing outside the garage since there wasn't enough room inside for a car. Somehow, they had managed to accumulate so much stuff that they had to store it in there.

Bikes, sleds, remodeling materials, gardening tools, moving boxes ... for some reason, they never got around to cleaning it all up. Supposedly, it was better for the car to be parked outside. Lars hoped that that wasn't just some rumor propagated by other people with garages full of stuff.

It wasn't raining especially hard, but there was still a hefty stream of water pouring down from the roof of the garage. That's right—he needed to repair the gutter. Lisa had been nagging him about that for a while, but as long as he couldn't move too well, there was no point in thinking about it. That would be his project for this weekend.

The drive to Liv's company was no problem. There was a bit of traffic at the two lights in Hässelby, but once Lars was on the freeway, things went smoothly. It was a typical November day: gray, windy, and rainy. It would probably never get fully light today. Lars was hoping it would snow soon, because that would instantly brighten things up. But it was still too early in the season for that. In the past few years, they were happy to just have snow by Christmas. Somehow, the season wasn't the same as what he remembered from childhood.

Liv's company was located in the industrial part, and finding it was easy. There was a row of visitor parking spaces in front of the building, and virtually all of them were vacant. Lars parked his car and hurried through the rain to the entrance. He pushed open the glass door and walked into the reception area. Sitting behind the reception desk was a young woman who was on the phone at that moment. She was wearing a headset and jotting something down on a notepad. Lars stood in front of her and waited until she hung up.

"Hej! How can I help you?" she asked.

"I'm here for a meeting with Liv Ulldahl. My name is Lars Olsson."

"Yes, I'll let her know." She pressed a button on her phone. "Lars Olsson is here," she said and paused. "All right." Turning to Lars, she told him, "Liv is on her way." And with that, she went back to her computer.

Lars looked about. It was a typical office building on the outskirts of the city: square, utilitarian, with lots of glass. One corner of the reception area had a comfortable sitting space with leather furnishings, and the walls were decorated with tasteful prints.

Martin appeared from around the corner. "Hey, Lars. So glad to see you."

"Glad to be here, Martin." They shook hands.

"Please come with me. Would you like some coffee?"

"Yes, please. I only had one cup at breakfast, and that was an hour ago."

Martin took Lars into a small kitchen, complete with a sink, dishwasher, and high-end, single-serve coffee maker. He showed Lars how to use it.

"You really know your way around here. Are you working here now?" Lars asked.

"No, today is my first day here," replied Martin. "Liv just showed me how the coffee maker works. We'll be meeting in her office. This way, please."

Lars followed Martin, coffee mug in hand. They stepped into a large office with a desk and conference table. Liv was sitting at the table. She looked a lot better than the last time Lars had seen her, although she did not seem happy.

They greeted each other.

"Thanks so much for coming," Liv said to Lars as she shook his hand. "How are you doing? Are you fully recovered?"

"Yes, thanks," he replied. "I've been back at work for two weeks now."

The three of them sat down, and Martin cleared his throat.

"Lars," he began, "we need your advice. Liv has a problem, but it needs to be handled with the utmost discretion. What she's about to tell you must remain between us."

"Not a problem. I'm sure you know that in our business, 'confidentiality' is spelled with capital letters."

"Yes, but we need to be sure that you'll speak to absolutely no one about this, not even the people at your agency."

"OK, I can guarantee that as long as you just want my advice." Lars studied their faces. They looked extremely serious. What was going on here?

Martin glanced at Liv, who nodded back.

"All right. Liv will now tell you everything. She'll be doing it in Swedish to make things easier. Afterwards, we can go back to German."

Liv then launched into a report on all that had happened. Lars was astonished. He hadn't expected anything like this. He also had Liv show him the text and the email.

When she had finished her report, Liv said in German: "And now I'm waiting to hear back from them. I have no idea why it's taking so long."

Martin agreed. "Yes, I also find it strange. It has to be in their own interest to pull this off as quickly as possible."

Lars was pondering their statements. "There could be a number of reasons for that," he said after a few moments. "It could be to get Liv upset so that they can manipulate her more easily. Or they may need some time to prepare. They probably also want to wait a bit to make sure you haven't brought the police into it." He looked at Liv. "We still don't know if it's about ransom, do we?"

"No, but what else would it be?" she asked.

Lars leaned back. "I'd like to first go through some other possibilities—at least, from a theoretical standpoint. The majority of child kidnappings are carried out by a parent, like when the two parents can't agree on the custody terms. And then, of course, there's the child sex trade, or trafficking, as they call it. Can we definitely eliminate those two options in this case?"

Martin pushed his coffee mug to the side. "But they wouldn't send a message in that case, would they?"

"It could be a ploy to gain time—to transfer the child out of country, for instance. I don't want to cause you any added anxiety, but can we completely rule it out? Liv, could anyone in your husband's family have an interest in your daughter? Because if that's the case, we should immediately report the kidnapping to the police. There are also a number of non-profit and professional organizations that can help in such cases. Liv, how are your relations with your husband's family?"

Liv knit her brow. "We had very little contact with them. My husband didn't get along that well with his parents. The ones we still visited the most were his sister and her family. Of course, we all saw each other at the funeral, but we hardly spoke. I think they were all ashamed for my husband or for what he did. His father was terribly shaken, and he was the only one who came up and formally apologized to me for what Thomas had done. On the other hand, Thomas's brother Erik was very unfriendly. I think he blamed me for his brother's death. But I can't imagine that anyone from that family would kidnap Saga. My husband's sister has her own children, his brother is single, and their parents are already over 70. None of them has a special relationship with Saga—they've hardly ever seen each other."

"OK, then that's probably unlikely. Can you think of anyone else who might have an unusual interest in your daughter? Someone at school, on the street, or in the supermarket? Maybe someone who didn't look Swedish?"

Liv tried to recall. "No, I can't think of anyone. But I can ask Mai-Li. She's our au pair."

"Yes, you should do that in any case. But wait just a minute!" Liv had already started to reach for her cell phone and now stopped short.

"You should also ask her some other questions," Lars continued. "The kidnappers wrote that you're being watched. Have you noticed anything that might be related to that—people walking past your home, cars parked nearby? Or was anyone tailing you on your way here this morning?"

Martin and Liv reflected. Finally, Liv said: "I have to confess that I haven't even thought about it. My mind has been completely focused on Saga."

"And I didn't get here until late last night. I haven't noticed anyone. I did watch extra carefully this morning to see whether anyone was lurking near the house or tailing us, but there was nothing suspicious."

"All right. Then, Liv, please call Mai-Li now and question her on both points: first, whether any suspicious-looking people had, for example, been watching Saga or had even spoken to her before the kidnapping; and second, whether she noticed anyone yesterday who was hanging around the house or near it and who didn't fit in."

Liv nodded and brought her cell phone over to her desk. While she was busy with that, Martin leaned forward and quietly said to Lars, "I'm glad we can talk to you. Those were good points. So what do you think?"

"Well," Lars answered, "it's already looking like a case of kidnapping and extortion. But we won't know for sure until they send a ransom demand. That's why I wanted to keep an open mind and consider the other options first."

They could hear Liv speaking with Mai-Li. Liv then lowered the phone and addressed them: "Mai-Li hasn't noticed anything. She wants to think about it some more and then call back. She also asked if she should take a walk around the block to see if anyone is watching the house."

Lars shook his head. "I don't know much about Mai-Li, but there's the risk that she could attract attention. And if the kidnappers are watching you, then they also know who Mai-Li is. It would be better if it were someone completely neutral."

Liv spoke briefly into the phone again and then hung up. She returned to the table and took her seat. "And now?"

"Lars thinks it looks like extortion. But without a ransom demand, we can't be 100 percent sure. Lars, what do you think? I originally recommended to Liv that she call the police, but she doesn't want to."

"Under no circumstances do I want anything happening to Saga," Liv interjected. "And the kidnappers were very clear that the police were to be kept out of it."

Lars looked first at Martin and then at Liv. Liv appeared frantic.

"Well," Lars said, "it's obviously your decision, Liv. I have just two more things to add. First, if it has to do with extortion, then it's one of a handful of cases in present-day Sweden. There have been a couple of kidnappings, but they were mostly of adult men. The names Erik Westerberg and Fabian Bengtsson come to mind. In those cases, there was a ransom payment, and they caught the perpetrators later. The police were involved in one of the cases, while in the other, they didn't call in the police until after the young man had been freed. Kidnappings of children for the purpose of extracting ransom are virtually unheard of. I think there was one case like that back in the sixties. Of course, there could be a dark figure, where the kidnapping never comes to light. But it doesn't matter. The fact is that the police have not had much experience with cases of that sort, which obviously doesn't mean that they can't be helpful. Because that's the other thing: the police have vastly more means at their disposal for tracking down the kidnappers and also for arranging and monitoring a delivery, for instance."

"What would you do, Lars?" Martin asked. "You have a daughter, don't you?"

"Yes, two, actually. Both are even younger than Liv's girl. That's why I can easily imagine what you're going through, Liv. It must be horrible. I would also want to be dead certain that nothing happened to my child. The problem is that once you involve the police, you may no longer have 100 percent control over the situation. Suddenly, you're dealing with a whole team of police officers and technicians, all of whom are informed and who have their own ideas and goals. There may even be a prosecutor thrown into the mix, and he'll also want to have his say. That means that you'll no longer be able to make your own decisions. So that, Martin, is why I can easily understand Liv's position."

"OK. Thank you for your honest assessment. So then what do you recommend that Liv should do? Just wait it out and go along with their demands?"

"We can do a bit more than that. I'm not here to pitch our services, but there are definitely a few things that we can do to support you. We could trace the origin of the email, for instance, and locate Saga's cell phone. Then we could also help with the ransom delivery and so on. And if at any point we feel it would be better to call in the police, we can always do that, too."

Martin looked at Liv. "What do you think?"

Liv brushed a troublesome strand of hair out of her face and wrapped it around her finger. "I'm not sure. Maybe a little help would be good. On the other hand, I don't want to bring even more people into this. It just increases the chance of a leak."

"Well, it would be a small team. I could get Elin on board, so that's someone you already know. And then I would have to inform my boss or at least give him a general idea. Any additional team members would just be performing technical tasks, and they wouldn't need to know the background information. What's most important is that you would be making all the decisions—for every move we make. We can give you advice and suggest ways of going about things, but we will do nothing without a stamp of approval from you."

"That sounds good to me," said Martin. "What do you say, Liv? I know that I would feel better with that kind of support."

"Yes, all right. Let's draw up a contract—or however you go about it."

"Well," Lars said, "let me call my boss first, and then we'll take care of the details."

39

Lars wasn't sure how Tobias would react. As far as he knew, they had never taken on a kidnapping case before. He had gone to his car to be able to talk it over in private. Luckily, Tobias picked up right away. Lars explained the situation.

"Lars, that's not exactly our line of work. You know that, don't you?"

"Yes, but I've worked with them both before, and it's important to me on a personal level to help them."

"But that has nothing to do with our agency. And our experiences with those two weren't exactly the best. You almost bit the dust, and you were out for four weeks. I have no interest in going through that again."

"Yeah, well, Martin and Liv couldn't help that, Tobias. They were victims, too. And last I checked, Liv paid us a good amount of money for that job."

Tobias seemed to be thinking it over. "OK, fine. But the minute you smell danger, I want to know about it! And in that case, I reserve the right to terminate the assignment."

"Agreed. Thanks."

"You and Elin can set up the contract."

"Great. Can I also use Elin on the assignment?"

"Yeah, she's always griping about getting out of the office, anyway."

"Thanks."

Lars was relieved. He hadn't promised them too much, after all. He immediately called Elin.

"Elin."

"Hey, Elin. It's Lars."

"Hey, 'Splosion Man." That was her new nickname for him. 'Splosion Man was a video game action figure who used explosions to finish off his opponents. After the explosion in Gävle, Elin figured it suited Lars. Lars thought it was in bad taste at first, but somehow he also felt flattered.

"'So, yeah ... 'Splosion Man needs a sidekick. How 'bout it, Elin?" Lars had no idea whether the character even had a buddy, but it didn't matter.

"What? Seriously? Field work? Chasing crooks?"

"Yeah, something along those lines. And it starts now. Draw up a standard contract for Liv Ulldahl: two associates, minimum three days. Then bring it with you right away. We're meeting at Liv's company in Vallentuna."

"Liv Ulldahl again? Already? Uh, and how am I supposed to get there? By cab?"

"No, take one of the company cars. You'll need it. And Elin, no 'Splosion Man quips or the like around Liv and Martin! I don't think they'd find that funny."

"Right, got it. I'll be outta here in a flash."

"Don't forget the contract!"

"How could I?"

She was gone.

Lars stuck his cell phone in his pocket. He leaned back and took a deep breath. Somehow, this new case was strange, almost like deja vu: Martin and Liv as clients, he and Elin as a team, a kidnapping. The fact that Liv had suffered another blow like that, and so soon ... that wasn't just bad luck. But there was no point in bemoaning the situation. Now it was time to plan and coordinate the next steps.

Lars went back into the building. The rain had stopped, but it was still gloomy outside. The young woman at the front desk was on the phone. Lars signaled to her and proceeded past the desk to Liv's office. He knocked and entered.

Liv and Martin were standing by the window and looked at him intently.

"All taken care of," he said. "Elin is on her way with a contract. Then we can get cracking right away. But I suggest we discuss our initial measures now. You haven't gotten any more emails, have you?" He gave Liv a questioning look.

Liv shook her head. "No, I just checked again."

Lars sat down at the table, where he was joined by the other two.

"The way I see it," he began, "there are four clues that we can pursue: the emails, Saga's cell phone, whoever may be watching you, and the school. There must be someone there who witnessed how Saga disappeared. She couldn't have been all by herself during the break."

"That's true," Liv said, "but asking around at the school is not such a good idea. I told them Saga was sick."

"Right. But I'm sure you know which of her classmates she normally hangs out with. We could contact them at home."

"Yes, of course. Well, at most, that would be three or four. But what will you tell them?"

"We'll come up with something. For instance, that Saga told us some strange story and that we want to verify it."

"Yes, that could work. Except that they don't know you at all."

"Right. That's why you should do it—by phone. I don't want you driving around the neighborhood and potentially ruining the plan."

Liv nodded. "All right, I can do that. But the girls don't come home until early afternoon."

"OK. I suggest that the two of us do it together later. You can call, and I'll listen, all right?"

"Yes, sounds good."

"Great! One other thing: I'm assuming the kidnappers will be getting in touch by email, but if they end up calling you, you need to insist that they let you speak with your daughter. We need to know that she's all right."

"Yes, I'll do that. I want to do that, anyway ... my poor little girl."

Lars cleared his throat. He had one more question. How should he present it? Or should he just forget it? He decided to go ahead and ask.

"Liv, I've had another thought. It may be completely off the wall, but I'd like to ask, anyway. Could there be any link between what happened to you in September and your daughter's kidnapping?"

Liv and Martin stared at him. Liv frowned and brushed another strand of hair from her face. At last, she looked over at Martin, who shrugged his shoulders. She turned back to Lars.

"I don't think so. What possible connection could there be? Thomas wanted to ensure the sale of the company. Even if I still can't grasp the means he resorted to, the fact remains that he almost succeeded. But then the whole thing got way out of hand, and he was killed in the process. The police have confirmed that as well, so that settles the matter. Why? What are you thinking?"

It was obvious that Liv had to get a grip on herself to be able to talk about it. She gulped, the corners of her mouth twitched, and she became teary-eyed.

"I'm sorry to stir things up again, Liv. I just find it hard to believe that you're the victim of a kidnapping for the second time in a matter of weeks. That's why I asked the question. But you're right. It's obvious that your husband was one of the kidnappers, and it's also been proven that he died in the explosion. But it's possible that there's someone else in the background, someone who may have even forced your husband to abduct you."

Liv stared at Lars, wide-eyed. "That hadn't occurred to me at all. And you're the first person to suggest anything like it. If that's true, I might even find it comforting. It means I wouldn't have been quite so badly mistaken about Thomas, after all."

"If there is someone else that we haven't run into yet," Lars added, "then there's a possibility that person has made contact with you in some way. Has there been anything unusual to do with your husband or the sale of the company? A strange enquiry or phone call?"

Liv thought hard. Finally, she shrugged her shoulders. "No, there's been nothing. A lot of people have expressed their condolences, but there's been nothing strange. And my notarized signature canceled the sale of the company. After that, I heard nothing more about it apart from a written confirmation that the contract was null and void."

"All right, thank you. If you think of anything else, please let me know immediately!"

Liv nodded.

"So where do we go from here?" Lars continued. "I would like to monitor your own and your daughter's cell phones, both the communications and the locations. Is that all right with you, Liv? I'll need both numbers for that and also the name of the provider. Could you write those down for me?"

"Sure." Liv stood and went over to her desk.

"Is it that easy?" Martin asked.

"No. The police can obviously do it without any major problems. Unfortunately, we can't."

"So how do you plan on doing it?"

"We're associated with an IT firm, and there's a guy there who can do that kind of thing. It's not exactly legal, but it's effective," Lars said, winking. "As soon as Elin arrives, I'll drive over there."

"Do you mind if I tag along?" Martin asked. "Otherwise, I'll have nothing to do but sit around."

"Sure, that's no problem as far as I'm concerned," Lars replied.

Liv came over with a slip of paper that had the information for both phones. Lars thanked her and excused himself to go make another call. Martin then told Liv about the hacker and that he wanted to go with Lars.

"Is that all right with you, or would you prefer I stay here?" he asked.

"Martin, if it's all the same to you, I'd really appreciate it if you stayed with me. I don't want to be alone when the kidnappers get in touch." She looked at him imploringly.

"You're right. I hadn't thought of that. Of course, I'll stay with you."

40

Lars took the Kista freeway exit. Carl was expecting him. It had been a while since they had seen each other. There had always been something enigmatic about the guy, which was why Lars had said nothing over the phone and had confined himself to asking Carl what they needed to trace the sender of the email. According to Carl, that was easy. Using

Outlook, they could call up the email properties and see the so-called header, which contained all the information about the IP address, etc. Liv had printed it out, and Lars had brought it with him to show Carl.

Meanwhile, Elin had also arrived at Liv's office. Liv had signed the contract, and then Elin had driven over to her house. Lars had sent her with some instructions that would allow her to identify a potential lurker without being noticed.

Lars turned into the industrial park near the center of Kista. There were a large number of technology companies there, including such large firms as Philips and Samsung. There were also a lot of smaller businesses that dealt with technology or IT. Lars was lucky enough to find a parking space near Carl's company—another Volvo had just pulled out.

On getting out of the car, Lars wasn't paying sufficient attention and stepped in a puddle. He cursed and shook his left leg. His boot would keep out the water, but it had splashed in such a way that half his pants leg was wet. A woman was hurrying by and gave him a sympathetic look.

Lars locked the car and crossed the street, studiously avoiding any more puddles. On making it to the building without getting his feet even wetter, he pushed open the glass door. He took the elevator to the sixth floor and rang the bell for IT Experts Support AB.

A short while later, a young woman flung open the door and stood there staring at Lars. She was dressed in jeans and a hoodie, with a pair of Birkenstocks on her feet.

"Hej. Who are you here for?"

"Carl. He's expecting me."

She turned to the left and called out in a loud voice: "Carl, visitor for you."

Carl came shuffling up. He was stocky, his hair was tied back in a long ponytail, and he was wearing horn-rimmed glasses.

"Hej, Lars. Come on in!"

Carl led Lars through an open-plan office with a minimum of twenty irregularly distributed cubicles. The whole place was buzzing. Some of the team members were on the phone. Others were sitting at their keyboards, frantically typing away. Carl's spot was in a corner, and he had a corner desk with four monitors and two keyboards. He had offered Lars coffee, but Lars had declined. He wanted to get out of there as fast as possible. The whole atmosphere just wasn't his thing—it was way too hectic.

Lars and Carl sat down on two swivel chairs.

"Do you have the email header?" Carl asked.

Lars handed him the printout. Carl glanced at it briefly and then laid the sheet aside.

"I'll take care of it, but it might take me a few hours. You said, you had something else for me?"

"Yeah, two cell phone surveillances. Here's the information."

"OK. How urgent is it?"

"I need it as fast as possible. For the first, I need to know its location over the last twenty-four hours and also where it is now. And I need the communications info for both of them: phone calls and text messages."

"No problem. I'm on it. Do you want to wait?"

"How long will it take?"

"If all goes well, I should have their locations in a couple of minutes."

"OK, I'll wait."

Carl moved over to one of the keyboards, opened a program, and started typing. Lars was already familiar with the process: Carl would hack the telephone service provider's server and extract the information. Carl was actually a "white hat"—a so-called "good" hacker, if there was such a thing. But Lars knew that Carl would occasionally go beyond that, so that the label "gray hat" was probably a better fit.

The computer beeped a couple of times. Carl entered some more data. He was working with at least three different windows at the same time. Then he finally opened another that showed a map, and he plugged in some coordinates that he had copied from one of the other windows. A red dot lit up on the map.

"Voilà! The first cell phone is in Vallentuna, in the industrial section."

"Right. I already know about that one, and that's correct."

"Oh yeah, right, you just wanted the communications info for that number. No big deal. OK, now for the other one …"

Carl went back to another window, entered the other data, typed something, and hit "Enter." He came up with some new coordinates that he copied into the map window.

"So this cell phone is probably off. I won't be able to find out where it is right now. But it was on the net yesterday— at 1:04 p.m., to be exact. At that time, it was in the Mörby Centrum shopping mall."

"Mörby Centrum. All right, thanks." That was just a few kilometers from Liv's house. "Can you find out where it was two hours before that?"

"It'll take me a little longer, but I'll figure it out."

"Great. Can you email it to me?"

"Sure thing. Same address?"

"Yup."

Lars said goodbye and walked back through the office to the door. Carl was already busy at work in front of his monitors—two at once, from the looks of it. Lars passed the woman in the hoodie, who was absorbed in her screen and filling out some template. She didn't look up even once.

41

Elin stuck the newspaper in the mailbox and kept walking. Lars had good ideas—you had to give him that. *Metro* was free in a lot of cities, including Stockholm, so Elin had gone to the hospital underground station in Danderyd and fetched a pile of papers from the stands. Now she was distributing them throughout the area around Liv's house.

Only a few people were out and about. Most were probably at work, and the rest were in their homes—the weather wasn't exactly enticing people to go out for a stroll. Elin had encountered only one woman who was taking her Labrador retriever for a walk, and she had explained that she was part of an ad campaign. Of course, that was utter nonsense. First of all, *Metro* had no need of ad campaigns, and secondly, it certainly didn't need them in this wealthy area, where every household was sure to have at least one daily newspaper subscription and little interest in *Metro*. Luckily, the woman hadn't questioned her story.

Before picking up the papers, Elin had made a quick stop at home, where she borrowed one of Maja's old parkas. After rummaging through the closet, she also found an old wig of her own with long, dark hair. She had worn it once to a Halloween party. With some girlish makeup, Elin was already looking five years younger. Now she was walking around in this disguise. No one would recognize her, which would also guarantee her usefulness for further actions on this case.

So far, nothing had stood out to her, but she also hadn't yet made it to Liv's house. She had parked her car at the school and had taken the shortest route to Liv's place, only occasionally inserting a paper in one of the mailboxes. Otherwise, there was the risk that her supply might dwindle too quickly.

Elin was happy to be out of the office again. Since the trip to Dalarna in September, she had done nothing but sit at her desk. Tobias had praised her efforts and promised to keep her in mind if another opportunity arose, but nothing had happened since then. And it wasn't because he forgot— she had reminded him enough times. That was why she was happy when Lars requested her, and she hoped she would get more assignments now that Lars was fully back on the job. Still, Elin never imagined that her second assignment would revolve around Liv and Martin again. Liv didn't look good at all—like she'd been through the wringer. That was understandable. The poor woman had experienced quite a bit.

Elin was now rounding the corner as the driveway to Liv's house came into view. Before starting out, she had looked it all up on Google Maps—the street view was really useful. She looked around. No one in sight. She slowly continued walking. After another hundred meters, she had a good overview of the driveway. It was empty.

No, there was nothing worth noting here. No people walking by, no cars on the street. And the plots all had plenty of room for several vehicles.

Elin decided to toss another paper in the mailbox for the property diagonally across from Liv's. The mailbox was right beside the driveway, and a BMW was sitting at the far end of the parking area. Elin opened the door to the mailbox, but the mailbox was pretty full, so she had to shove the paper inside to get the door to shut.

"Strange," Elin thought, "didn't these people empty their mailbox, or were they out of town?"

She was about to go on when she noticed a movement inside the car, and something lit up. Someone was apparently sitting in the car, lighting a cigarette. She took her cell phone out of her pocket and pretended to make a call, but before she put it back, she took a photo of the BMW. Then she pondered her next move. Lars had impressed upon her that she was to do nothing but observe. Elin, however, decided to act. She walked over to the car and knocked on the driver's window. A man was sitting inside it with a cigarette dangling from the corner of his mouth. He lowered the window and stared suspiciously at her. Balding head, stubbly beard, on the heavier side, scruffy leather jacket—possibly not from this area.

"Hi!" Elin began. "We're conducting an ad campaign today. Would you like a free *Metro*?"

The man shook his head and waved her off. The window went back up.

Elin dropped the paper and made a big production out of picking it up, taking longer than necessary. The man ignored her and stared straight ahead, so she used the moment to stick a GPS tracker on the underside of his car. She had activated it the moment she left her own car. Now she hoped that the guy actually had something to do with the kidnapping.

Elin continued walking down the street but couldn't see any more suspicious-looking people or cars, so she headed to the school and gave Lars a call.

42

Martin watched helplessly as Liv paced back and forth in her office, her high-heeled boots making a staccato sound. She was a nervous wreck, constantly checking her inbox for new messages. The conversation with Lars had done her good. The questions and the discussion had kept her distracted, but after Lars was gone, she could no longer hold herself together. Martin was at a loss as to what to do—he felt so useless. So far, the only way he had managed to help was by bringing in Lars. He had also tried to calm Liv down, but without success. In his opinion, she should be taking a calmative. Instead, she kept drinking one cup of coffee after another, although she claimed it had no effect on her nerves—at least, no negative effect.

Martin looked at the clock. It was nearly half past eleven in the morning. He couldn't understand why the kidnappers weren't communicating. If their intent was to make Liv nervous, then they had already fully succeeded. There was no need to wait any longer.

There was a knock at the door. It was Lars, who now entered the room. It was a good thing, too. Hopefully, his presence would help to calm Liv's nerves.

"Hi, any new messages?" Lars asked.

Liv shook her head. "No, nothing. Damn it all, why are they taking so long? It's killing me."

"Have a seat. I'll fill you in on what we've got so far." Lars went to the table and sat down beside Martin. Liv hesitated at first but then sat down across from them.

"The cell phone surveillance is in progress," Lars began, "and we're also in the process of tracing the source of the emails. I'm hoping we'll have the results by this afternoon. What we already know is that the last time Saga's cell phone appeared on the net was yesterday at 1:04 p.m."

Liv glanced at her cell phone. "Yes, that's the exact time I received the text message."

"At that time, her phone was at Mörby Centrum."

"Where's that?" Martin asked.

"That's the shopping center closest to Liv's house. It's just a few kilometers away."

"Is that helpful to us?" Martin asked.

"No, not really. And it doesn't necessarily mean that Saga was there, because it was already two hours after the kidnapping. The person who sent the message could have made a point of being there at that time to avoid giving away his actual location. But at least it's nearby, which means that we can probably assume that Saga's location is not too far away."

Liv let out a deep breath. "That's good. Then at least she's not that far from here."

Lars continued: "Also, I just spoke with Elin. She noticed a conspicuous car parked diagonally across from your house in Danderyd. It was actually parked on the neighbor's property, and there was someone sitting inside it, smoking. The mailbox also hadn't been emptied for several days."

"What number was that?" Liv asked.

"Number 8."

"Yes, that's the Melander couple. They're both retired and are out of town this week."

"Elin is in the process of checking the car's license plate number," Lars added. "She was able to slip a tracking device onto the car so that we can follow its movements."

"Wow! Great!" Liv was excited.

"Well, we don't want to get too enthusiastic too soon. The man and the car may not have anything to do with the kidnapping, but if they do, we've got the guy by the collar. In any event, Elin is going to do another round once you're home. I've looked around here at the industrial park, but it's hard to pinpoint anything. There's a lot of activity here and a lot of parked cars, some with drivers in them. It's possible that one of the kidnappers is here. All in all, that means that what they said about watching you could be true. In other words, we need to be extremely cautious."

"And what does that mean in practice, Lars? Should we be doing anything differently now?" Martin asked.

"No. First of all, they'll be keeping an eye out for the police, but they also know that the cops won't be coming around in a patrol car. We should keep meeting here and not cause any commotion at your place. My only question is whether it wouldn't be better if the two of you went to Liv's so that the kidnappers see that you're staying put."

"Sure, we could do that," Martin offered. "But you should also know that you have a genuinely calming effect on Liv. Until you came in, she was pacing back and forth like a tiger in a cage."

"Yes, and I don't want to go home right now," Liv added. "I would go stir-crazy there."

"All right, then we'll stay here. At the moment, though, all we can do is wait."

43

The email arrived at one in the afternoon, exactly twenty-four hours after the first one. They had just finished eating the lunch they had ordered, although Liv had hardly touched any of hers. She had set her phone so that it would beep whenever an email came in. Until now, they were always other emails, but this time, it was the one they had been waiting for. Liv read it and shook her head in disbelief.

She sat down at the table, handed the phone to Lars, and buried her face in her hands. Martin stared at her, horrified. What had happened now?

Lars was breathing heavily as he read the email.

"This is unbelievable," he said. "They want 100 million kronor." That was more than 11 million euros.

"Are you sure there isn't one zero too many there?" Martin asked.

"No, they also wrote it out. There's no doubt about it."

"God, that's a ton of money. What else did they write?" asked Martin.

"I'll translate: 'Your daughter is fine. Stick to our instructions. No police! We are demanding 100,000,000 SEK. Get the money together and contact us at this email address. At that time, we will give you the number of the account to be used for the funds transfer. We will shortly be sending another email with a video.' That's all they wrote."

Martin looked at Liv. That was a huge amount. Would she be able to raise that much? She hadn't budged at all but just sat there with her elbows on the table and her face buried in her hands.

Martin turned to Lars. "Lars, how much did they demand in other cases?"

"In Fabian Bengtsson's case, I think it was 55 million kronor, but the family never paid it. Of course, that was ten years ago. But the Bengtssons are one of the richest families in Sweden. At that time, they already had billions in capital. They could easily have forked over that amount. So Liv, what's the situation with you?"

Liv slowly lowered her hands. Her face was wet and her makeup smeared. She fumbled around for a tissue to wipe her nose and eyes. Then she shook her head.

"No," she replied softly. She cleared her throat. "I could never get that much together."

Martin and Lars looked at each other. Martin had no concept of Liv's financial situation. It was obvious that she had a lot of money, but 11 million euros was another scale altogether.

Martin turned to Liv. "Liv, it's none of our business, but maybe it would be good if you outlined the exact situation for us. How much cash do you have available, and what could you sell to increase the amount?"

Liv stared at the table. Then she quietly answered: "Yes, I have no problem telling you. I have a bit in savings—just under two million kronor all together. And then there are the houses and the two companies. And the two cars."

She looked up. Her big blue eyes were filled with tears.

"Everyone thinks we're super rich, and yes, I have enough money and can afford plenty of things for myself. But that amount? Back when I took over the company, it was already running well. And then we bought the house in Danderyd. We took out a mortgage for half its value. But then the financial crisis occurred, and the market stagnated. We had hardly any business, so I also took out a mortgage on the house in the Archipelago. That would let us pull through and also make some critical investments. Once things picked up again, we decided to take our time with paying down the mortgage. It's actually due now."

"All right, so even if you sold both of the houses here—I mean, the one in Danderyd and the one in the Archipelago—how much would you get from that?" Martin asked.

Liv thought for a moment and then replied: "Prices have gone up dramatically, so that being the case, maybe 10 million for our house in Danderyd and 5 to 6 million for the summerhouse in the Archipelago. That's minus the mortgages, although I would still have to pay taxes."

"In Germany, we pay no tax after ten years of use. Is that not the case in Sweden?"

"No," Lars answered. "You always have to pay tax on your capital gains—22 percent."

"All right, but do you have to pay it right away?"

"No, not until you file your tax return."

"OK. Liv, what about the house in the mountains and the one on Mallorca?" Martin asked.

"The one in Åre is just a ski cabin. I might be able to get two million for it. The finca is worth more, probably 20 million. But it's on leased property and is hard to sell for that reason. We had already toyed with the idea and looked into it. That's how I know."

Martin had been adding it all up in his head. "So the sum total of all of that doesn't amount to even half the ransom demand. What makes them think Liv can pay 100 million?"

"And besides," Lars added, "it's impossible to sell all those properties in such a short a time. Even with a buyer already in place, it still takes a couple of weeks to wrap everything up and for the funds to clear."

"And a loan is out of the question since the combined value of the houses is not enough to use as collateral. So what can we do? Should we make them a lower offer?" Martin looked at Lars.

"You could try that, of course, but whether they believe that Liv is incapable of paying more is another question. What about your company, Liv? Could you borrow against that?"

Liv shook her head. "Not for that amount. The sale price was just about 100 million."

"Well, wait a minute. The canceled deal was for the same amount, wasn't it?" Martin asked.

Liv nodded.

"Was the price public knowledge?"

"No, at least not through us, except that the buyer, agent, and notary were obviously all privy to it."

"Yes, I can confirm that," Lars threw in. "In September, Elin and I tried to find out the selling price but without success. We didn't try all that hard, and there are better sources than the Internet, but still."

"Right. So maybe the kidnappers got wind of the amount and now believe they could siphon off the money," Martin mused.

"Do you think they're unaware of the canceled deal?" Lars asked.

"Either that, or they imagine that Liv can somehow realize the value of the business," replied Martin

Liv gave him a despairing look. "But how?" she asked.

For a while, there was silence. Finally, Lars asked: "Is selling the company still an option?"

Liv looked off into the distance. "I have no idea. Maybe the buyer has set his sights on something else in the meantime. I can check, though. Do you both think I should?"

Martin nodded. "As far as I can see, that's your only chance to come up with the ransom amount. And since a draft of the contract already exists and has already been signed, you could finalize the deal pretty quickly." Finally, a topic he knew well. "You just remove the passage about the objection period, change the signatures and the date, and it's done."

Lars agreed. "Yeah, at least ask about it."

Liv stood and walked to her desk. "All right, then I'll call the agent right away."

Martin turned to Lars. "What else was in the email? They said they're sending a video?"

Lars nodded.

"What do you think it's about?" Martin asked.

"I'm reasonably sure it will be a video with Saga in it," Lars replied. "If not, then we should insist on some sign of life, regardless. But let's wait for the email to arrive!"

Liv was talking on the phone with someone. She had apparently managed to reach the agent. After several more comments, she ended the call.

"The agent will get in touch with the buyer," she told them. "I made it clear to him that it's urgent."

44

Elin was getting bored. Even the office was more exciting. She had driven past the house another two times, but there was nothing happening. The BMW was still parked on the same property, although she could see that from the GPS program on her laptop. She wanted to avoid driving past it too often since that would definitely stand out—assuming the guy was in fact watching Liv's house and whatever was going on there. Then again, why else would he be sitting in his car for hours end?

Maja had just called. She wanted to know if Elin was interested in seeing a movie that evening.

"I don't think so, love. I'm on assignment, and it could take a while."

"What? And you're telling me this in passing? That's great!"

"Yeah, I'm seriously happy about it. Lars asked for me again."

"Your 'Splosion Man?"

Elin chuckled: "Exactly! Now I'm his sidekick."

"I had no idea there even was one ..."

"There isn't in the video game, but for Lars, there is."

"That's great! Good luck! You'll tell me all about it tonight, right?"

"Well, yeah, but it might be pretty late."

"OK, I'll see you then."

Elin always felt so good after talking to Maja. She was so supportive of her goals. But right now, Elin wanted to see some action. She called Lars.

"Hey, Elin."

"Hey, 'Splosion Man."

"Elin, chill on that."

"Yeah, I know, but there's no one listening, is there? I just wanted to ask you what we're doing next. There's nothing going on here. And I can't just keep trudging around the place."

"Yeah, hang on a sec! I'm going outside."

Elin could hear footsteps and then a door.

Lars was back. "OK, now I can talk. So there's nothing new on your end? What about the car at the neighbor's?"

"Same as before. Hasn't budged."

"OK, then come on over here. We just got an email, and we're waiting for the second one."

"Oh? What's in it?"

"I'll tell you when you get here."

"OK, see you soon."

Elin hung up. This sounded interesting. She put the car in gear and started it. She was itching to learn more but decided to observe the speed limit.

A half hour later, Elin pulled up at Ulldahl Bygg, Liv's construction company. Lars was standing in the doorway. He had his jacket on and came down the steps. He had apparently been waiting for her, and now he sat down in the front passenger seat and shut the door.

"Do you want me to drive?" Elin asked.

"No, no, you can turn off the engine. I just wanted to give you a quick briefing before we went in."

Elin turned off the ignition, and the sound of the engine died down. She looked at Lars expectantly.

"Shoot, 'Splosion Man."

Lars rolled his eyes. Elin giggled.

"So the first email came in an hour ago. In that one, the kidnappers were demanding 100 million kronor."

"Holy moly!" Elin's eyes opened wide.

"Yeah, exactly. We've already discussed how Liv could come up with that amount. She doesn't have much cash—it's all tied up in houses and businesses. There are partial mortgages on some of the houses, and selling them would take a while. The only viable solution we've come up with so far is to sell the construction company, assuming the previous buyer is still interested. We're looking into that now."

"OK."

"A couple of minutes ago, we got the second email with a video attached. It shows Saga with a copy of today's paper."

"Did she say anything?"

"Only that she was fine and that she wanted to go home. That upset Liv a fair amount. Martin is doing his best to comfort her. That's why I wanted to give you a heads-up so that we don't stir things up again."

"When do they want the money?"

"Liv is supposed to let them know when she has it all together, and then they want it transferred to their account."

"That's odd, isn't it? Usually, they want cash."

"Yeah, that's right. They seem awfully sure of the situation. Although from a purely logistical standpoint, delivering such a large sum in cash could present a real problem. It wouldn't fit into a suitcase and would also weigh a decent amount."

"True. Especially if they wanted it in smaller bills." Elin chuckled. She could just see some guy using a shovel to unload a luggage compartment full of bank notes at the delivery site. "So what do we do now?" she asked.

"We're waiting to hear from the buyer and also from Carl about his findings. But we should still keep an eye on the BMW near Liv's house—I mean through the GPS program."

"Yeah, no problem. Should I do that from here in the car, or are we going inside?"

"We're going inside. I hope Liv has gotten a hold of herself in the meantime."

Elin took her bag and laptop and followed Lars inside, past the reception desk, and into the large office. Martin waved at her. Liv was sitting at her desk, staring at the computer screen. Lars motioned to Elin to sit down at the big conference table. She decided to keep her mouth shut for now and immediately opened her laptop and went to the GPS program. The blinking dot was still in the same spot, which in itself seemed suspicious. Who would sit alone in a car for hours on end, and in that area?

Martin came over to the table and whispered to them: "She's watched that video five times already. But at least she's not crying anymore. Any news?"

"No," Lars said. "Now we just have to wait."

45

The first messages came an hour later. The agent called to say that he had spoken with the buyer, who was interested in finalizing the deal, even on short notice. But now he only wanted to pay 90 million. Liv was already on the phone with her bank to procure the remaining 10 million for the ransom.

Lars's cell phone rang. It was Carl. Lars took his phone and went outside. After a few minutes, he came back in. Liv was still on the phone.

"Any news?" Martin asked Lars.

"Yes, but no progress. I'll tell you both once Liv is done with her call."

Martin went to get himself another cup of coffee. In spite of all the excitement, he couldn't help noticing that he was starting to feel tired. It had been a long night.

Liv had just hung up as Martin reentered the room. Lars and Elin were both sitting in front of the laptop.

"How are things looking?" Martin asked Liv. "Will you be able to get the money?"

"Yes, I can take out additional mortgages on the two houses in Stockholm, so together with the money in my account, it will be enough. I spoke first with my contact at the bank and then with the head of the loan department. He hasn't yet confirmed it 100 percent, but he was optimistic. In any case, I have to go to the bank to sign the application forms. If I do that today, I can have the money tomorrow, assuming everything goes smoothly."

"All right, that sounds good! If we can finalize the sale tomorrow, then you may also be able to deliver the money tomorrow." Martin was trying to cheer Liv up. He turned to Lars. "Lars, you had news?"

"Yes, but nothing that gets us any further—unfortunately. My IT expert Carl called me. Saga's cell phone was never turned back on, so there's no way we can get a location. We also can't trace yesterday's email. Carl has tried everything, but he's only been able to get as far as an elite server in the Seychelles. I don't know how much of this you understand—I can't say that I fully understand it myself—but that's apparently a server that ... how can I explain this ..."

"I can do it." Elin had a mischievous smile on her face. "An elite server," she went on, "is a totally anonymous proxy server. A proxy server acts as an intermediary server between the Internet and your own personal network or computer. You can use it to cloak your IP address."

Liv and Martin appeared to not be completely following her, so Elin expanded on her explanation. "The IP address is the address that identifies your computer and through which you do all your communications. An anonymous proxy server replaces that address so that you can't be identified, although the server identifies itself as a proxy server. An elite proxy will also make you anonymous, but you would need a specific type of special software to identify it as a proxy."

"Thanks, Elin. I couldn't have explained it better myself."

Elin rolled her eyes.

Lars continued. "Anyway, Carl has this special software and was able to identify the server as an elite server. But that's where it stops. The only way we could get any further is by getting the server operator to release both the communications and the IP addresses. Of course, you can forget about that for the Seychelles, which means that we won't get any further with this. Elin also sent Carl the headers for both new emails, but I'm not too hopeful that tracking them will reveal anything new." He looked at Elin. "What else have we got? Oh, yeah, the BMW in front of your neighbor's house is still parked in the same spot. So unfortunately, there are no further clues for us to pursue."

"I'll pay. I've already confirmed with the buyer of my company, and he's ready to sign the contract tomorrow. The sooner I pay, the sooner I'll have Saga back. Anything else will jeopardize that." Liv placed her hands firmly on the table.

The room was silent for a moment. Then Martin turned to Lars with a worried look.

"Are we doing everything right here? Will they actually free Saga once Liv has paid this enormous sum?"

Lars grew very serious. "There's no way we can know for sure, Martin. There are unfortunately no guarantees. But I'm encouraged by the fact that, so far, everything has been done very professionally. The kidnappers haven't let their guard down at any point, either in their communications or with the actual kidnapping. That gives me hope that they'll also behave professionally when it comes to keeping their word."

Once again, there was silence. Then Lars said: "Liv, earlier, we talked about Saga's friends. Shouldn't we at least call them to see if they've noticed anything?"

Liv furrowed her brow. "I still have to go to the bank. I don't want to do that too late. Otherwise, the loan may not go through until tomorrow."

"Yes, I understand, although it wouldn't take long to talk to Saga's friends, and you could head out right after that. I also suggest that one of us drive you to the bank."

"All right, then let's try it!" And Liv immediately reached for the phone.

46

Martin was steering the car through the intersection on the way to Liv's house. Liv was sitting in the passenger seat beside him, slumped down and totally exhausted. Who could blame her? It had been a nerve-racking day. The phone calls with Saga's friends had yielded little. Only one of the girls had seen Saga being approached by a man during the break in the schoolyard. Saga had vanished with him into the school building and had not shown up for her next class after that. The girl could give no further description of the man except that he was wearing a long coat and a hat.

After the phone calls, Martin drove Liv to the bank. Elin had driven ahead of them and shown Martin the way. Now she was ahead of him again.

At the bank, everything went smoothly. Liv had signed the mortgage agreements, and the money was expected to be in her account by the next day. The sale of the company would also take place the next day at 11 a.m., and by then, the notary would have made the relevant amendments to the text. In other words, everything would be ready.

In spite of that, Martin still felt anxious. Would the ransom payment get Saga back? And then there was that huge sum. He himself had never possessed even remotely that much money—he hadn't even paid off his condo yet. That was why he had trouble thinking on that scale. Liv seemed to have no doubts. She would do everything in her power to get Saga back. Nothing else mattered. And the consequence would be that she would lose the company, after all.

Elin pulled off to the right. They had agreed beforehand that she would not be accompanying them all the way to the house, and from here it was easy to find. Martin drove past her and waved. She waved back energetically and grinned. It was nice having Elin on board. She never seemed to lose her good mood. Then again, she wasn't directly affected. Still, her good cheer was something they all could certainly use.

Martin didn't know what they would do between now and the morning. He hoped that Liv would be able to calm down and get some sleep. Then he would also have a chance to lie down for a while.

Liv's new cell phone rang with its old-fashioned ringtone. Lars had given the phone to Liv and Martin so that they could communicate with him by some other means than Liv's number. Liv picked up. Lars wanted to find out how things had gone at the bank. After a few comments, Liv hung up again.

"Lars says hello. He thinks I should take a sleeping pill so that I'm in good shape tomorrow. Might be a good idea."

"Yes, do you have any here?"

"I think so. There was a period last year when Thomas was having a hard time sleeping. There are probably still some left in the box."

Liv thought back to that time. Back then, the world was still in order—at least, compared to now. Thomas was alive, and Saga was at home. They hadn't had any major arguments yet, although Thomas had become more distant. Liv never did find out why he had so much trouble sleeping. Something was troubling him, but he insisted that it was nothing. Was that when their problems had begun? She didn't know. She wondered whether her life would ever be normal again. She tried to beat back the tears—self-pity just wasn't appropriate right now. Her sole purpose was to rescue Saga. After that, everything else would sort itself out.

Liv looked over at Martin, who was concentrating on driving. She was glad he was there. And he had been right about bringing in a private detective. Discussing the whole matter with other people had been good. They were all so capable, too. Liv couldn't imagine how she would have handled that day by herself. She reached over and placed her hand on Martin's. He turned his hand over and squeezed hers. He smiled at her. It felt good to be by his side.

47

Elin was staring at the screen. The red dot was moving. She immediately called Lars.

"The BMW is leaving."

"OK, in which direction?"

"He should be passing you soon."

Lars was sitting in a roadside parking spot on the other side of the school. "OK, just as we discussed, you tell me where he's driving, and I'll tag along behind him."

Lars's car also had a GPS tracker, which showed as a green dot on Elin's map. The red dot was passing it right at that time. If Elin did a good job guiding Lars, he wouldn't need to drive too closely behind the other car and could still follow it without attracting attention.

Elin kept Lars informed as to how the BMW was moving on the map. First, it went to Mörby Centrum. From there, it proceeded onto the freeway to Stockholm and turned onto Route E18 heading west. Then it went under the E4 bypass. For a little while, Elin questioned whether the BMW would be turning onto the ramp, but it soon became clear that the car was staying on the E18. It kept driving straight until County Road 279, where it turned left into the Bromsten district. The car then stopped midway on Duvbovägen. Elin let Lars know.

"OK, I'm driving past it now," Lars told her. "Yeah, I see the BMW, and the driver is getting out of the car. Wait, I need to find a parking spot."

Elin heard the car sounds in the background. Finally, Lars came on again.

"So I'm parked on a side street. The driver is crossing the street as we speak. He's going to No. 122a. There's a pub on the ground floor of the building, and he's now in the entryway to the apartments and is plugging in a door code."

In most multi-family dwellings in Sweden, the main entrance door was always locked but could be accessed through a four-digit code. This code was known to all residents and naturally also to the mailman and the building management. Normally, there was no doorbell for the individual apartments. Visitors would either receive a code in advance, or they would need to use their cell phone to call the apartment once they were down at the main door. The resident could then press a button inside the apartment to let them in.

"The man has now disappeared into the building. Either he lives there, or he's visiting someone."

"If he lives there, wouldn't that be listed in the BMW's ownership information?"

Elin had sent in the car's license plate number to Transportstyrelsen, the central office for transportation. Transportstyrelsen had a text messaging service that worked quickly and without any issues. You simply sent a text with the license plate number, and you would receive a message with the vehicle and owner information. Each inquiry cost three kronor. Thank God for Swedish transparency!

The BMW belonged to a Bengt Persson in Nacka, a district in the southern part of Stockholm. So far, it had not been reported stolen.

"Yeah, I know," said Lars. "Maybe he borrowed the car. Or it was stolen, and the owner doesn't realize it yet ... So now a light has gone on in the apartment on the top floor, which is the third floor. I think he lives there. Elin, I'm going to wait a while longer, and then I'll end the surveillance."

"Don't you want to check out the apartment? Saga could be in there."

"No, I don't think so. We're definitely not dealing with a single individual here. And if we force our way in and Saga isn't there, then we could jeopardize the entire rescue mission. And that's totally apart from the fact that Liv gave us clear orders not to interfere."

"Got it. So what do I do?"

"You can drive home. That's all for today."

"OK, what's on for tomorrow?"

"Head over to the office first, and I'll get in touch with you then."

"OK, talk to you tomorrow."

Elin hung up. She had finished earlier than expected. Now all she needed to do was drive home. She lived on Kungsholmen, one of the islands in the center of Stockholm. It was rush hour, and even if most of the traffic was headed out of the city, it would still take some time to slog through it.

But first, Elin wanted to drive past Liv's house one more time. Somehow, she just couldn't imagine the surveillance as being completely done. She started the car, reversed direction, and turned onto Liv's street after a short stretch. She drove slowly past the property where the BMW had been parked. And she was right: an Audi now sat in its place. She memorized the license plate number and kept driving, repeating the number out loud so she wouldn't forget it.

After the next bend in the road, Elin pulled over to the right and took out her cell phone. She entered the license plate number and sent another text message to Transportstyrelsen. Then she set off for Stockholm. Shortly before Mörby Centrum, her phone beeped. She looked at the screen. It was a text from Transportstyrelsen:

> Audi A4 2.0, black, 2012
> Registered September 1, 2012,
> to Eva Carlsson, Örebro
> Reported stolen

Bingo! The car was hot. Elin laughed to herself. Now she was sure that both the BMW and the Audi were related to the kidnapping. She thought for a moment. She had an extra GPS tracker, but how could she attach it to the Audi? She didn't want to repeat the trick with the newspaper. The two guys watching might be in communication with each other, so that would be too obvious. It would be best if she didn't show up there anymore, with or without a disguise. Ha, she had an idea! She pulled out of the traffic and into Mörby Centrum's parking garage. She would call Maja and ask if she could do it. With a little disguise on her part, a totally different person from Elin would appear at the Audi. No one could possibly mistake one for the other since Maja was much taller than Elin. And after that, they could go straight to the movies. It was a win-win situation.

Wednesday, November 18

48

Martin was sitting at a large table in a wood-paneled conference room. This truly was a law office in the traditional, venerable style. Such places also existed in Berlin, but this one looked genuinely old. He hadn't been to the men's room yet, but he expected to see gold faucets.

The contract appeared to be in order. He had read through the entire thing and found no errors. He wasn't particularly used to dealing with long English-language texts since he rarely had international cases. But the notary had done a good job: everything was correct and in its proper place. He looked at the clock. It was shortly before 11 a.m., which meant that the others would soon arrive.

Martin stood up and opened the heavy door—not the easiest task since its handle was mounted too high. He stepped into the hallway and looked around. Liv was sitting on a leather couch in the corner seating area and was speaking with the notary. Martin walked over to them. They both looked up.

Martin said in English: "The text is excellent. Liv can sign it. Have the buyers arrived yet?"

The notary shook his head. "No, but they called and said they were on their way. I suggest that the two of you wait in the conference room in the meantime. Would you like something more to drink?"

Both Liv and Martin declined. They hadn't yet finished what they had. Liv rose and went into the conference room with Martin.

"How are you feeling? Is everything all right?" Martin asked her.

Liv looked at him, a serious expression on her face. "Oh, Martin," she said, "I feel like a zombie. I just want to bring this to a close. The only thing that matters is Saga."

"I understand," he replied. "It will soon be over."

Martin sat down beside her. He knew that she hadn't slept well. The night before, she had wanted to sleep near her son, but she had showered him with so much affection that he eventually began to wonder what was going on. He had asked where Saga was and was surprised that he hadn't seen her at school. It was also unusual for Saga to spend several nights in a row at a friend's, especially during the week. In short, the whole story was on the verge of being exposed. In the end, the boy disappeared into his room. Liv then decided to go to her own room and had taken a sleeping pill. But it only worked until 4 a.m., at which point Liv actually went to his room. Under any other circumstances, he would have been glad about it, but with the way things were, he found it disturbing. Liv had laid her head on his shoulder and wept. After that, it was hard to think about sleeping. Eventually, Liv and Martin had breakfast with the au pair and Liv's son until Mai-Li took the boy to school.

Soon after that, Lars had gotten in touch to inform Liv and Martin that he and Elin had most likely identified the two watchers. At least one of them was using a stolen car.

That was a real win, but Liv still didn't want them to endanger Saga's life by interfering in any way.

The door opened, and the notary entered, followed by two men. One was tall and powerfully built, while the other was short and slight. The notary introduced them as Boris Melnikov, the buyer, and Nicholai Novikov, his lawyer. Martin was introduced as Liv's lawyer. They all shook hands and murmured "Nice to meet you" in English. Then they sat down, and the notary explained that Martin had already reviewed the contract. He then handed a copy to the Russian lawyer, who began reading it. Martin tried engaging in small talk with the buyer, but he apparently spoke no English. And so, they sat at the table in silence and waited for the other lawyer to finish.

Martin made use of the time to scrutinize the two Russians. Both were well-dressed in dark suits with matching vests, starched white shirts, and ties. Melnikov, the buyer, was the powerfully built of the two, with a paunch and double chin. He had to be in his mid-fifties. He had dark, thinning hair, a receding hairline, a clean-shaven face, and pockmarked cheeks. His small, deep-set, dark eyes flitted restlessly back and forth. Martin did not find him likable. The lawyer was significantly younger, maybe in his early to mid-thirties, with dark-blond, short hair and a goatee. He was intensely focused on the contract, and every time he turned the page, he would moisten his thumb. Finally, he nodded and said something to the buyer in Russian. After the latter responded, the lawyer said in English: "Everything is correct. We can sign."

"Good," the notary replied. "Then I would like to examine the buyer's and seller's IDs."

The Russian lawyer translated. The Russian buyer presented his passport, and Liv brought out her ID. The notary reviewed them both and made a note of their numbers. Then he handed Liv and the buyer a copy of the contract and asked them to sign. Each page of the contract had to be initialed. After that, the parties exchanged copies.

"The sale agreement is now legally binding," the notary informed them. "I'll report the transfer to the Bolagsverket—the Swedish Companies Registration Office. The full payment of the selling price is due immediately."

The Russian lawyer nodded. "My client will make the transfer today." He then translated what he had said to the buyer.

The buyer said something in Russian and reached for his briefcase. He placed a bottle of vodka on the table.

"According to Russian custom," the lawyer explained, "my client would like to make a toast. Do you have some glasses?"

The notary stood and fetched four glasses from the cabinet. The buyer opened the bottle and filled each glass halfway. He gave one to each person and then raised his own. He was grinning.

"*Nastrovye!*"

The others raised their glasses in response, whereupon the Russian buyer drank the entire contents of his glass in one gulp. Martin only took a sip of his, and he noticed that Liv did the same. The Russian lawyer drank one mouthful and then rose from this seat.

"Thank you for the good business," the lawyer said in parting. The large Russian nodded, stood as well, and took his leave. The door closed behind them. They had left the bottle of vodka behind.

Martin and Liv looked at each other.

"Strange people," said Martin.

Liv nodded. "Yes, I thought that already when we signed the first contract. Come on, let's go!"

It was almost noon as they stepped out onto the street, although the sun was still low in the sky. The days were shorter than in Berlin, and the sun never rose too far above the horizon. At least, it was a clear day, with only a few clouds.

"Would you like to walk a bit and have lunch somewhere? Or would you like to go home?" Martin was feeling hungry. Was that because of the vodka?

"That sounds like a good idea. There's no one at home, and I would just be brooding the whole time. And I don't want to go to the office today. Let's go down to Strandvägen. That's just a short stroll from here." Liv slipped her arm in his.

They only needed to make one left turn and then walk 100 meters before arriving at the street with the lovely housefronts overlooking the water. The quayside was full of hustle and bustle, partly from tourists and partly from people who were probably enjoying their noontime break. An icy wind was blowing across the pier, but the view was stupendous. The splashing waves, the ships, the buildings that graced the other islands: the whole scene was one of harmony.

"Stockholm is incredibly beautiful," Martin exclaimed.

"Yes," replied Liv. "You have to come sometime to see the sights. Have you been to the Vasa Museum?"

"No, I've only been to the Old Town and on a boat tour through the Archipelago. I enjoyed both a lot, but I haven't yet made it to the museums. What kind of museum is that?"

Liv shielded her eyes against the sun with her left hand and pointed across the water with her right.

"You can see it from here—the big building over there with the two ships' masts jutting out from the roof. Inside it is the Vasa, a seventeenth-century warship that sank in the Stockholm harbor on its short inaugural voyage. They recovered it more or less in one piece fifty years ago and then brought it to the museum. It's fascinating. You could spend the entire day there without losing interest."

"Yes, I remember now. I read about it in a brochure about Stockholm. I'll add that to my list."

They continued walking toward the city center, where they found a small restaurant that served lunch. You had to line up at the counter and pick out your food and drinks. There was a choice of salad and three main dishes, and you would place everything on a tray and pay at the end of the counter. Liv paid for the whole meal, but it wasn't expensive at all—about ten euros per person. She explained to Martin that those were lunchtime prices and that they were only available on workdays between 11 a.m. and 2 p.m. That was the cheapest option for eating in a Swedish restaurant. Dining à la carte outside of those hours usually cost three times as much or more.

Liv and Martin found themselves a table by the window and sat down.

"I'm really hungry, although I don't know why," said Martin. "I usually eat later. But I think that sip of vodka might have given me an appetite."

"Yes, I feel the same way. But I also haven't eaten much these past few days, so it's no surprise that I'm hungry."

"I'm glad you're eating in any case."

"Yes, it felt good to walk around here. And anyway, I have the feeling I've done everything I can. I've sold the company, and the mortgages have been approved, so the money should show up in my account by tomorrow at the latest. Then I'll immediately transfer it to their account. How long do you think it will take before they release Saga?"

Martin was glad that Liv was now asking about "when" instead of "if."

"Well," he said, "I'm assuming they'll wait until they have the money. And I'm not assuming that you'll be transferring the money to a Swedish account. I suspect it will be to an account in a tax haven somewhere. I don't know how quickly a transfer like that can happen." Martin was afraid it would take several days, but he didn't want to say that.

Liv seemed content with his answer. She nodded and turned her attention to her meal. Martin had already informed Jürgen that he would be staying the rest of the week—at least that wasn't a problem. But he was dreading the next few days. If it took another three to four days before Saga's release, it would be a terrible wait.

They wound up their meal with a cup of coffee, which was included in the price. The customers would simply fetch it themselves from a small table. There were even cookies to go with it.

They had just taken their first sip when Liv's cell phone rang. "It's my bank," Liv explained apologetically before accepting the call.

Martin couldn't understand what she was saying, but something didn't seem quite right. Liv was clearly agitated. Once she hung up, he anxiously asked: "Is there a problem?"

Liv shook her head. "No, not at all. My administrative assistant just wanted to let me know that the money from the mortgages has now cleared my account. At the same time, she informed me that another 90 million has been deposited. I find that hard to believe since we just finalized the sale. They were super fast."

"But that's great. That means you can transfer the ransom money today."

"Yes, all we need is the account number. I have to write and tell them that I already have the money."

"Right. But hang on a minute. I'd like to ask Lars if he can give us any tips."

"Martin, this is not a major issue. I just need to let them know that the money is available and that they need to send me the account number."

"OK, well, let me still give him a call. It will only take a minute."

"Fine." Liv reluctantly gave in. Martin could understand her impatience.

Martin called Lars on the cell phone that Lars had given them. "Hi, Lars, it's Martin. We have all the money, and we'd like to let the kidnappers know."

"All of it? Even the money from the company sale?"

"Yes, it's just been transferred."

"That's crazy. That was fast."

"Yes, we were also surprised. But it's good for us since Liv obviously wants to wrap up the transfer as fast as possible. We'd now like to ask for the account number. Do you have any tips for us?"

"Hmm, no. It's pretty simple. The only thing you might think about is requiring some new sign of life from Saga."

"OK, I'll talk it over with Liv. Thanks."

Liv gave Martin a questioning look as he ended the call. "Lars thinks we should ask for another video or something similar from Saga," he said.

Liv raised her eyebrows. "Do you think that's a good idea? It could drag things out even more."

"Yeah, maybe by a few hours. We could put it more delicately. Something to the effect that we'd like to transfer the money today but that another video or photo of Saga would give us more assurance. What do you think?"

"I don't know." Liv was looking down at the table as she thought it over. Finally, she said: "Yes, that's a good idea. I'll write that."

She picked up her smartphone, accessed her email, and typed for a while. Then she read everything through one more time and hit "Send."

"There. That's done," she said. "I hope they respond quickly. I can't use online banking to transfer a sum that large. And the bank is only open until 4 p.m. today. I've already told my assistant that I plan on transferring that amount today."

"Didn't she ask what the money was for?"

"Yes. I told her I had bought an overseas company." Liv had an embarrassed expression on her face. She apparently felt uncomfortable about having to lie.

49

Elin was jiggling her foot up and down. She was back in the office again, sitting at her desk. It wasn't her thing at all. Lars had been more than pleased when she told him about the other car and also about her success with the GPS tracker, but there was nothing more for her to do at the moment.

Of course, Maja had gone along with Elin's idea. She had even found it fun. Before going out, she had gotten all dolled up as though she were about to make a gala appearance. Elin almost didn't recognize her when she picked her up at the Mörby Centrum underground station. Maja usually wore her long hair in a braid or pulled back somehow. But that night, she wore it down and had apparently curled it. Add to that her eye-catching makeup and miniskirt with boots, and she was a real knockout. As they were walking to the parking garage, Elin could see the effect that Maja was having: she had almost every single man turning his head. Elin, on the other hand, went completely unnoticed in her old parka.

Next, Maja had strutted up to the house across from Liv's and rung the doorbell. When no one answered, she had walked back and acted like she hadn't seen the person in the Audi, who had bent down to avoid just that. Maja had then stopped beside the car and fumbled around with one of her boot zippers. To do that, she had to lean against the Audi, which made it easy to stick the GPS tracker on the underside of the car.

Afterwards, Maja was in high spirits and could hardly sit still at the movies. She and Elin spent a great evening together. Maja was even of the opinion that Elin should use her much more often. Elin had to laugh as she thought about it.

On arriving at the office, Elin had immediately fired up her computer and accessed the GPS program. The red dot that represented the BMW was showing it as parked in front of Liv's house again, while the Audi, whose tracker had been assigned a yellow dot, was now in Södertälje. The town of Södertälje was seventy kilometers south of Stockholm, where there was quite a lot of organized crime. It seemed to Elin that a stolen car would fit in well there.

In any case, the two watchers had apparently switched places again. Maybe the other one lived in Södertälje, or maybe that was where they were hiding Saga. Elin had an overwhelming urge to investigate the matter, but Lars had been very clear on that. So there she sat, watching the dots. The good thing about the program was that you could both see where the transmitters were at any moment and also trace their movements from the time the tracking began. Of course, Elin had already checked that. Early that morning, at 5 a.m., the BMW had driven from Bromsten to Danderyd and had taken its place in front of Liv's house again. Then, the Audi had driven to Södertälje and was now parked at a large park-and-ride next to the Östertälje commuter rail station. From there, the driver had probably transferred to the train. That meant that there was nothing more Elin could unearth about the man (she was assuming they were dealing with a man here as well).

It was a different situation with the driver of the BMW. Elin had used the Internet to find out who was living in the building the man had gone into earlier in their surveillance. There were five units, the sixth being the pub. Unfortunately, it was impossible to see the exact location of each apartment in the building, which was why Elin decided to use the exclusion principle to pinpoint who he was. There was an older married couple, both over seventy. Then there was a young couple in their early twenties and a single woman in her fifties. None of those were a possibility. Elin guessed that the balding man was in his mid-thirties, and there were only two men who might fit that age group. One of them lived in the building with his girlfriend and was thirty-three years old. The other appeared to be living alone and was thirty-six. Elin was betting on the bachelor, but she had no way to be sure. She had googled their names, but unfortunately both names were common in Stockholm, so that led her nowhere. Several of the residents had Facebook pages, but none of their photos resembled the balding man. She would have to do some more probing at the actual location.

The phone rang. It was Lars calling to tell her that the sale of the company had been concluded and the money had already cleared. Maybe something would happen by tomorrow, and once Saga was released, they would try to get the money back from the kidnappers.

Or would Liv call in the police at that point, after all? That would be bad, Elin thought, because as private detectives, they would then be out of the game. And Elin fervently hoped to be able to work on the case some more.

50

Liv was desperate. She was pacing up and down the living room.

"Martin, it's been more than two hours already. What's taking them so long? Was it wrong to ask for the video?"

"I don't get it, either. I also expected a faster reaction. It can't take that long to shoot a picture or video. But aside from that, they could at least have already sent the account number, after all we did get two emails in a row yesterday."

"Should I send them another email?" Liv had already sent a second email an hour after her first one. In it, she said that her bank was only open until 4 p.m. today, which meant that she needed the account number soon. But the kidnappers hadn't budged.

"No, I don't see how that could help," Martin told her. "They have your two emails, and now they need to respond."

"This is driving me insane. I've gotten all the money together—and I was so happy that everything went so smoothly. And now they're not getting in touch. Damn it all, I don't want to lose another day."

"Liv, by when do we need to leave to make it to the bank? Maybe it would be better to wait for the email there."

Liv stopped in her tracks. "I think we need to allow twenty minutes, and then we'll need some time at the bank to make the funds transfer. So by 3:30 at the latest." She looked at the clock. "That means in just under half an hour."

"Shouldn't we slowly start getting ready?" Martin suggested. "It makes no difference where we wait."

"And what if they never get in touch?"

"Well, then there would have been no point in going. But what do we have to lose? If we wait here and they email us just before four, we'll never make it to the bank in time."

"You're right. I'll tell Mai-Li." Liv disappeared upstairs to the children's room. Mai-Li had just fetched Hampus from school and returned home with him.

Martin picked up his phone and informed Lars, who was also surprised that they still hadn't received any messages from the kidnappers. But he thought it was a good idea to go to the bank now.

Martin retrieved his jacket and put on his shoes. Finally, Liv came back downstairs and got ready.

As they were leaving the house, the sun was an orange ball that lingered just above the horizon.

"Is it sunset already?" Martin asked

"Yes, at around a quarter past three, which is right about now."

"Wow, that's early." In Berlin, the sun would be going down an hour later.

"Yes, by the winter solstice, it will even be setting a half hour earlier. After that, things will start to improve again."

They got into the BMW i3, Liv's city car.

"So where is the bank, anyway?" asked Martin.

"In the city," Liv answered, "but not too far in. I had set up an account there back when I lived in Stockholm. After we moved, I never switched branches since I do most things over the Internet, anyway. I could make the transfer at another branch, but with such a large sum, there might be complications. Besides, I've already told the people at my branch, so it shouldn't be a problem."

Liv started the car. There was no sound from the electric motor. The only noticeable thing was that all the lights went on. Martin had offered to drive, but Liv thought it would be faster if she drove, and she also needed to keep herself occupied.

They made it to Stockholm in good time even though the rush-hour traffic was slowly starting to pick up on the other side of the freeway. Martin looked about. Even from the freeway, there was still a lot to see: water again and again and, to the left, a large building that was the natural history museum—even he could translate that much. At that point, things got a little more modern with the university. As they exited the freeway, they had to wait at several traffic lights, and there was also more traffic, but that didn't delay them much.

At last, they arrived at their destination, and Liv found a parking spot on a side street. The small car was practical in that way since it didn't require a lot space. There was a ticket machine where Liv could pay for parking, but instead, she simply typed away on her smartphone. She explained to Martin that there was an app where you entered your license plate number and the parking zone, and then you started the parking, which could be stopped at any time. Martin had heard that that existed in some parts of Berlin, but he hadn't tried it yet. It sounded useful, and he made up his mind to download the app.

Martin and Liv went into the bank. One corner featured a seating area with couches and armchairs, and there was a machine where you could get yourself a cup of coffee. Liv asked Martin what he wanted and came back to the couch carrying two cups of the steaming brew. They sat there sipping their coffee, which was cool enough to drink. Martin was watching the activity in the room. There was a whole line of people waiting their turn. Martin had already noticed a number of times that, in Sweden, you had to take a number to get in line. That was also the case here at the bank. As soon as a customer left the counter, the number would change on the large display, and there would be a soft dinging sound. Then the next customer would step up to the counter. An elderly lady, all bundled up in a scarf and warm hat, had just finished. After her, a young man rushed up to the counter. He seemed to be in a hurry but had still dutifully waited his turn.

"Do we need to take a number?" Martin was worried that they would have to wait a long time, after all.

"No, we're not going up to the counter. We're going to an area in the back, where we'll get immediate service. My assistant is waiting for me there."

They drank their coffee in silence. Liv checked her phone once again, but every time, she would just shake her head. There was no email.

After quite a while, Martin looked up at the clock. It was almost a quarter to four. He couldn't understand it. Had something gone wrong? Were Liv's emails not getting through? Maybe the cloaking through the proxy server had created a blockade of sorts. He understood nothing about that sort of thing, but he could easily imagine that something might not be working as it should. Or was this just a way of pressuring Liv? But then why do it over the release of the account number? That made no sense. Quite the opposite—it gave him doubts about how things would go with Saga's release.

Liv was sniffling. She looked at him with tearful eyes and sighed. "We'll never get this done today," she said.

Right at that moment, Liv's cell phone rang. She held it up, and Martin could see that the call came from Saga's phone. They both held their breath. Were the kidnappers planning on transmitting the account number over the phone? Or would there be new instructions?

"Hello? This is Liv Ulldahl."

Martin couldn't understand the rest, but he could see that Liv was thoroughly agitated. She was speaking very rapidly in Swedish, and the tears were streaming down her face. She seemed to be firing off one question after another.

Finally, Liv turned to Martin excitedly. "It's Saga. She says she's free. We're supposed to pick her up at Mörby Centrum."

"What?" Martin couldn't believe it. "But we haven't paid them a thing."

"I know. Let's go now!"

They dashed out of the bank to the car. Liv switched her phone to handsfree mode and insisted on driving herself. Unfortunately, things weren't moving as quickly as they had hoped. There was a lot more traffic heading out of the city, and the traffic lights were taking a long time to change. Sometimes they would be lucky and make it through, and other times, they would have to wait a long time.

Martin was listening to the conversation between mother and daughter. Liv had gotten herself under control, and Saga also seemed composed.

During one of the pauses, Martin told Liv, "I'm calling Lars. Is there anything I should know about Saga?"

"She says she's fine and was treated well. She was never tied up or anything like that."

Martin took out the dedicated cell phone and entered Lars's number.

"Lars."

"It's Martin. Lars, guess what? Saga is free. We're on our way to Mörby Centrum, where we'll be picking her up."

"What? I mean, how did you manage to transfer the money so fast?"

"That's the thing. We haven't transferred anything."

"I don't get it. Go through it with me one more time. Did you get a message?"

"No, nothing. We were waiting at the bank, and then all of a sudden, Saga called and asked us to pick her up."

"You spoke with Saga herself?"

"Yes, she's still on the line."

"And I'm keeping her on the line until I'm there with her myself," Liv threw in.

"I heard that," Lars said. "Which phone is Saga using to call?"

"Her own cell phone."

"OK, that's great. All right, you pick up Saga, and Elin and I will meet you at Liv's. I absolutely want to speak with Saga. If anything else happens, call me! Good luck!"

Lars seemed skeptical, and no wonder—Martin could hardly believe it himself.

It took them twenty minutes to get to Mörby Centrum. The traffic on the freeway was brisk, but downtown it was moving slowly. Liv didn't waste any time on a parking garage but parked instead in a small pull-off between the taxi stand and the buses. She and Martin leapt out of the car and ran to the entrance, pushing their way through the swinging doors. And there she was, standing in the middle of the hall by a large column with a bench, where she had said she would be waiting. Liv rushed up to Saga, and they fell into each other's arms.

Martin scanned the area. Was there anyone else there watching them? It was virtually impossible to know. There was so much going on there. There were two supermarkets, a hallway that led to the parking garage, an escalator to the second floor, and another one that went down to the underground station. There were people walking every which way. Three young girls were standing by the column, laughing. At the post office in one of the supermarkets, people were waiting in line—there were apparently no numbers to take.

A crowd of people had noticed that this was no ordinary reunion and had gathered around Liv and Saga, both of whom were crying and holding each other. Saga's cell phone had fallen, so Martin picked it up. He put his arm around Liv's shoulders and said: "Come on, let's go. We're drawing a crowd here."

Liv looked up and nodded as the tears streamed down her face. She clasped Saga's arm as they left the shopping center. They hurried to the car, and Liv and Saga climbed into the backseat. Martin started the car. He would figure out the way to Liv's house.

51

Lars was sitting across from Saga and Liv, who were seated close together. Liv had laid one arm around her daughter's shoulders. Saga was pale, but she seemed in reasonably good shape. Liv and Saga had already spoken at length with each other, and the au pair had made pizza for everyone. Saga had practically wolfed it down.

The BMW was still parked on the neighbor's property, so Martin had picked up Lars and Elin in downtown Danderyd. While driving down Liv's street, the two of them had ducked down to avoid being seen. Martin had then driven around, and they had gone in through the terrace at the rear of the house.

Liv had wanted to spare Saga all the questioning, but she had ultimately agreed to it. Lars's argument that her memory would be at its freshest now had made sense to everyone.

"Saga," Lars began, "we would like to know what happened during the past three days. Can you tell us about it? Your mother will stay beside you the whole time, and if it gets to be too much for you, we can take a break. Is that OK with you?"

Saga nodded.

"On Monday, when you were at school, what happened there? Did someone speak to you during the break? Is that right?"

Saga nodded again.

"Who was that?" Lars asked.

"A man," Saga answered. "He said I was supposed to go with him to see the principal."

"Did you know the man?"

"No."

"Can you describe him?"

Saga thought about it. "He was really big, and he was wearing a long coat and a hat."

"And his face? Did he wear glasses or have a beard?"

Saga shook her head. She couldn't describe him any further.

"What happened then?"

"The man walked over to the school building, and I followed him. We went in, and he held the glass door for me. I went through, and then all of a sudden, he pressed a cloth against my face. It smelled horrible. I don't remember anything after that."

"Saga, you're doing great. Did you notice anything unusual before the man appeared? Anything in the schoolyard or on the way to school?"

Saga looked at her mother and thought. "No, I don't think so."

"And where did you wake up?"

"In a playroom."

"Was it nice, this playroom?"

"Yes, it had everything. Dolls, Playmobil, a Wii. But I was all alone. And the room was small."

"Did anybody come to see you?"

"Yes, a woman. She would bring me food. And sometimes she would play with me."

"What kind of games did the two of you play?"

"Bowling, on the Wii."

"What did the woman look like?"

"She had long red hair."

"Was she fat or thin?"

"Uh, normal, I think."

"What was she wearing?"

"Um, some kind of jogging suit. A pink one."

"And she also brought you food?"

"Yes."

"What kind of food?"

"Hamburgers. And pizza."

"For breakfast, too?"

"No, for breakfast they had corn flakes, but they didn't have my pops."

"What did the woman say about why you were there?"

"She said that Mama had to go out of town and that Mai-Li was sick. That's why I had to stay there a few days. But I didn't believe it."

"Smart girl! How did they take you out of there?"

"I had to wear a blindfold over my eyes. They told me they were bringing me back to Mama. And then, I got into a car."

"Were you wearing the blindfold the whole time?"

"Yes, I wasn't allowed to take it off until I got to Mörby Centrum."

"Who brought you inside Mörby Centrum?"

"It was the same man."

"What did he say?"

"He gave me my cell phone and said I should call Mama and tell her to come pick me up."

"All right." Lars leaned back in his chair.

"Is it OK if I ask you a few questions, too?" Elin was squatting beside the coffee table.

Saga nodded.

"Was there a window in the nice playroom?" Elin asked.

Saga shook her head.

"Hmm. And can you tell us about the video they made of you? The one where you were holding the newspaper?"

"They said it would make Mama happy if I sent her a greeting. Mama would be sure to send one back, but she didn't. And I also wasn't allowed to have my cell phone."

"Yes, I see. Did you see the car that brought you to Mörby Centrum? Maybe when you got out?"

Saga shook her head and looked at her mother. "Mama, can I go to my room?"

"Yes, soon, just one more question!" said Elin. "How long did the car ride take? Was it short, or did it take a long time?"

"I don't know. It took a while. And I couldn't see anything the whole time."

"Do you think it was as long as a school lesson?"

Saga stared straight ahead. She seemed to be thinking. "I think so, yes, definitely that long."

"Thank you, Saga!"

Elin looked at Lars, who nodded at Liv.

"I would say that's enough," Lars said. "It's fine if she goes to her room now."

Saga disappeared up the stairs. Lars then translated the conversation into English for Martin.

"So what have you concluded from it all?" Martin asked.

"Not much," Lars replied. "They evidently treated Saga well. On the other hand, they made sure that she wouldn't be able to reveal anything about the place where they were holding her. It's also highly unusual that they had a woman taking care of her. That was where they took a risk."

"Yes, but maybe the woman was wearing a wig and heavy makeup, which would make her hard to recognize," Elin interjected. She was speaking from experience as she thought about Maja's disguise.

"Yeah, that could be. Children are also not very good as witnesses. They have a hard time giving good descriptions of people," Lars added.

"Why did they let Saga go without first having the money transferred?" asked Martin. "I still have trouble believing that."

Elin and Lars looked at each other.

"We've already discussed that," Lars replied. "In our view, there are two possibilities."

Liv had appeared somewhat absent during the entire conversation, but now she was suddenly wide awake as she turned to look at Lars.

Lars continued. "Either they cut their action short for some reason—although I'm having a hard time coming up with a good reason for that, especially since they were so close to getting the money ..."

"Or?" Martin asked.

"Or they had achieved what they wanted," Lars replied.

"What do you mean by that?"

"Well," Lars said, "Liv was forced to sell the company. That may have been the real reason for the kidnapping."

"You mean, it was never about the money?" Martin asked. "They only wanted the company?"

"Yes," said Elin, interrupting. "They probably knew enough about Liv's financial situation to realize that she had no way of raising that amount without selling the company."

"But that would mean that the buyer of the company was behind the kidnapping," said Martin.

"Yes, you're right," said Lars.

"But then shouldn't we be able to nail them?" asked Martin.

"In theory, yes. Except that to do that, Liv would have to call in the police."

They all turned to look at Liv, who immediately shook her head.

"No, no way. I just want to put it all behind me. The company doesn't matter to me. All I want is a normal life."

"Is there even a chance that Liv could get the company back? I mean, from a purely theoretical standpoint."

"A chance, yes—if you can prove that the buyer blackmailed her. But that's hard to do. They handled everything very professionally. It would be very hard to establish a connection to the kidnapping. On top of that, they're based in Russia. It would be different if they were in Sweden."

Elin didn't like this at all. The case seemed to be hastening to its end. "But that's exactly what the kidnappers were counting on," she said, "that Liv would be happy to have her daughter back and not have to pay ransom on top of it. Why should she look into it any further? But what makes me mad is that they can get away with it so easily. They did kidnap a young girl, you know."

For a moment, they were all silent. Then Martin began to speak. "Liv, what do you plan on doing over the next few days? Will you be sending Saga back to school?"

Liv spontaneously shook her head no. "Absolutely not. And most certainly not tomorrow."

"Yes, but at some point she'll have to go back."

"Yes, I know. I can ... I don't know what to do." She covered her face with her hands.

"We could keep a close eye on her," Lars offered.

"I think that's a good idea," Martin said. "What do you say, Liv?"

Liv looked relieved. "Yes, that would help. Preferably both children."

Thursday, November 19

52

It was time now. The car should be coming at any moment. It was sure to have the same destination as the day before. Elin shut her laptop and got out of the car. She positioned herself next to the entryway to the train station. From there, she had a good view of the entrance to the parking lot—and yes, the Audi was turning into the lot. Elin followed it with her eyes. The driver found a spot a bit farther to the left at the rear of the parking lot. The man got out of the car, pulled his jacket over his dark hooded sweatshirt, and rummaged around in the car before setting off for the train. Elin took out her cell phone and acted as though she were phoning someone. Instead, she took a picture of the man. Unfortunately, his face didn't come out too well—everything under the hood was dark. She let the man pass and then followed at a safe distance. She noticed that he bent forward and also teetered a bit as he walked. Just as she expected, he made his way to the platform for the trains heading to Södertälje.

Elin had to wake up early to get to Östertälje in time to wait for the man. The night before, she had noticed from the tracking program that the two cars had switched places again, so she decided to find out the other man's identity. She had arrived at the parking lot at 6 a.m. and nearly frozen her feet off just waiting there. But things were now finally moving again.

The train was due to arrive in ten minutes. Meanwhile, Elin was watching the man out of the corner of her eye. Unfortunately, he was inconspicuously dressed in a dark jacket, jeans, and black Western boots, and she didn't want to get into the same train car, so that meant she would have to watch him like a hawk every time the train came to a stop.

The train pulled in. There were not many people on the platform. It was probably too early for most, which Elin completely understood. A couple of passengers got off. The train was nearly empty. Elin watched to see exactly where the hoodie man got in and then chose the car directly behind his. She stood near the door so that she could quickly exit the train.

It was only a few minutes before they arrived at Södertälje Hamn, the next station. Elin got out and watched closely. The guy had already disembarked. He hurried to the other side of the platform where another train had pulled to a stop. There was a lot going on here. Everywhere, there were people walking and standing around. Elin pushed her way through to the other side and leapt onto the train. Once more, she managed to get into the car right after the man's. Just as she made it, the doors closed and the train pulled out. Wow, that was close.

They arrived at the next station about two minutes later again, and Elin did the same thing. And once again, the guy was walking in front of her on the platform. He was heading down the stairs to the exit. Elin followed him at a safe distance. The man marched over to a large glass door and out the building, straight to the large parking lot in front of it. Crap, thought Elin, it was also a park-and-ride—the man had probably parked his car there. Elin looked around. Of course, there was not a single cab in sight. Damn, there was no way she'd be able to stay on his tail.

Elin stopped at the underpass and followed the hooded man with her gaze. His car appeared to be farther to the back of the parking lot, and there might be another exit on the other side. Elin had never been there before, so she didn't know. She ran down the street behind him. She wanted to at least see which car he got into. At last, the guy stopped.

It was a low car, a roadster that was painted yellow and black. Elin paused to see which exit he would take. Damn it all—of course, it had to be the one she just came from. All right, well, back we go again! But now she could see his license plate number. She took another quick picture with her cell phone and immediately shot off another text to Transportstyrelsen.

The car exited the parking lot and sped away. Powerful-sounding engine, thought Elin. She walked back to the train station and took the next train back. The reply from Transportstyrelsen came after she had transferred trains. The car was a Ford Mustang, registered in 2004; the owner was Per Brorsson of Södertälje. It had not been reported stolen.

That might fit. Elin immediately checked and found only one person in Södertälje under that name. He was thirty-one years old. She would look into this a little more closely.

The first thing she had to do now was to retrieve the tracker from the Audi. That was actually the task Lars had assigned her to, but she doubted he would be sore if she managed to also identify the driver. Tonight, she should also get the tracker from the BMW, which had since been reported stolen. That was the reason Lars didn't want the trackers to stay on the cars. If the police got involved, they would be able to trace things back to Lars and Elin, and that could lead to some uncomfortable questioning. And so, she decided to keep watching the BMW on her screen today so that she knew where the car was parked.

It was almost noon now. The BMW was still dutifully parked near Liv's house. Elin had adjusted the GPS program settings so that she would hear a beeping sound the minute the car moved. That would give her a chance to work on other things at the same time. So far, she hadn't found much on Per Brorsson. He had managed to remain pretty anonymous on the net. He had also been extremely cautious with the stolen Audi.

Finally. It was Lars calling.

"Hej, 'Splosion Man."

"Hey, Elin. Did the thing with the GPS tracker work?"

"Is Norrland in Sweden? Of course—and there's more." Elin told Lars about how she had followed the guy and the results of her pursuit.

"But we never discussed this, Elin." Lars sounded more amused than mad.

"I know, but it got results."

"I hope the guy didn't notice you."

"No, no need to worry."

"OK, well, if we could get the name of the other guy—I mean the driver of the BMW—then I could pull a few strings with some contacts of mine, and maybe something will come of that."

"So should I try to find out his name?"

"Yeah, if you want. But no more initiatives, OK? You know what Liv told us."

That was cool. She would have a chance to take off again. And she would find a way to get the other guy's name.

Saturday, November 21

53

Martin had woken up early. He was sitting alone at the breakfast table and had already made himself coffee. He had used fewer grounds this time because he found Swedish coffee to be too strong, but now the stuff was too weak and still didn't taste good. It would probably work better to make it strong and then dilute it with milk.

And why was he awake so early? Well, he had had plenty of sleep in the past two days, so his sleep requirements had been met. But there was also another reason. He felt a bit as though he were in a vacuum, as though he were hanging in mid-air.

Martin had booked a return flight to Berlin for the following day, but he wasn't at all sure that he wanted to go. On the one hand, Saga was back safe and sound, and there was no longer anything he could do to help. Also, his work was waiting for him in Berlin. And, of course, there was his daughter. On the other hand, he would love to spend some normal time with Liv—a time without kidnappings and other worries. When exactly that would happen was another question.

For Liv, it would be a long time before she found closure with the whole affair. That much had become clear to him. Saga had stayed home on Thursday, and Liv had watched over her like a mother hen. Not that Martin couldn't understand that. On Friday, Saga had wanted to go back to school, and Lars's agency was there to monitor the situation: his co-workers were working shifts around the clock. Of course, they couldn't go with them into the school, but they watched out front, and both children were equipped with GPS trackers. But Liv was still ill at ease whenever the children were gone. Upon hearing her cell phone ring, she had immediately become alarmed and imagined the worst, but it was just someone from her company. She then drove over there at around noon to inform her employees of the completed sale and that the transfer of ownership would take place on December 1. They weren't too enthusiastic about it. After all, they had no idea what types of changes it would bring. Liv didn't exactly come home in a good mood.

Martin and Liv had spoken again that evening. Liv was even more up in the air than he was. With the sale of the company, she had lost her career and now needed to regroup, which was not so easy given her constant fear for her children. It would be best if she could go on vacation for a couple of weeks, but the children had school, so that was out of the question.

And now Martin, too, would be leaving. After all, he couldn't stay away from his law practice any longer. He would probably return to Sweden for Christmas, and he hoped that things would be back to normal by then.

Little Hampus was coming down the stairs at that moment, still in his pajamas. He had taken in very little of all the commotion and was probably wondering why his mother had been crying so much and what all the strange people had wanted there.

Hampus uttered a "hej" as he came into the kitchen. Then he went straight to the fridge and took out a carton of milk. Once he had found a bowl and the corn flakes, he sat down and started eating his breakfast. Martin asked him about Saga, but the boy just shrugged his shoulders. He had his own room—how should he know what his sister was doing? Saga had spent the past few nights in Liv's room, which was surely the best solution for them both.

Martin decided to take a quick stroll, and he hoped the rest of the family would be up by the time he came back. He pulled on his boots and jacket and was about to open the door when he remembered the alarm. That was something Lars's agency had installed, including video monitoring of the driveway and yard. He entered the six-digit code. The unit beeped twice, and the LED light switched from "armed" to "alarm off."

Martin opened the door and breathed in the fresh morning air. It was still dark outside, but the sun was visible just above the horizon, and the scattered clouds were deep red in color. It was cold and damp, probably barely above freezing. He walked down the driveway and turned onto the street. The parking space on the property diagonally across the street was vacant. Lars had already informed him that the watchers had not shown again since Thursday.

It felt good to get out and walk a bit. Most of the houses were old and big and, without exception, constructed of wood. Some of the properties were hidden by hedges, but most were easily seen from the street. It was lovely here. It must be even more beautiful in the summertime, when the trees were green and the flowers in bloom. Martin thought about how they would spend his last day there. Maybe they could take a drive somewhere and do something together. It was looking as though it would be a sunny day—so far, there were only a few clouds in the sky. And it would do everyone good to be outside. Martin quickened his pace.

54

"So one more time, from the beginning!"

Maja wasn't as thrilled as Elin had hoped.

"You're telling me you want to solve the case in your spare time?" Maja continued. "Even though that rich bitch hasn't paid a single cent of the ransom and she doesn't want people looking into it any further? Did I get that right?"

"She still had to sell her company," Elin countered.

"For how much? Ninety itty bitty millions? Oh yeah, I really feel for her."

"Well, regardless, those guys kidnapped a ten-year-old girl and held her hostage for three days. They shouldn't get away with that so easily."

"OK, fine. But how do you expect to nail these guys? Without a ransom payment, it's just not going to be that easy to prove, is it?"

"Maja, I just want to find out if the company sale was the real motive behind the kidnapping. So far, that's been nothing more than conjecture."

Maja laid her index finger on her lower lip and said, "OK, let's assume we can find a connection."

Elin was glad she said "we."

"What do we do with that info?"

"Well, for me, that would solve the issue. We would tell Liv, and she could decide whether she wanted to do anything with the information or not."

"OK, so it's mostly about your wanting to know how it all fits together?"

Was this a setup? Elin decided to tell the truth, anyway. "Yes."

"To satisfy your curiosity."

"Yes," Elin replied, uncertain.

"And play a little private detective at the same time?"

Elin nodded vigorously.

"OK, then I'm in."

Great—it wasn't a trap, after all! Elin gave Maja a huge hug. "Cool! This is awesome."

"Wow, you really are passionate about this." Maja laughed. "But I'm not going along with just any old bullshit."

"Yeah right, gotcha."

The two of them started getting ready. They brought along various paraphernalia for their disguises and also a couple of self-defense items since you never knew what could happen.

Elin wanted to take a closer look at the hooded man from Södertälje. She had also managed to identify the other guy, which was easy. She had chatted with the elderly woman who lived in his building while she helped her with her shopping bags. Elin had asked about the balding man on the top floor, and the elderly lady had instantly recalled his name. Lars then had an old police chum of his run both names through the police database. There was nothing on the balding guy, but the guy in the hoodie had been placed on probation a year ago for illegal drug possession. That was probably why he had been so careful about the stolen car. In any case, that was why Elin thought it would probably be more worth her while to check him out rather than the other guy. She didn't yet have a concrete plan, but she figured it would come to her.

Finding his address was easy. He lived in an eight-story apartment building on the outskirts of Södertälje. Since they didn't know exactly which apartment he lived in, she and Maja had simply watched the entrance. And they were lucky. After just shy of half an hour, the guy emerged minus his hoodie, so that Elin was unsure at first. He was wearing jeans and a long green parka. But his slightly hunched-over posture and his limping gait seemed familiar, and when the man walked over to the Mustang, that clinched it for her.

Earlier, Elin had slipped a tracker onto the underside of the Mustang, which made following good ol' Per Brorsson an easy task. He drove to downtown Södertälje and pulled into a parking garage whose entrance was next to an O'Leary's pub. Across from the entrance, the wind was rippling over the waters of Maren, a connecting arm between the Baltic Sea and Lake Mälaren. Thanks to this arm of water, Södertälje had a small harbor and several promenades that ran along the water's edge.

Elin stopped in front of the entrance. "I'll follow our friend on foot," she said to Maja. "Can you stay close to the car? We may still need some wheels."

"Sure, no problem."

Elin had stuck a tracker in her own pocket so that Maja could find her more easily if she needed to. She had also hung her camera around her neck. It had a telephoto lens and in that way was far superior to her smartphone. And besides, it made her look more like a tourist.

Now Elin got out of the car and took her place beside a kiosk on the promenade. From there, she had a good view of the entrance to the parking garage. There were lots of people out and about, which was typical of a Saturday afternoon. She wouldn't stand out.

Maja turned on the engine and started to drive away. It didn't take long before Per came down the long stairway. He looked around on every side and finally headed Elin's way as he walked along the water.

Per seemed somewhat wary. Had he noticed something? Elin had to be careful, so she followed at a safe distance. Per was walking at a brisk pace along the water. It wasn't easy keeping him in her sights: there were people heading in all directions and children running this way and that. It was a sunny Saturday, and there was clearly a lot going on.

The guy continued past the backside of a parking lot, where he turned onto a street that curved away from the water. This made it easier for Elin to pursue him since there were fewer people on the sidewalk, although there was also a greater risk of being noticed. She decided to switch to the other side of the road. Per crossed the street at the next intersection and turned into a small park. The sign read *Stadspark,* or "city park."

Elin followed the guy to a small fountain, where he sat down on a bench. She kept walking and finally took a seat in a small glass booth that served as a bus stop. From there, if she craned her neck, she could see across the bush to the bench where Per was sitting. She then phoned Maja and described her location. Maja said she would come and park nearby.

Elin stretched her neck some more and noticed a teenager joining Per. They exchanged something between them, but it happened so quickly that Elin couldn't tell what it was. By the time she had her camera in position and had removed the stupid cap from the lens, the teenager had already gotten up and left. What a pile of crap—she had missed it. But Per remained seated, which gave Elin hope that something more might happen. And she was right. Not five minutes had passed when a man in a suit came sauntering by, looked around, and sat down next to Per. This time Elin had her camera in place and could make out every detail. She switched it to video and filmed what happened. The two of them were talking to each other without looking at one another, but Elin could clearly see that their lips were moving. Then the man reached into one of his side pockets, pulled out a couple of bills, and slipped them to Per, who put them in his own pocket. Per then took out a small plastic bag that contained something white and passed it to the man. After the man had pocketed it, he looked both ways, rose from his seat, and sauntered off again.

Good ol' Per had remained true to his career: he was still dealing.

55

It was a beautiful day, so they took the children to the ABBA Museum. The museum had only been around for two years, and until now, Liv hadn't had a chance to go. Saga had been really excited to see it. Martin liked ABBA's music, but he had been skeptical about what more a museum could offer him. The main point, though, was to do something together, and since the zoos and the amusement park Gröna Lund were closed at this time of the year, he was OK with the museum.

It turned out to be a pleasant surprise—it really was very well done. Of course, there were the typical items on display: pictures, gold records, and other memorabilia. But the interactive exhibits were the best part. You could take a seat at a mixer in a sound studio, climb into a helicopter, or rock out on the dance floor. The children loved the last part the most. And in the end, even Martin joined in.

After the museum, they went to a nearby restaurant. The kids had hamburgers and french fries, while Liv and Martin had the most deliciously prepared fish.

The children had now gone to their rooms. Hampus was at his PlayStation and was racing cars. Saga was tired and was sleeping. Liv had been somewhat quiet since they had returned. Maybe she was also tired. She was opening a bottle of red wine while Martin, after his third attempt, had finally managed to get the fire going. He didn't have a fireplace at home and had imagined the whole process to be easier. After Liv had explained to him that you had to leave enough space between the logs to let the air through, it had finally worked. Now they were sitting in front of the fire sipping their wine.

"Are you tired?" Martin asked her.

"No, not really." Liv shook her head without looking at him.

Martin waited, but she said nothing.

"You're quiet tonight. Is something bothering you?"

Liv hesitated. She glanced at Martin and then looked back at her glass.

"Yeah, I don't know." She took a sip of her wine and stared at the fire.

Martin didn't want to pry, but this was his last evening there. If she had something on her mind, then he would love to know what it was.

"Do you want to talk about it, Liv? Can I help in some way?"

She took another sip. Then she glanced at him briefly again. Something was not quite right. Finally, she cleared her throat.

"You're taking off tomorrow," she said.

So that was it.

"I am," replied Martin. "I'd love to stay longer, but I have my law practice, and my daughter is also coming to visit."

"I understand that, Martin." Liv was now looking him in the face. "I'm very grateful to you for coming, especially on such short notice and without hesitating. And also that you were there for me. I have no idea how I could have managed without you."

Martin could feel himself blushing.

"But that's a given, Liv."

"No, it isn't. I can't think of anyone else who would have done that for me."

"Well, regardless, I'm here for you if you need me."

Liv looked back at the fire, shifted in her seat, and started playing with a strand of hair, just as she always did when she was nervous. She cleared her throat again.

"That's very sweet of you. But, well, that's also what's bothering me." She paused and looked at him. There was a question in her big, blue eyes. "Exactly why are you here for me?"

What should he say to that? Martin felt a bit uncomfortable. What was she driving at?

"I mean, you already rescued me once—in the fall. Do you now feel responsible for me? Like in the Chinese saying: once you've saved another person's life, then you're responsible for that person forever afterwards because you intervened in his fate?"

Wow, now things were getting complicated. Martin had the feeling that no matter what he said, it would be wrong. Better to keep quiet. He smiled, shook his head, and looked into her blue eyes.

"Or to put it another way: what exactly am I to you? Am I like a little sister who's always in need of help?"

"No, not at all." Martin plucked up his courage. He had to tell her what he felt. It was obvious it wasn't clear to her.

"Liv, I would love to tell you what you mean to me. I just didn't trust myself until now because the conditions were never right. There was always some kind of danger or stress. And then there was your family and the bit with your husband. I didn't want to get the timing wrong."

Liv looked at him expectantly.

"I'll be honest with you," he continued. "I fell in love with you the first time we met."

There. Now it was out.

Liv stared at him in disbelief. "Really?"

"Yes, and the feeling has only grown stronger. I think you're a wonderful woman and that you've done an amazing job dealing with all these tough situations. And yes, I ... I would love to be with you. But I don't know how you feel about that."

"Oh, Martin."

He could see the tears welling up in her blue eyes.

"I also liked you from the very beginning," she said. "And I was so impressed that you risked yourself and did so much for me without even knowing me. And I also feel so safe with you. That's why I felt I needed you here when that happened to Saga. But ... what I don't understand is ... well, not that long ago, I went in to you during the night. And please don't misunderstand me: it was nice lying next to you, and I felt very safe. But ... didn't you want me as a woman?"

So that was it. No matter what he did, it could be taken the wrong way.

"Liv, of course! I had to fight to restrain myself. Because I didn't want to exploit the situation. You were desperate, and the relationship was too important to me to start getting intimately involved with you. If something ever did happen between us, I wouldn't want it to be out of desperation but out of love."

Martin looked at Liv, who nodded. A tear was trickling down her left cheek. She wiped it away with the back of her hand.

"That's what's so wonderful about you," she said. "You're so considerate. And I thank you for that. But for once, could you please just stop and take me in your arms?" Liv was beaming at him.

Martin's heart was pounding madly. He rose from his seat and walked toward her with outstretched arms. Liv threw herself into them so hard that he nearly lost his balance and had to take a step back. As he did so, he bumped against the coffee table and knocked over the wine glass, which rolled clear across the table, spilling the wine all over the tablecloth. He tried to bend down to get it, but Liv wouldn't let him go.

"Leave it! It doesn't matter. Kiss me instead!"

She didn't have to ask twice. Martin turned around and kissed her. Liv held him tight and pressed herself against him. Their lips parted, and their tongues touched. Martin could feel himself getting hard, and this time he would not be able to restrain himself. Although now, he no longer needed to. A feeling of happiness flooded his entire body. Finally—he was holding Liv in his arms, just as he had always wanted.

56

Elin flung open the front door and plunked herself down on the passenger seat.

"You won't believe this! I got the whole thing on video. We have to bust this guy!"

Maja looked puzzled. "Hang on a second. I have no idea what you're talking about."

Elin told her about the park and what she saw there. "There were five people that stopped by, one after the other: a teenage kid, some dude in a suit, a young girl, and two young guys. They each bought something different. I don't know much about this stuff, but the white powder is definitely cocaine, and there were some white and blue pills. The guy is like a drug warehouse."

"OK, so what do you plan on doing with this? I mean, do you think it's related to the kidnapping?"

"No, of course not—that's ridiculous. But don't you get it? We can use it as a way of pressuring him."

Maja looked at her incredulously. "How did you come up with that one?"

"It's obvious. We nab the guy and tell him that the photos are going to the police if he doesn't tell us about his part in the kidnapping."

"Hang on. This is getting to be a bit much for me. What do you mean by 'nab' him?"

Elin explained her idea. At first, Maja didn't want to go along with it, but when she realized that Elin would go ahead and do it on her own, she finally gave in.

Elin then suggested they go to the parking garage and wait for Per at O'Leary's. For the moment, he was still sitting on the park bench dealing, and they would be able to work out their plan in more detail at O'Leary's. Maja started the car.

They didn't need to wait long. They had had a bite to eat and had just finished their coffee when they saw Per approach. Elin had been watching the stairway to the parking garage the whole time. The lower part was not enclosed, so Elin had a good view of it from O'Leary's. She and Maja had also paid in advance, which allowed them to immediately get up and follow the guy.

Elin and Maja raced up the stairs and flung open the steel door to the parking garage. Per was walking up ahead. They hurriedly pulled on their ski masks and started running after him. Luckily, there was no one else in sight. Just as they had almost caught up with him, he suddenly turned around. When he saw the masks, his eyes opened wide, but before he could react, Maja had already felled him with one quick blow. Elin had the cable ties ready and bound the guy's hands and feet. Maja grabbed the parking receipt that the man had dropped—he had evidently just paid at the ticket machine. His car key was in his parka pocket, and the Mustang was parked just two spaces away. Together, they dumped the guy onto the backseat, which was not a problem for them. Elin then climbed in on the passenger side, and Maja got the Mustang going.

Maja and Elin had chosen a wooded area near the Södertälje Syd train station, and they quickly found a secluded spot that would allow them to interrogate good ol' Per in peace and quiet. Per had already come to, so Elin was keeping a watchful eye on him. He asked them twice what they wanted, but the girls didn't answer.

After Maja turned onto the woodland road and found a place to park about 100 meters later, both she and Elin turned to Per.

"So listen carefully," Elin began. "We know who you are, Per Brorsson, but you don't know us. We also know that you're on probation. And now we have the proof that you're still dealing, you little dumbshit."

"What do you mean? What kind of proof?"

Elin showed him the video on her camera. Per looked on, speechless.

"Yup, and then there are also a couple of little bags in your parka pocket, and your fingerprints are bound to be all over them. And ours are obviously not. Trust me, the police will love this. That'll put you in the joint for a few years."

Per gulped. "OK, what do you want? Stuff?"

"No. We just need some information."

He stared at her, astonished. This guy was seriously ugly. He had a big nose, his face was covered with acne scars, and he had a squint.

"What information?"

"About your job in Danderyd."

Per looked dumbstruck. "What job?"

"Listen, don't try and play dumb here! You spent days lurking around in that stolen Audi, and I want to know everything about it—who hired you and whatever else."

"I don't know anything about it."

"OK, then let's go to the police."

Elin nodded to Maja, who started the engine. By the time she had turned the car around, Per was protesting.

"Now hang on a second! Man, I could be in deep shit if I told you about that. He said he'd finish me."

Maja stopped the car but left the engine running. Elin gave him an intense look through her ski mask.

"No one needs to know what you said. We just want information. And that means everything you know!"

Per nodded. And then he told all. One of his clients had offered him the job. Per was supposed to procure a car and then watch the house in Danderyd 24/7. He had split the job with a buddy of his. They had been given a phone number, and they were supposed to call right away if anything unusual occurred. He had no idea what all of this was about, but the client had made it clear to him that discretion was critical. The payment for the job had happened at the park bench—yesterday, in fact.

"What's the client's name?"

"Not a clue."

Elin stared at him and waited.

"No, for real. I don't know any of my clients' names."

"But you still have his phone number, right?"

"Yeah, on my cell phone."

Per tried to get to his phone with his wrists bound, but it didn't work.

"Can't you guys untie me?" he asked.

Elin didn't answer. Instead, she leaned over and fished his cell phone out of his inside jacket pocket. Per entered his code and, after a brief search, gave her a cell phone number.

"What does the guy look like?"

"Tall, dark hair, strong."

"How old?"

"Early 40s maybe."

"What else?"

"Nothing. There isn't anything else."

Elin looked at him.

"There really isn't!" Per looked at his cell phone.

"I don't believe you. I think we'll go see the police after all." She signaled to Maja, who started to drive.

"OK, OK. There's one more thing, and then that's really it."

"What? Spit it out!"

"I have a picture of his car. Took it yesterday."

He entered some stuff on his phone and then showed Elin a picture. It was a black Land Rover. You could see the license plate number, but you couldn't make out the first letter. It was either a C or an O. It didn't matter—that wasn't a problem. Elin entered the number on her phone.

"OK, you can go."

Per leaned back, relieved. Maja drove out of the woods and parked the Mustang near the Södertälje Syd train station. She and Elin got out, turned away from the car as they immediately removed their masks, and walked through the glass door. They waited until the Mustang drove off. Per had apparently done a fast job of undoing the cable ties. He probably had a knife in his car.

Maja looked at Elin. She was proud of her. Elin was short and slight, but she had given him a seriously tough time.

"You were amazing. I didn't think you could do it. You're gonna be a great detective someday."

Elin gave Maja a light punch on the shoulder. "Thanks for coming." Then she leapt into the air. "Yay! We finally have a real clue."

They took the train back to downtown Södertälje to pick up their car. Elin was content: the initiative had paid off. Now she just had to figure out how to break the news to Lars about her solo foray.

Sunday, November 22

57

Martin couldn't take his eyes off her. She was lying on her side, sound asleep, her face turned toward him. Her blond hair was spread out across the pillow, and the light that streamed in through the slits in the curtains made it glow like gold. He had noticed that she had risen several times during the night to check on the children, especially Saga. It was the first night that Saga had slept in her own room again. But the rest of the night, Liv had slept—except, of course, during those times when they had made love. Last night had been very passionate, and afterwards, Liv had fallen asleep in his arms. Then, this morning, they had explored each other's bodies more thoroughly. It felt amazing. It had been some time since Martin had been with a woman, and he hadn't realized how much he had missed it. He and Liv were so close, and yet everything was so new.

So why did he have to leave today? Should he change his reservation? But then he would have to ask Jürgen to cover for him again, and there were some cases that he wanted to follow through on himself. Also, next weekend, Lara would be visiting. Otherwise, he would have flown straight back.

Liv stirred and opened her eyes—those wonderful blue eyes.

Martin smiled. "Good morning, my love."

"Hello, Martin." She pulled him close to kiss him.

"Did you sleep well?" he asked.

"Yes. It's so nice being in bed when you're here. I haven't slept this well in a long time."

"Me, neither. Even if I did wake up a couple of times."

"Yeah, but that last interruption was the best, wasn't it?"

Martin nodded and held Liv close.

"I don't want to leave—now that we have such a nice thing going."

"I don't want you to leave, either. But you have to work, don't you?"

"Yeah, I don't want to put it off one more time. The problem is that my daughter is visiting next weekend, which is why I can't come here."

"How old did you say she was? Four?"

"Yeah, she'll be five in February."

"Bring her along! Saga would play with her. I'm sure of it."

"I just have to check with my ex. She can be a bit difficult on that point."

Martin's ex-wife always wanted to know exactly what he had planned for Lara. A trip to Stockholm would not go over so easily.

Liv shook out her hair and wove it into a braid. "Then we'll come to you. How much space do you have?"

Martin thought it over. He had a three-room apartment. Liv could sleep with him in his king-size bed. Lara always used the guest room, where she had a closet with toys. That room also had a sleeper sofa.

"Lara's room has a couch that can be made into a double bed. Do you think that would work for the three kids?

Otherwise, one of them could always sleep in the living room."

"That would work. But think it over. And now, let's just enjoy the day! You're not taking off till this evening."

Liv leapt out of bed and flung the curtains wide open.

"Look! It's another beautiful day!"

Monday, November 23

58

Martin was digging through his mail. Even if most of it was handled via email, there were still some written documents that arrived at the office by conventional mail. He had gotten there early because he had had a feeling there were a number of things to review. Besides, he had woken up early and hadn't been able to go back to sleep with Liv being constantly on his mind.

The front door to the law office opened. That had to be Jürgen.

"Hello?"

Martin went out to greet him. "Hey, Jürgen."

"Man, am I glad you're here. It was getting to be a bit much. Welcome back!"

They exchanged a vigorous handshake. "Thanks for covering for me. From what I've seen so far, everything looks great."

"Well, there were no major problems and just a few conflicts related to my own cases. But I got through it all. How did things go for you? Did you manage to achieve what you wanted in Sweden?"

While Jürgen was getting himself a cup of coffee, Martin gave him a rough idea of what had happened during his week in Stockholm. Jürgen was wide-eyed with astonishment.

"Man, you went through a lot there. At least, you didn't come back with a bunch of bumps and bruises this time. But what do you make of the kidnappers' choice to not withdraw the money?"

"The only explanation we could come up with was that the kidnapping was tied to the sale of the company. Maybe the Russians were behind all things and were content with the fact that they were able to buy it."

"At a lower price?"

"That, too."

"So now what?" asked Jürgen. "Don't you want to go to the police?"

"Liv doesn't want to," Martin replied. "She's happy to have her daughter back safe and sound. And she did get the money in return for the company, even if it was probably too little. In any case, she doesn't want any more stress."

"I can see that," Jürgen said. "But I would still be ticked off if someone played me like that."

"Yeah, but for now she doesn't care. Maybe it will be an issue for her later on."

Jürgen gave Martin a penetrating look. "So, uh, what's up with you and the Swedish lady?"

Martin turned red. "Um, well, how can I put this? I think we're a couple."

"Seriously? That's great! I'm happy for you, Martin." Jürgen clapped him on the shoulder. "I had a feeling from the start that you had a thing for that woman. It'll be good for you. So how are you two going to handle this now? I mean, Stockholm isn't exactly around the corner."

"We're not quite there yet. At first, we'll just travel back and forth. She'll probably come here next weekend."

"By herself or with the kids?"

"With the kids, of course. She would never leave them at home after what just happened."

"Yeah, I can see that, too. So then it won't be a super-romantic weekend, will it?"

Martin smiled. "Yeah, Lara will also be staying. More alone time with Liv would be great, but it's better than not seeing her at all. And maybe Lara will enjoy being around other kids."

"True. You're right. It will all work out. Listen, I've got an appointment coming up, but could we meet at 10:30 to review the cases?"

"Yeah, sure."

Martin went back to his office. Until then, he hadn't made a final decision about the weekend, but now he was sure: he wanted Liv to come. He would tell her that right away. He picked up the phone and dialed her number.

Liv answered after the second ring. "Hello?"

"Good morning, Liv. It's me, Martin."

"I was hoping it was you. I still need to save your office number to my contacts list. Did you sleep well?"

"No. I miss you."

Liv let out a loud sigh. "I miss you, too. It's nice that you're calling. The house is empty. The children are in school, and Mai-Li is out. I feel so alone."

"I can imagine. Listen, I've been thinking. I would love it if you all came here for the weekend. Even if we won't have much time to ourselves, I absolutely want to see you. And the children might have fun, too, even if they have a hard time understanding each other." Lara spoke only German, while the two Swedish kids didn't.

"Wonderful! I'm so glad. I'll book the flight right away."

They agreed on the times and said goodbye.

Martin hung up. He already felt better. Now he had something to look forward to. The workweek would go by quickly—he had a lot to do.

Martin had just come back from lunch. He and Jürgen had gone to a pizzeria, where they had a chance to swap more stories. Jürgen had naturally been curious to hear more of the details. Now Martin was bent over the files pertaining to an old case that was always taking on a new spin. He would have to discuss it with his client again. He was about to reach for the phone when his cell phone rang. He could see from the display that it was Lars.

"Hello, Lars."

"Hello, Martin. Sorry to bother you. Do you have a few minutes?"

"Sure. What about?"

"Well, it's about the kidnapping again."

"Really?"

"I know that Liv didn't want us to investigate it any further. But Elin is very committed and has tracked down another clue. I'm somewhat uncomfortable with this, since we always adhere to our clients' instructions, and I've already had a serious talk with Elin on this subject. So it won't happen again—I promise you that. But what I wanted to tell you was that she's discovered something that I don't want to keep from you and Liv. The two of you will need to decide what you want to do with the information."

"I see. OK, shoot!"

Now what? Lars had Martin in suspense.

"So you remember the two guys who were watching Liv's house. We were able to find out their names. Over the weekend, Elin put some pressure on one of them without revealing who she was. In my opinion, she was very smart about it, and I don't see any chance of it being traced back to us or you."

"OK, so what did she do?"

"Well, Martin, it wasn't exactly by the book, so I'd rather not say any more."

Martin raised his eyebrows. Whatever was going on here was certainly interesting.

"I see. So what did the guy say?"

"He led us to the man who hired him. Not directly, but by way of his car."

"Now I'm curious. And he's based in Russia?"

"That's the thing—he's not. We were able to identify him as Erik Lind." Lars paused.

Lind, thought Martin. Why did that name sound familiar?

Lars resumed. "That's the brother of Thomas Lind, Liv's husband."

Martin was dumbstruck. He needed a minute to let this tidbit sink in.

"Martin? Are you still with me?"

"Yes, I'm just stunned. I hadn't anticipated anything like this."

"Neither had we. But there's no question about it."

Martin's head was spinning. "Now hold on a second," he said. "I'm still having a hard time piecing this all together. You're saying the brother kidnapped Saga but didn't collect the ransom money. Did he get cold feet? And that would also mean that the Russians are clean, wouldn't it?"

"We don't know all of that yet. Either he cut the kidnapping short, or he's working with the Russians. But to get him convicted and to understand the background, we need to keep working on the case. Elin is ready and willing to do so, but we'll only do it if you assign us the job."

Martin thought it over. This would come as a shock to Liv—he was sure of it. And Liv had no desire to dig deeper into the whole affair. This was not something he would be able to discuss with her over the phone.

"Lars, I need to talk to Liv about this. And I'd like to do it in person, not over the phone. I'm sure you can understand that. I'll be seeing her this weekend. She's coming to Berlin."

"Aha."

"Yeah, something has developed between us. In any case, I'll discuss it with her, and we'll get back to you this coming Monday. Will that work, or could something have eluded us by then?"

"No, I don't think so. That should be OK."

They said goodbye.

Martin leaned back in his chair as he pondered this new bit of information. That was some great family Liv had married into. First, her husband tried to kill her, and then her brother-in-law kidnapped her daughter. Unbelievable.

59

Lars hung up and looked at Elin. She was sitting across from him and was pretty damn nervous. Her right foot was crossed over her other one, and it was jiggling up and down at a rapid rate. She hadn't been able to follow the phone conversation, which was in German.

"Was he pissed?" she asked.

"No, I don't think so," Lars replied. "At least, he didn't say anything to that effect. Although he was pretty shocked by our clue about the brother."

"So what now?"

"Well, as I already told you, Liv is the bigger problem, which is why I talked to Martin. There's a good chance that she could make our lives a living hell because of your solo action. But he's going to tell her and discuss it with her, so that's good for us. I think Martin knows how to handle her. Especially now that what I've suspected all along has come about." Lars grinned at Elin.

Elin gave him a blank look. "I don't get it. What are you talking about?"

"Simple. From the beginning, I've been wondering why Martin had gotten so deeply involved in this case. I mean, he had only had two brief encounters with the woman before she disappeared. But he still followed her trail to Stockholm, hired us to search for her, and went to Dalarna himself. You don't do that kind of thing just because you think some woman is nice. I told him to his face that there was more going on, but he firmly denied it. So what's happening now? He just told me that they're together. This weekend, Liv is flying to Berlin to visit him."

Elin giggled. "When love comes along ... But if you ask me, they were already coming across as a couple when we had that meeting at her company. I think they work well together."

"Yeah, and now Liv is available again."

"Oh, come on, Lars! Don't you lay that on her."

"No, no! I didn't mean it that way. If anyone is to blame for her husband's death, then that would be me. I was the one who tied the guy up inside the house before it blew up."

Elin leaned forward and put her hand on his arm. She had to bite her lip: she had almost blurted out "'Splosion Man," which would not have been appropriate just then.

"Lars," she said softly, "that wasn't your fault. The guy placed the explosive there himself, and you had no idea."

"I know. But the stupid feeling is still there ..."

"I understand. So what happens next with Martin and Liv?"

"Martin will be discussing it with Liv this weekend. He doesn't want to tell her over the phone. I wouldn't, either. Then he'll let us know if we should keep digging."

"OK. So for the time being, we do nothing?"

"Elin! Have I not made myself clear? We only take action when someone hires us to do so. Tobias will fire you if he ever catches wind of this. That means that you will now stay put!"

"Yeah, OK. I won't do a thing. Cross my heart."

"All right. I'm not saying anything to Tobias, but if Liv makes a big fuss over this, I won't be able to help you. Do you understand that?"

Elin nodded and sheepishly answered, "Yeah, I understand."

Lars rose from his seat and patted her on the shoulder. "No need to hang your head. It'll all work out. I have full faith in Martin. And anyway, like I already said, great job on Saturday. It's just too bad it wasn't official."

Lars left the office. Elin was staring blankly into space. Yeah, right: 'Too bad ... so sad ...." If there had been an official job, there was no way they would have given it to her. It would surely have gone to Lars. They just never let her take part in the interesting stuff because they didn't think she was up to it. But then how could she ever prove herself?

Still, she would once again refrain from forging ahead on this case. Lars had been really pissed when she told him the story this morning, and Lars was the only one there who ever gave her a chance. She had no desire to ruin what she had with him.

Saturday, November 28

60

Martin was observing Liv. She was sitting on his sofa with a glass of wine in her hand, and she seemed at peace with herself. They had spent a pleasant day together. When Liv and the children had arrived the day before, things had been somewhat reserved at first. He and Liv had felt uncomfortable about indulging in a passionate greeting in front of the kids. And the children were tired and had eyed each other with suspicion. But Martin had ordered pizza, and eating together had broken the ice.

Today, they went out and spent the day sightseeing around Berlin. In the morning, they went to the *MACHmit!* Museum, which was a lot of fun for the kids. Then it was off to McDonald's—always a sure bet—and in the afternoon, to the Christmas fair. By the end of the day, the children were exhausted, and once supper was done, they went happily off to bed. All three of them slept on the sofa bed in the guestroom, and they even enjoyed it. Somehow they managed to communicate, too. They each spoke their own language and also made signs with their hands. Martin almost got the feeling that Lara could understand the two Swedish kids' wishes better than he could.

The evening before, he had already had a chance to have Liv to himself for a couple of hours, but he hadn't wanted to spoil her first day in Berlin, which was why he hadn't told her about his phone call with Lars. Now, however, he could no longer put it off. He set a small cheese platter on the coffee table and sat down across from Liv. He started to speak but then stopped to take another sip of red wine.

"Don't you want to come sit next to me?" Liv patted the spot beside her on the couch.

"I will. But I need to tell you something first."

Liv looked at Martin uneasily. "Is something wrong?"

"No, no, it has nothing to do with us. It has to do with Saga's kidnapping."

Liv said nothing. Her big blue eyes were trained on his face. Damn it, this was no fun at all. Why did he have to be the one to tell her?

"I got a call from Lars this week." Martin paused. Liv kept looking at him expectantly. "They've found out something new."

Liv set down her wine glass and leaned forward. She reached for a strand of hair.

"And why is that? They weren't supposed to pursue this anymore. Did you hire them for another job?"

Martin raised his hand in defense.

"No, no," he protested. "I wouldn't do that without your consent. And as I understand it, it also wasn't Lars. It seems that Elin has developed a bit of personal initiative."

Liv became agitated and held both hands to her mouth.

"Martin, are we in danger?" She looked terrified.

"No, not at all. Liv, it's nothing bad. Well, it is in a way, but at least it's not a danger to you or your kids or any of us. Lars didn't agree with what Elin did, but he said that she executed the operation very skillfully so that no one could make a connection to any of us. He didn't want to give me the details, but they have a lead."

Liv took her hands away from her mouth. Martin had evidently succeeded in calming her down. Her expression had now changed to one of curiosity.

"You're not going to like this," he said, "but you need to be aware of it."

"So tell me already!"

Martin swallowed hard. "They spoke with one of the men who was watching your house, and he told them who hired him. We thought the Russians were behind it, but that's apparently not the case. The man who hired him was your husband's brother."

"Erik?" Liv looked utterly mystified.

Martin nodded.

"That can't be ..." she said. "I don't believe it."

Martin took a sip of wine, set down his glass, and moved over to the couch beside Liv. He took her hand in his.

"Are they sure?" she asked.

"Lars says they are."

She leaned her head on Martin's shoulder, and he laid his arm around her.

"I'm sorry," he said.

Liv shook her head in disbelief. "How could Erik kidnap his own niece? And why?"

"We don't know. We can only speculate. Maybe the Russians hired him."

Liv had tears in her eyes. "I still can't believe it. Not that I've ever had a good connection with Erik or that I think too highly of him. I just don't think he's capable of that." She looked at Martin. "Why did you wait until now to tell me?"

"I didn't want to tell you over the phone. And last night, I just couldn't bring myself to do it."

Liv nodded. "Yes, that was probably smart of you. But what do we do with this now?"

Martin shrugged his shoulders. "That has to be your decision. If you want, Lars can keep digging and pin Erik down. At that point, we can turn the case over to the police."

"I don't know."

"Well, before you make any decisions, we can discuss it with Lars again. He can explain things better."

Liv was staring into space.

"Did you have much contact with Erik?" Martin asked.

Liv shook her head. "No, virtually none. We saw each other at some family get-togethers, but that was just a couple of times. He's an odd person."

"In what way?"

"Well, how can I say this? He's quite volatile and somewhat cynical. He's not very approachable."

"Is he married?"

"No, he was usually with some girlfriend or other. But he came alone to his brother's funeral."

"What does he do for a living?"

"He works in the IT department at Saab in Linköping, which is two hours south of Stockholm."

"Right, so IT. Don't want to say anything, but it fits."

Liv looked at him. "You mean because of the emails and that ... what do you call that camouflaged server again?"

"An elite server, I think. Yeah, that's what I meant."

"Yes, that's true. But why did he do it? For the money? He didn't get any."

"Lars believes that things either got too hot for Erik and he aborted the kidnapping or that he was working with the Russians and their goal was to buy your company."

"You mean the Russians paid him to do it?"

"Yes."

"That bastard!"

"It doesn't matter which version you choose. There's no argument about this guy's character."

Liv looked into Martin's eyes. "You must think I'm a complete idiot. I marry a man who first has me kidnapped and afterwards tries to murder me. And then I refuse to believe that my brother-in-law is behind my daughter's kidnapping." The tears were running down her face. Martin wiped them away with his finger.

"There's nothing to worry about. I love you. This whole mess has nothing to do with us or my feelings or my opinion of you. And you're not responsible for your brother-in-law's actions. No one can see inside a person's heart. You wouldn't believe some of the things I've witnessed. As a lawyer, you experience quite a few surprises."

"Yes, but I lived with Thomas for many years. It never occurred to me that he could do this." Liv was sobbing.

Martin pulled her close. "Some people are good actors. You're not the first to be so thoroughly deceived by someone."

Martin let Liv cry a while. He could easily see how this latest disappointment could tear open an old wound. And he knew that it must be hard, but he hoped she would manage to compose herself, just as she always had before. She was sensitive, but she was also strong.

All of a sudden, Liv sat up. She took a tissue out of her pants pocket and wiped her nose.

"He's going to pay for this! Thomas destroyed himself, but I'm going to nail Erik. He kidnapped my daughter. And that was after everything else. What a miserable, filthy swine!"

There she was, the strong Liv. Martin hadn't figured on that fast a turnaround.

"You know, Martin," she said, "this past week has not been an overly pleasant one for me. I mean, you left, and all my fears returned. The surveillance by the security company is definitely a good thing, and so is the alarm system, but I still spent the entire time worrying. I just can't be with the children all the time. And then—well, I thought that if the Russian Mafia was behind all this, then ... they always find a way. The danger isn't over, you know? I've already thought about leaving Stockholm and moving here to be near you. Of course, not just because I'm afraid but also to be with you. You're so good for me—in every way." Liv smiled at him.

"And," she continued, "it was in fact that miserable little brother-in-law of mine who did this to Saga and me. He obviously knows a lot about me and can approach us at any time without raising eyebrows. This is just incredible."

All of this came gushing out of her, leaving Martin struck by how she managed to channel her fear and disappointment into anger and indignation.

"But you know what we're going to do, Martin?" she added. "We're going to forget all about this for now! I want to spend time with you and enjoy this day before we fly back to Stockholm tomorrow. I'm so proud of our children. The three of them are getting along so well, aren't they? Tomorrow, we'll also have a lovely time. And next week, I'll meet with Lars, and we'll call you. And then we'll finish that scum!"

Martin was glad to see the change. "That's my Liv," he said. "That's what we'll do."

"I love you, Martin."

"Jag älskar dig, Liv."

Martin had practiced that sentence last Wednesday in his Swedish class, and now he could say it flawlessly.

Tuesday, December 1

61

Lars walked over to Elin's desk in the office and sat down across from her. Elin gave him an anxious look.

"Hej! How did it go?"

"Well, you lucked out again. Liv is not going to give us a hard time over your actions."

"Phew!" Elin breathed a sigh of relief. She didn't want to admit it, but she had had some serious jitters. She had no wish to lose her job.

"Yeah," Lars continued, "she even wants us to put the guy behind bars. She's really pissed at him. And it's easy to see why."

"Great! When do we start?"

Lars looked at her. His expression was serious. "I don't think you're on the team."

Elin's jaw dropped as she stared at him in shock.

"I have to be able to rely on the people I work with," he said. "They can't constantly be pulling off some solo initiative."

"Lars, you can't do this … OK, I promise that things will change now. I'll do whatever you tell me. And no more special excursions. I swear! Please let me be a part of it!" Elin was begging him.

Lars looked her in the eye and waited. Finally, he nodded.

"All right, last chance. Anything like that again, and that's it. Got it?"

Elin nodded energetically.

"And I'm not saying that your initiatives haven't been good. I just want you to run things by me first! No stepping on the gas until I've given the OK. Got that?"

"Yeah, thanks. You won't be sorry."

Lars shook her hand.

"All right, then that's settled. So now you're going to sit down and find out everything you can on Erik Lind. We'll get started right away with the surveillance. I'm driving over there now, and you'll come tomorrow."

"To Linköping?"

"Right. See you tomorrow."

Lars turned around and walked out. It looked like the message had gotten through. Of course, he wanted her on the team—the kid had done a great job in Dalarna. She was the best partner in the whole agency. She just needed to learn some discipline. But he would make sure of that.

Elin gradually calmed down. Lars had given her a real scare. She badly wanted this case. She knew that she could solve it—together with Lars, of course. This time, she really would get her act together.

She started typing, which reactivated the monitor. She had actually already collected some info on Erik Lind. True, she wasn't supposed to be working on it until now, but no one would notice that little bit of Internet research. And now it would save her some time—now that she had official permission to work on it.

Wednesday, December 2

62

Lars was happy to see Elin arrive. Sitting there, waiting in front of the Saab building was a pretty boring pastime. It was a long, two-story, red building with a yellow roof, and it was located on the outskirts of Linköping, not far from the freeway. Erik Lind was on the job. His black Land Rover was parked in the company parking lot, which was open to the public. That allowed Lars to take up his station there. Unfortunately, the entrance was on the other side of the building, which made it impossible for him to keep an eye on it. But the assumption was that Erik would be using his car for every excursion since there was nothing within walking distance.

Elin pulled into a vacant spot and walked over to Lars.

"Hey, 'Splosion Man."

Lars grinned. "Hey, Elin. Good to see you."

She sat down beside him. "So what's up?"

"Not much. I kept an eye on Erik last night, and he left shortly after 5 p.m. Drove right home to the address you sent me. It's a three-story apartment building with six households. He stayed there the whole time, so I quit at 11 p.m. During that time, at around 6 p.m., a woman came by and went into the same building. She drove off again at around 10 p.m. But I don't know which unit she went into. Did you find out anything else?"

"I asked for his tax records—nothing too exciting. Salary fits the job. He bought the apartment five years ago and is in the process of paying off his mortgage. So other than just buying a new car, there's nothing that stands out."

"Did you check to see where he bought it?"

Elin rolled her eyes. "Does a fish swim in the water? Of course, I checked. Sweden has nine Land Rover dealerships, and one of them is right here in Linköping. I want to drive over there now to see if they can tell me anything."

Lars would have gladly taken on that job. A little variety would have done him good, but Elin might have an easier time getting the information. Car salespeople were usually male. There was a good chance that she would be able to get something out of them just by batting her eyelashes.

"OK. Anything else?" Lars asked.

"No, Erik Lind hardly shows up at all. He's mentioned in some publication to do with Saab and in connection with his dead brother, but beyond that, there's squat."

"Well, nothing we can do about that. So go ahead and drive over to the Land Rover dealer, and after that, you can take my place for the remainder of the day, all right?"

Elin nodded. "Yup. So are you driving back to Stockholm?"

"No, I want to poke around a little and see what I can find out about the woman from last night. I got her address through her license plate number. She lives a little ways outside of town. I just want to check this lady out."

"So you think she was at Erik's place?"

"That's what it looked like. I think I saw her in the window of the same apartment where the light went on after Erik disappeared into the building. But I'm not sure."

"OK, well, I'll head on over to the Land Rover dealer now," Elin said.

"Yeah, great. Good luck! Maybe you could pick up some food on your way back."

"Sure, what would you like? A three-course French meal?" She grinned at him.

Lars laughed. "No, it doesn't have to be that fancy. I'm fine with a burger."

"With or without cheese?"

"The works would be great."

"OK, so a cheeseburger."

"Right."

Elin got out of the car and returned to her own vehicle. Before opening the door, she waved at Lars. Having her there was definitely a good thing—she brought momentum to the case.

Elin had scrutinized the area. The car dealership was located in an industrial park on the outskirts of Linköping. The courtyard was surrounded by large trees and a lawn, which clearly set it apart from the other businesses. In addition to Land Rovers, the company also dealt in other makes, including Mercedes and Fiat, a combination that didn't make much sense to Elin. She had seen on the Internet that, along with a few general salespeople, the dealership also had a representative for each specific make. She was now waiting for the Land Rover representative to finish his phone call.

Finally, he hung up. "Hej! Sorry about the wait. What can I do for you?"

Elin explained that she was interested in a Land Rover, in particular, a Discovery Sport, which was the model Erik Lind had bought. The salesman took her to the Land Rover section of the large showroom and pointed out a model in silver. After examining the vehicle in detail and enquiring about the price, Elin asked about delivery time frames.

"Right now, we have four of this model here. Those are immediately available. Otherwise, it takes three to four months."

"What colors are available for the cars you have here?"

"Aside from this silver one, we have two in white and one in red."

Elin made a disappointed face. "Oh, that's too bad. I so wanted one in black. You know, for us ladies, color is always critical."

The salesman nodded. He seemed to have no trouble understanding that.

"Yes, unfortunately, we don't have the Sport in black. We could either order one, or you could choose a standard Discovery. We have that here in black. Of course, it's a bit pricier."

"No, I really want the Sport. And I also don't want to wait that long. Why don't you have that one in black? Is that not a popular color?"

"Well, yes, it is. We had a black Sport, but I sold it last week."

"Oh, bummer! So I came a week too late. Any chance the customer will return it?"

The salesman laughed. "I doubt it. The man had his eye on that car. He even paid cash for it."

"What? The whole amount?"

The salesman nodded.

"Do you get that a lot?" asked Elin.

"No, it's pretty unusual. And our company doesn't like it, but we'll obviously do it if the customer insists."

"And the customer was trustworthy? Not some Mafia type who was trying to launder his money?" Elin smiled and winked at him.

"No, he was from around here. He works at Saab. We weren't worried about it."

Elin had found out what she wanted. She asked a few more questions, told him that she needed to think about it, and said goodbye.

63

Lars was thrilled to get his hamburger—or rather (he corrected himself in his head), his cheeseburger.

"So how did it go?"

Elin told him what she had found out.

"And they just told you that outright?"

She explained how she had gone about it.

Lars was impressed. "Great job. You really are talented."

Elin smiled. "Thanks, but the sales guy made it easy for me. I was surprised he even took me seriously. I don't look at all like someone who would buy a Land Rover."

"Oh, I don't think there are any clear-cut standards for that kind of thing these days."

"Yeah, maybe. Anyway, we now know that Erik bought the car new and that he paid cash. That makes him even more suspect, doesn't it?"

"Absolutely. A sudden windfall like that is always suspect, and in his case, it doesn't match his financial situation. What does a Land Rover like that cost?" Lars asked.

"Around 500,000 bucks."

"Yeah, right. Why would he have that much in cash?"

Elin nodded and started chowing down on her hamburger.

When they were done eating, Elin headed to her car. She was supposed to continue monitoring Erik Lind's movements. Lars had taken a picture of him and sent it to her cell phone.

Lars's plan now was to drive to the house of Erik's potential girlfriend, so he started the car and drove out of the parking lot.

The house was easy to find. It was more of a summerhouse, but it was listed as the woman's address, and from the looks of it, she lived there year-round. It was situated on a gravel road at some distance from the nearest neighbor. Lars had driven past the place and parked two roads farther down. Now he was standing by a tree, observing the house. There seemed to be nobody home. There was no car in the driveway and no sign of movement. Lars looked around. The street was also completely deserted. He slowly moved closer. His leg hurt, especially in this kind of weather. He stood by the first window and peered inside. The room he was seeing was the kitchen. There were some dishes lying around, but there was no one there.

Lars walked around the outside of the house. From the rear of the house, he could see into the living room. No one here, either. He was wearing his leather gloves, so he pulled on the terrace door handle. To his amazement, the door was unlocked. That meant he could enter the house, but it also might mean that the occupant was not too far away. Lars hesitated. Should he risk it? He figured he should be able to hear in time and disappear out the back in case a car drove up. He looked around the garden. There was a lawn beside the small wooden porch. Behind that stood a greenhouse, and behind the greenhouse were some trees. There was not a house in sight. In a pinch, he should be able to escape here unnoticed.

Lars opened the door all the way and went in. He carefully wiped his shoes on the mat to avoid leaving tracks. He listened intently, but all he could hear was a sound like the ticking of a clock. He was right: there stood an old grandfather clock in a large wooden casing with pictures painted on it. The living room was simply but comfortably furnished with a wooden chair and couch from IKEA and a big flat-screen TV. A couple of landscape paintings hung on the walls. To the left, a dining table stood directly next to the service hatch to the kitchen.

Lars stepped into the narrow hallway. Going left, it led to the little kitchen, inside of which was a small table for two with the leftovers from breakfast. Going right were some stairs to the upper level, although from what Lars could tell from the outside, there couldn't be more than one room up there. There were two more doors in the hallway. One had a sign that unmistakably indicated a toilet. Lars cautiously opened the other door. There was no one inside the room, and it was otherwise also fairly empty. It was small, maybe three by two and a half meters. There was a bed on one side. Two cardboard boxes stood in front of it, and a large drywall panel was leaning against the wall. Were they renovating the room? Lars examined the walls but could see nothing that needed repairing. Then he saw the holes, and a chill ran down his spine. He stepped over to the window. Yes, indeed, on either side of the window were three holes that had held some screws. He inspected the drywall panel. There they were—the six screws—and the spacing matched the holes on the wall. Someone had covered the window with the panel. There couldn't be too many logical reasons for that.

Lars sat down on the bed and pulled over one of the boxes. He pushed the flaps apart and examined the contents. A wig with long, red hair was lying on top. Beneath that were several dolls, children's books, and a Playmobil farm with a number of different figures. It all matched the description Saga had given of her prison cell. Lars looked inside the second box. This one was smaller, and all it contained was a Wii with every conceivable type of cable and two remote controls. Lars knew all about this. His daughters also had a device like this. He had set it up and played on it many times with them, even if he had to admit that he stood no chance against his kids. So this was where they had held Saga hostage. The kidnappers had probably moved the TV from the living room into this one so that Saga could play with the Wii.

As Lars was pondering whether to immediately inform the police or first speak with Liv, the door flew open to reveal this woman from the night before. She stood there and glared at him, a large kitchen knife in her hand.

"What are you doing here? What business do you have snooping around?" she demanded.

Lars raised his hands in the air as he reviewed his options. He had no wish to fight someone with a knife, and the woman looked determined. She had an athletic build, was about thirty years old, and was wearing a pink jogging suit. All she had on her feet were thick socks, which explained why Lars hadn't heard her footsteps. But he still had no idea where this woman had come from so suddenly. Was she already here in the house? Even with no car outside?

Lars started to stand, but the woman snapped at him: "Sit down and don't move! You and I are going to have a little chat."

64

Elin knew that Lars had planned to drive to the house of Erik's potential girlfriend, but he had not been too forthcoming about where that was. In Elin's view, he could easily have let her in on it. But the obligation to share information apparently only applied to her end. She didn't want to whine about it, though. She was happy to just be part of the team.

Elin shifted her position in the front seat—one of her legs was tingling and starting to fall asleep. Erik hadn't shown yet, and the Land Rover was still parked in the same spot. It had started to rain again. While the weather this November had been surprisingly mild with lots of sun, usually rare for that month, December seemed to be getting worse: for two days, all they had had was rain.

Elin took a sip from her water bottle. That hamburger had been awfully salty. But it had tasted good. She didn't eat that kind of thing too often. Fast food wasn't Maja's thing.

Suddenly a man burst out of the building. Was that ...? Yes, it was—Erik Lind. Elin set her water bottle back in its holder and got ready. And, yes, he was sprinting to the Land Rover, with the key already in one hand. The Rover's blinkers briefly lit up, and the man jumped into the driver's seat. The engine started, and the car backed out of the parking space and took off like a shot to the exit. Wow, he was in a rush.

Elin followed at a distance. She had stuck a tracking device on the Land Rover and now had her laptop on the passenger's seat beside her, a procedure that had already proven effective and was almost routine for her. This way, there was no way Erik could get away from her.

The man was headed toward Linköping and was not observing the speed limit at all. Elin followed him at a leisurely pace, and the Land Rover soon vanished in the distance. As she watched the dot on the screen, she saw the car turn right toward downtown Linköping. She continued to follow at her own speed as the distance between them increased.

After a while, Elin noticed that the dot was no longer heading downtown but had switched to a more southbound course. Finally, it came to a stop. Elin was sitting at a red light, so she took the opportunity to read the location: Rättaregatan. That was where Erik had his apartment. Why was he in such a rush to get home, especially now, when it was way too early for quitting time?

The light turned green, and Elin resumed driving to Erik's apartment. She had almost arrived when the dot began to move again. Now Erik was heading north to the university. Elin decided to turn around. That way, she could take a shortcut if Erik changed his mind and drove back to Saab. At first, it did in fact look like he planned on heading back when he turned west before the university. But then he took County Roads 23 and 34 heading north and eventually passed under the freeway. It still seemed like he was trying to make warp speed, because the distance between them was rapidly growing again. Elin followed as well as she could while sticking to the speed limit.

Finally, the Rover turned west, took a few more turnoffs, and came to a halt in a residential area near the woods. Elin continued to follow, although it took her more than five minutes to reach the destination. There, she saw the Land Rover sitting in front of a small house. She drove another fifty meters, parked the car on the side of the road, and raced to the house. If the guy had been in such a hurry to get there, whatever it was must be important, and she didn't want to miss it.

There was no one in sight as Elin approached the house. She crept up to the Land Rover to use it as a cover. Then she heard voices and noticed something moving in the window to the left. She hunched down and ran over. She couldn't make out what they were saying, but she could hear the voices of two men. One of them sounded like Lars. Was that possible? She peered cautiously through the window. Yes, there was Lars, sitting on the bed. But what did that mean?

Elin knew that she had to get in there. She slunk over to the front door and pulled down on the handle. The door was unlocked. Now she could hear more clearly what the other man was saying.

"Let's make short shrift of this snoop. There's no guarantee he won't talk. Move it, pal—up!"

That didn't sound good. Elin darted into the hallway. One of the doors was wide open, and Erik was standing inside the doorway with his back toward her. It looked like he was a holding gun. Damn it all—Lars's life was in danger. She had to do something now.

Elin got a running start and rammed the man full force from behind. The impact thrust him forward, and he stumbled and crashed into the woman, who was standing by the wall. The shot that went off from the gun in that small space was deafening. Elin fell to the floor in front of the couch. Lars was lying next to her. She sat up and grabbed him by the shoulder.

"Oh my God, Lars, are you hit?" she cried.

Lars reached for the gun, which had also fallen to the floor. "No, I'm OK. I just dropped to the ground."

Right at that moment, the woman shrieked, "No, no! Erik!"

Elin looked up. Erik was slowly collapsing onto the floor. The woman was staring at him, horrified. Then Elin saw the knife: it was sticking out of his stomach, and the blood was gushing forth. Erik had turned as he was falling and was now sitting with his back to the wall. He was groaning.

The woman was squatting beside him. "Oh my God! This is not what I wanted!" she wailed.

She tugged at the knife. Erik screamed, but by then, she had already pulled it out. Erik was moaning loudly, and his face was contorted. The blood was spurting out of the wound and had already formed a large pool on the floor.

Lars pointed the gun at the woman. "Drop the knife!" he ordered.

The woman stared back at him, a blank expression on her face. Then she looked at the knife and threw it into the corner. She was kneeling next to Erik in the pool of blood.

"We have to help him—fast!" she screamed.

Lars ripped the blanket off the bed and threw it to her.

"Here!" he cried. "Press down on the wound as hard as you can!"

Elin had already grabbed her cell phone. "I'll call an ambulance," she said.

Lars sat down on the bed, still holding the gun in the crook of his arm. He looked at Elin.

"It's a good thing you came," he said. "And not one second too soon. Thanks."

Friday, December 4

65

Martin had arrived at Liv's an hour ago. Lars and Elin had just made it there. Martin had already heard over the phone about some of what went on, but now he and Liv would be getting a coherent version of the whole story.

After everyone had gotten their drinks, they all sat down on the group of sofas in front of the fireplace. Martin was looking at Elin and Lars. They seemed tired.

"When did you two get back to Stockholm?" he asked.

"Just a few hours ago," Lars answered. "The police had a lot of questions. They didn't let us go until noon today." Addressing both Martin and Liv, he added: "We had to tell them everything—about the kidnappings, too. They also want to speak with both of you."

Liv nodded. "I know. They already came by today and questioned me. Next week, they want to talk to Saga."

"What happened with the kidnappers?" Martin asked. "Did they confess?"

"Well ..." Lars started to answer, but Elin jumped in.

"Erik Lind is dead. The police just told us today. The knife severed the abdominal aorta, and they weren't able to save him. By the time the ambulance finally arrived, he was already unconscious and had lost so much blood that the hospital could no longer do anything for him. No surprise, the whole room was swimming in blood."

Liv put her hands to her mouth and her eyes opened wide. "That must have been awful."

"Yes, it was," Elin said. "And it's my fault. I was the one who shoved him toward the knife."

Lars laid his hand on her arm. "Elin, there's no need to blame yourself. You had no idea the woman was holding a knife in her hand. Besides, I probably would have died if you hadn't jumped in."

"I know," replied Elin. "But I still don't feel good about it."

Martin turned to the two detectives. "Now tell us the whole story from the beginning."

Lars and Elin told Liv and Martin about their day in Linköping, and they listened without interrupting.

"So that means that my Saga was held hostage in that summerhouse? Is that certain now?" Liv asked.

"Yes," Lars answered. "It's certain. We found all the paraphernalia that Saga described to us. Also, from what the police have told us, the woman confessed. Yesterday, they still weren't giving us any information, but today they were reasonably sure that we were just witnesses, and they believed our account. At that point, they gave us more information."

"Did those two pull the whole thing off by themselves?" Martin asked.

"Yes," Lars replied. "That's what the woman claims."

"But that would mean that Erik was the one who kidnapped Saga at her school. So why didn't she recognize him?" Martin looked at Liv.

"I've been thinking about that as well," Liv said. "As I told you before, we had very little contact with my husband's family. I believe Saga only met Erik twice, and they never talked at all. Saga always immediately went off to play with her cousins. And I only saw Erik from a distance at my husband's funeral."

"Right, and if he changed his appearance and disguised his voice ..." Elin added.

"I don't know the woman at all," Liv continued. "The police showed me a picture, but I've never seen her before."

"But why did they kidnap Saga?" Martin asked. For him, that was the central question.

"Someone apparently paid them to do it," Lars replied. "We don't yet know who it was, but I'm assuming it was the Russians who bought your company. Who else would have a motive? And since you never paid ransom, Erik must have been paid by someone else—especially given the fact that he paid cash for his Land Rover, and the police found even more money later on."

"How much?" Martin asked.

"They wouldn't tell us."

Liv was staring down at the coffee table. "So then it was all about the company?" she asked.

Lars nodded. "That's what we're assuming," he said.

Martin gave Lars a questioning look. "So what's the scenario here?" he asked. "Were the Russians initially in contact with Liv's husband, and then, when that didn't work out, they turned to his brother?"

"Yeah, it could have played out like that," Lars answered. "They may have also been pressuring Liv's husband in some way, since they wanted to buy the company at a cheap price. I'm afraid we'll never know exactly what happened. We can no longer ask Thomas and Erik, and the Russians will never tell us anything."

"But then why didn't they just go straight to Liv?"

"We can only guess. They may have been aware of her attitude from her husband. And they may have found out that she would never have even considered their price."

For a moment, there was silence. Then Elin turned to Liv.

"I'm so sorry it all turned out this way. Losing two members of your family must be a terrible thing, even if they had such bad intentions."

Liv shook her head. "To be honest, I don't know whether to be happy or sad. I still find it impossible to believe that those two were capable of that. It's probably better that I'll never have to deal with them again."

In spite of her words, Liv had tears in her eyes. Martin placed his hand on her arm.

"The good part," he said, "is that it's finally over. The company has been sold. The Russians have what they want, and the two Linds can no longer do you any harm. You can now look to the future."

Liv nodded her head, but without any great conviction.

Lars looked around the group.

"Well," he said, "we have nothing more to tell you. The case is now closed. If anything else comes up, we'd be happy to discuss it with you. You probably also don't need anyone guarding the children, do you?" He watched Liv carefully as he said that.

"Actually, could we please continue that for a while? I won't have any peace otherwise." Liv had a pleading expression on her face.

"Of course," Lars replied. "We're glad to do it. It's totally up to you."

That was a relief to Liv.

"Then we don't want to keep you any longer," said Lars. "And we want to go home, too. My family is waiting for me."

They all rose from their seats, and Lars and Elin said goodbye as Martin and Liv thanked them both for their efforts and their excellent work.

Liv and Martin were sitting by the fireplace, each holding a glass of wine. This time, Martin had managed to light the fire on his first try, and it was blazing. Liv's hair glowed like gold in the firelight. She was relaxed, but she also seemed pensive.

"What are you thinking, my love?" Martin asked.

Liv took a sip of wine. Her free hand was playing with a strand of hair. "I'm thinking about what you said."

Which statement was she referring to? Martin gave her a questioning look.

"You know, that I should look to the future," she said. "I haven't processed everything yet, but it seems to me that my entire life has fallen apart. Nothing is now as it was before. My husband abducted me, and he's dead now. The company that I was so involved with has been sold. And since Saga's kidnapping, I no longer feel safe here. I think I need a new start."

Liv paused and took another sip of wine. Then she looked into Martin's eyes with an earnest expression.

"What would you say if the children and I moved to Berlin?"

The question took Martin completely by surprise. He hadn't figured on this at all.

"That would be wonderful!" he answered. "I would love that. But are you sure you could leave Stockholm?"

Liv nodded. "Yes, I've thought about it a lot lately. There just isn't much keeping me here anymore. I've already told you that the house and the surroundings give me an eerie feeling now. I no longer feel safe. My parents are dead. I have nothing to do here, and there's no chance that I'll lose my female friends—I don't have that many, anyway. And Stockholm won't go anywhere. I can come back here whenever I want, and I'll keep the place in the Archipelago."

Liv seemed to have thought this through in detail. In fact, Martin was having trouble believing it.

"I didn't expect this at all," he told her. "This is a huge surprise. Well, would you like to move in with me? You're all more than welcome."

Liv edged over and took him in her arms. They kissed.

"Yes," she said, "of course, it's about you, too. I feel so much better when I'm with you. And I like Berlin. It's so different from Stockholm."

"And when did you want to come?"

"As soon as possible. If I can make all the children's school arrangements by then, as early as January."

"That would be great!" Martin responded. "I'll help you with all of it."

"And you don't feel that I'm pressuring you in any way?" Liv asked. "I mean, it's all happening so fast, and I've dropped this on you all of sudden."

"No—stop it. Not at all! This has been my deepest wish. I love you, Liv."

"I love you, too, Martin."
And Liv put her arms around him.

Epilogue

Two months later

66

Martin was on his way to the office. The traffic was crawling, and he had to stop once again. But none of that bothered him. His thoughts were somewhere else.

Martin's life had totally changed. It was less than half a year ago that he had traveled to Sweden for the first time to reflect on his life and on how to deal with his failed marriage and maintain contact with his daughter Lara. He had barely had time to think when his new adventure with Liv began, that whirlwind of events that he at first chose to be involved in but that then increasingly drew him in beyond his control.

And now, he had a family. Liv and her two children were living with him, even if only for the time being. Lara was naturally also a part of it, even if only every other weekend.

Still, none of it had been easy. The Swedish police had spoken with them multiple times and also reopened the subject of Liv's kidnapping. And Erik Lind's girlfriend, who had taken part in Saga's kidnapping, had evidently come clean and told them everything she knew.

Erik, it turned out, had already previously been in close contact with his brother Thomas, who had piled up a lot of gambling debts. Thomas had first frequented a number of casinos in an attempt to increase his capital, with the intention of reinvesting the money in his businesses. Unfortunately, after some early wins, he kept losing more and more money. He then switched to Internet casinos and private poker games, but there, too, he only increased his gambling debts. In the end, they probably amounted to several million euros. Finally, the Russians entered the game and bought up all his promissory notes. They then offered to eliminate his debts if they could acquire the construction company at a favorable price. Thomas had agreed and had hoped to convince Liv to go along with it. But when she resisted, he resorted to the kidnapping, with all its unforeseen consequences. After Thomas's death, the Russians had contacted his brother and offered Erik five million kronor if he would kidnap Saga for a few days.

And so, the whole mystery was finally solved, which was a great relief to Liv, who now had the explanations she had been seeking.

But the one who suffered from the clarification process was Saga. The police had interviewed her twice, and that had not been easy for her. She had been doing fine after the kidnapping, so that no one was prepared for her reaction. But the interrogations had stirred the memories up again.

Of course, the police had shown her pictures of the room and the woman, and after that, Saga had panic attacks, was afraid to go out, and would wet her bed at night. She underwent psychotherapy for a number of weeks, and except for the occasional panic attack, it seemed to be working. Saga was also the one who had welcomed the move to Berlin. She felt much better on the weekends they spent in Berlin, while in Stockholm, her entire surroundings seemed to close in on her with memories of the kidnapping.

Her brother Hampus, on the other hand, did not want to leave his friends and resisted making the move. But he quickly made friends at his new school and was now content. Liv had been lucky there: the Scandinavian school in Berlin had had a place for Hampus right away, and Saga was also finally accepted after being on the waiting list. As of January, both children had been placed in the appropriate grades and had adjusted well.

The traffic moved ahead a bit, but Martin was forced to step on the brakes because a white delivery truck was intent on changing lanes. Of course, after that, they were sitting beside each other in the middle of a traffic jam. If this kept up, Martin would have to call the office to cancel his 9 a.m.

Liv was doing great. She had left everything behind, or so it seemed, at least. She was often highly emotional, but Martin was always impressed by how good she was at organizing her life once she had decided what she wanted. She had hired a CEO for the property management firm so that her only function now was to be on the board. She had already sold the house in Danderyd—for an excellent price, no less. That was easy to do in Stockholm, where there were too few houses and apartments. She had also rented the finca on Mallorca to a travel agency that now used it for tourist accommodations.

Liv had bought a huge two-story apartment on Potsdamer Platz, in the heart of Berlin, and they would all be moving in there a couple of weeks from now. The upper floor, where the children could make themselves at home, had four rooms and a small pantry. The lower level included a large living room, a bedroom, and a study. That way, they would all have plenty of space. At the moment, the apartment was being renovated, and after that, everything would be ready to go. They had agreed that Martin would keep his apartment for now, but he was sure they wouldn't need it. He and Liv also got along well on a day-to-day basis, and in the past few weeks, their relationship had deepened. Liv was looking for a new job, but there was no financial pressure, so she was able to take her time. For the moment, she had plenty to keep her busy between organizing all the changes and taking care of the children. Every day, she would accompany them on their way to school and back—it was easy taking the underground.

The traffic inched forward again. Now Martin was right in front of the red light. Once it turned green, things should move at a faster clip.

What Martin liked best of all was that, every day, he looked forward to the end of the day. He loved coming home, where Liv and the kids would greet him. Liv would have often fixed some food, or they would quickly prepare their dinner together. That was a major change from his bachelor existence.

And Martin would not repeat his old mistakes. His law practice was important, but his new family was more so. He would never confuse his priorities again.

Sweden would also not be lost to them. They planned on spending their summer vacation in the Archipelago, and they were already looking forward to it. Martin had diligently continued with his Swedish studies and could already hold a simple conversation with the children—with Liv's help, of course. But he noticed the children were making faster progress in German than he was in Swedish. The Scandinavian school had German lessons, and some of the children had a German parent, so you heard a lot of German on the playground.

Martin was happy, probably happier than he had ever been in his life. How lucky he was to have seen that ad back then: "Vacation home in Southern Sweden"—even if at the time he could never have guessed how much that vacation would change his life.

Green. It was off to the office now—and another day at work that would bring him closer to the weekend and to spending time with his new family.

My Thanks to the Reader

I am thrilled that you have chosen to read my book. I am even more thrilled that you have read it to the end.

I especially hope that you liked it. If so, I would like to ask a small favor of you: please take a few moments to rate my book on Amazon.

If you did not like the book, please tell me directly! Your feedback is extremely important to me since it gives me the chance to learn about my readers' preferences.

You can reach me at
contact@christertholin.one
or
www.christertholin.one

My heartfelt thanks,
Christer Tholin

About the Author

Originally from the Schleswig-Holstein region of Germany, Christer Tholin and his family have spent many years living in Stockholm, Sweden, where the author works as an independent management consultant. He is a great fan of Swedish crime literature and for a long time had been planning to make his own contribution. That has now come to fruition with *VANISHED?*, his first book in the "Stockholm Sleuth Series" and where we meet the two detectives and main characters, Elin and Lars. *SECRETS?*, the second book in the series, tells about their next case. You can read more about it on the following page: www.christertholin.one

Read the second book of the
Stockholm Sleuth Series!

SECRETS?

"Damn! She had made a huge mistake. She would never make it out of there. They were going to kill her."

In this Swedish crime novella, fledgling private investigator Elin Bohlander takes on what at first glance looks like an easy assignment: to determine whether her client's boyfriend is having an affair with another woman. Elin follows him to a secluded cabin in the woods, where she soon discovers that what's actually happening there is stranger than anyone thought. Having ventured too far, she now sees that she has stumbled upon a hornet's nest and placed her life at risk. But it's too late. Will Elin be able to win the uneven fight against a gang of brutal child molesters?

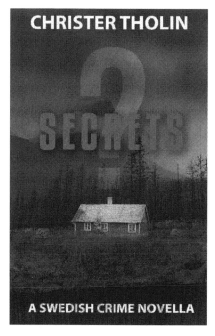

11567750R00187

Printed in Great Britain
by Amazon